OUT OF THE FRYING PAN AND INTO AN APOCALYPSE

THE FINAL BOOK IN THE
KINDNESS IS ENCOURAGED
TRILOGY

DAVID ALLAN BROWN

ISBN: 979-8-37044-496-8
OscMay Publishing, Douglasville, GA

Cover design by Matthew Morse
Printed in the United States of America

DEDICATION

Dedicated to the unparalleled services of the St. Jude Children's Research Hospital who provide advance cures, and means of prevention, for pediatric catastrophic diseases through research and treatment. No child is denied treatment based on race, religion, or a family's ability to pay. Regardless of the duration or the cost of care, families never receive a bill from St. Jude for treatment, travel, housing, or food, so families can focus on helping their child live. Thanks to St. Jude's noble efforts, their treatments—many invented at St. Jude— have helped push the overall childhood cancer survival rate in the United States from 20% to more than 80% since they opened in 1962.

CONTENTS

1

A SHOCKING DISCOVERY

He woke in complete darkness. One moment caught up in the pandemonium of the violent invasion and the next, a cloud took form and blotted out all senses. Marcus woke to Tiny licking blood from his face. The room was silent; the moon provided a patchy, diffused lighting. He propped himself up on one elbow and glanced across the room. Janey lay unconscious; her body stretched across the threshold of the foyer. Marcus climbed from bed and struggled to stand. A person lay motionless with a halo of blood bordering their body next to where he once lay. Suddenly, his pain meant nothing; he felt his face go pale, while his heart threatened to jump from his chest. Waffa was the one lying next to him when he drifted off to sleep earlier that evening.

God almighty, I implore you! Please let her be all right.

He placed his fingers on her neck, pressed lightly, and whaled in pain. No pulse, she was cold and as he rolled her body over, he realized rigor mortis had already set in. He laid his head on her chest and sobbed, then just as suddenly, gasped; he ran his hands over her very flat stomach and a flicker of hope fluttered through him. Marcus studied her closely, and after a brief examination, quickly determined this was not Waffa at all. His wife was pregnant and proud of her baby bump. At first, an overwhelming joy replaced his sense of agonizing loss and he smiled.

She may be alive. Waffa may be alive! He celebrated; however, his jubilation was short-lived. The lifeless body was that of Fila.

He stumbled forward, fell to his knees, and shook Janey lightly. She was out cold; a large gash in the back of her head explained the blood that outlined her torso, but her pulse was strong. Marcus laid her on the couch and then ran back to Fila. He hoped he was wrong, but once he examined her up close, there was no doubt. Her throat had been cut; her body battered. He moved from room to room in search of the others, but the house was empty. After cleaning and bandaging Janey's wounds, he began feeling faint and before he could sit down, he tumbled to the ground. So concerned about the others, he never took a moment to notice the two jagged wounds just above his belt line. As he struggled to remain conscious, he noticed two large military-style boots come into view. Not sure if it was a dream or one last sensory function, he was lifted from the ground and whisked away.

2

UNEXPECTED DEPARTURE

In an instant, Marcus sensed the end of hope and a return to the destruction of the past. Yes, the Nill had been defeated—perhaps for the last time—but now another more nefarious enemy rose from the newfound peace, a stealthy, unknown, yet lethal enemy from within.

"Clear that table and lay him here! Get the doc. And where's Ferris? Let him know we have Martyreon."

Marcus could hear everything going on around him, but he was unable to react or move no matter how hard he tried. He couldn't speak and was immobilized as if paralyzed. He couldn't bear the thought of being a quadriplegic, but even in his current despair, he felt a bolt of joy when he heard Ferris's name mentioned.

"His eyes are open, doctor."

"Anesthesia, we need more anesthesia!"

"We have an arterial bleed!"

"Hand me the Haemostatic Forceps, stat! I need some more suction. I can't see the bleeder, nurse. Sponges so I can get to the artery!"

"I'm trying doctor."

"More suction! Got it! Sutures, Angela. Sorry things got a bit tenuous."

"Whatever it takes doctor. He is a friend. Is he out of the woods yet?"

"Should be now that we have repaired his liver."

Angela looked at Ferris and Leeba with a thumbs up, while Eowyn and Raghba waited on Janey in the critical care ward. Her brain swelled from the head wound, and she was rushed into emergency surgery to relieve the pressure. Both Marcus and Janey faced high-risk procedures, but Janey had much less chance of survival.

Ferris grabbed Leeba's hand content that Marcus was all right and they headed to see how things were going with Janey. He had just stepped into the hallway when he collided with Celeste.

"Sowwy, Ceweste! Wanted to check on Janey.

"Me too," she retorted as they stepped into the observation room. All were fixated on the operation going on below.

"How are things going so far?" Celeste inquired. She didn't get an answer other than Eowyn and Raghba crying in one another's arms.

"What is it wadies?" Ferris stepped between them and took their hands.

"She coded Ferris. I mean she was dead for almost a minute, but they brought her back," Eowyn sobbed while Celeste consoled, and Leeba sat with her face cradled in her hands.

"I can't believe that out of our victory, something like this has occurred. What happened, Ferris?"

"I stiww don't know evewything, but I know the intwudews wewe capitow guawds. We wewe attacked by ouw own peopwe! I hate to say it, but I think Sewima is behind this."

"No, I can't believe that! Selima wouldn't do such a thing."

"Weww, someone fwom the capitow owdewed the attack. We'ww get to the bottom of it. I pwomise you that. I'm just gwad that aww of you wewe abwe to get out."

"They marched right on by us and directly to Waffa. They dragged her out even before we had time to react. Once they had her, they went right to Marcus and started beating him. He'd be dead right now if it wasn't for Janey," Eowyn finished while staring intently as the doctor drilled a second hole in Janey's skull. "Angela called the procedure a **Ventriculostomy**. See they are inserting a tube that is supposed to drain some of the fluid from around her brain."

"What do you mean she saved him?" Leeba asked.

"Just before I ran out the back, I saw a guard slam Marcus to the floor, and another stabbed him. I wanted to help, but I couldn't get around the gunfire. There was nothing I could do!"

"It's okay, Eowyn. We know you wouwd have hewped if you couwd've." Ferris pulled her tight and whispered, "Thewe's nothing you couwd have done."

"Anyway, Marcus was down and if it wasn't for Janey jumping onto the intruder's back, he would have stabbed him to death. She fought so hard that he tossed her across the room. She saved him. There's no doubt! She would do anything for her dad."

Eowyn finished, collapsed onto the couch next to Leeba, and the room fell silent.

It sounded like a predictably melodic beep. The sound was soothing as the operation extended into the second hour and became a reassuring beacon that informed those listening that Janey was alive. All but Ferris had long since dozed off when the persistent beep unexplainably morphed into a persistent and wretched shrill tone that brought Ferris to his knees as if the oxygen was suddenly sucked from the room. The sound of Ferris's knees hitting the ground snapped the others from their stupor and they rushed to the observation window to see nurses scrambling and the doctor frantically performing CPR. The sound of the monitor cut through the chaos taking place on the floor below. Doctors barked orders while intermittently administering an electric shock, but after several minutes, their efforts were futile, they discontinued lifesaving efforts.

Eowyn slammed her fists against the glass in agony while Ferris wrestled her to the couch. Leeba embraced Raghba; the entire group eventually consoled one another in one large ball of sobbing souls, loving, consoling, and supporting one another.

—Janey Martyreon was dead—

3

A RECOVERY & A FAREWELL

May the Lord make your love increase and overflow for each other and everyone else, just as ours does for you.[1] "This quote from Thessalonians was a favorite of Janey's, and she modeled her life in accordance with this passage. As we have already shared, Janey was one of the most giving and loving friends anyone could have. We have shared our testimonies today, the many stories of her amazing life, and out of those, a common theme has emerged, a theme that will not surprise any of her family and friends. Words like selfless, heroic, loving, courageous, sweet, caring, and the one characteristic that repeatedly surfaced, loyalty, were all used to describe this amazing young woman. Loyalty—what a powerful trait to possess. Janey epitomized loyalty. As I listened to your testimonials, I was reminded of how Janey selflessly sacrificed her life for her father as her final act on earth. She could have run, she could have hidden, but no, she didn't hesitate to thrust herself into danger to save him. This young woman, Janey Martyreon lived a life that we should all admire; we should all aspire to be as selfless, loyal, and loving as she was. As we depart and end our fellowship today, I

---

1   Thessalonians 3:12

want to remind everyone that Leeba has prepared a luncheon for everyone who would like to further celebrate Janey's life."

As Janey's body was laid to rest, Marcus simultaneously woke from a three-day coma-like state to find Adiva sleeping with her hand clutching his, her head resting on the bed next to him. He glanced across the room to find it empty as nurses and doctors scurried by in the hallway. His mind immediately returned to the brutal attack. Waking to find Waffa swept away, Fila struggling with an attacker, and Janey coming to his rescue.

"Adiva." He shook her gently. "Adiva, how long have I been here?"

She jumped to her feet and embraced him. "Well, it's about time you returned to the land of the living. Everyone has been worried sick! How are you feeling?"

Marcus sat up and grimaced in pain.

"They had to perform surgery to stop internal bleeding. You're going to be sore for quite some time." Adiva smiled as she stared at Marcus.

"What?"

"I'm just so glad you are awake and healthy. For a while, it was touch and go. I mean you were close to death." She leaned in and kissed him on the cheek.

"Where's Waffa?"

Her smile transformed into an immediate frown as she stumbled over her words. "I...ah...you don't remember?"

"They took her, didn't they?"

"Yes, but we are still unsure by whom. Ferris is investigating, but he feels confidentand, I know this may be shocking to you—that Selima is behind the attack."

"No, I know her too well. She isn't capable of such a thing." He finished his sentence and stared off into the distance as if unsure of his statement. "Then again, I didn't think she would ever have a person executed either. As much as I hope it's not true, Ferris may be on to something. Where is he anyway?"

Again, Adiva nervously tripped over her own words. "He... he's at your home to...uh...check on..." She took a deep breath, placed her hand on his knee, and looked him in the eye. "He and the others are with Janey—her service."

Marcus immediately recognized her evasive reply and focused on the later part of her comment; "her service." His mind searched for all the possible services that she could be referring to, but the obvious and only sensible answer was a funeral. He was having difficulty making sense of anything, especially regarding Janey. A flood of thoughts careened like an out-of-control car crashing through his mind. His already fragile psyche was hit with a rapid barrage of devastating rights and lefts. Waffa being dragged away, Fila being murdered, he being thrashed, and finally, Janey springing onto the back of his attacker.

"What happened to her? Is she going to be all right?" He slid to the edge of his bed, but as soon as his feet hit the floor he collapsed in agony.

"Holy fuck! What did they do to me?"

Adiva assisted him back into bed. "I told you that they performed the surgery. You were in bad shape and by no means should you be moving around."

"What about Janey?"

"She fought so hard, Marcus!" Tears welled in her eyes as the words peeled from her lips. "They did everything they could, but the damage was extensive."

Marcus swallowed hard and for a moment, wavered as if faint while Adiva tried to steady him. The years of loss and sacrifice that he thought had desensitized him from feeling, deceived him. The tears didn't come slowly, but instead, as if an ancient dam suddenly gave way, waves of grief slammed him repeatedly. He gasped for air while grabbing the bed rails to keep from tumbling to the floor. Adiva laid him back in bed.

"Just breathe, Marcus. Deep breaths!"

A few moments later, a nurse entered and injected something into his I.V. and his eyes closed soon after.

"Is that you, Nayla?" Adiva did a double-take. "I didn't know you were working here!"

"I had to occupy my mind, somehow keep my thoughts from obsessing on Maria." Her eyes watered just mentioning her name.

"You loved her, didn't you?" Adiva brushed her hair from her face. She was lucky that you entered her life."

"No, I was the lucky one. She gave me purpose and helped me through some of the toughest times of my life, and she is the only person to love me without reservation despite my foibles. Yes, I loved her more than she probably was aware. A part of me died when she did."

"But here you are, Nayla! You are a strong independent woman. You made it through the war unscathed physically, and you will make it through this very difficult time as well. I'm confident! Besides that, Maria hasn't abandoned you spiritually; she's right here and always will be." She took Nayla's hand and placed it gently over her heart. "She will always be with you."

Nayla brushed a tear from her cheek and recomposed herself. "Thank you, Adiva. Yes, I will be fine; I just hope I am not alone for the rest of my life. Maria was my chance at happiness!" She finished and departed before Adiva could reply.

Within seconds after Adiva's departure, Raghba and Eowyn arrived.

"Was that Nayla I just saw?" Eowyn asked as she took a seat on the bed next to Marcus and brushed the hair from his eyes.

"Yes, she's working as a nurse."

"Is she doing any better? I mean the last time I saw her she was a mess. I felt so bad for her. She took Maria's death as hard as her own family did." Eowyn laid her head on Marcus's shoulder.

"You do know she was in love with her, right?" Adiva asked a bit surprised.

"I suspected as much, but I wonder since Maria made it clear that she was a devoted mother and also straight as an arrow if you know what I mean."

"You know as well as I do, Eowyn, that living in isolation and extreme fear can easily change any person's values, desires, and beliefs. Remember, Maria thought her husband was dead, and from what Nayla has shared with me, Maria and she were isolated together, subject to abuse, and they went through hell together. They were raped and physically abused throughout their captivity. Those sorts of things pull people together, even those who might not normally care for one another."

"I can relate to that. I've never shared this with anyone, but when Marcus and I went through the whole nuclear plant meltdown and later, being trapped in Nill Headquarters ready to burn to death, I rethought my whole belief system. For a while, I thought I was in love with Marcus. Can you imagine? I, a lesbian, and yet those harrowing experiences had me questioning everything about myself. I would have jumped his bones if given the chance at that time, but as time passed, I realized I loved him, but only as a brother or as a confidante—at least that is how I compartmentalized it. Sharing stressful situations and surviving daunting experiences can profoundly change a person."

"Hey, Raghba. We were just talking about how difficult situations can cause people to act in strange ways. You know, those times when in extreme danger or when your life is threatened."

"Those same types of scenarios can also cause people to lose all sensibilities; cause them to make some stupid choices," Raghba replied then hung her head and waited for a reply.

"Do you want to share a story? Tell us a little bit about yourself before you met Celeste?"

"No, I am too ashamed to share the awful things I have done for love. Just know that in my experience, love, as well as traumatic situations, can lead people to do monumentally stupid things."

"We all have things that we regret in life, Raghba. You're not the only one. What counts is what we do with those mistakes. Do we use them as a tool to help us become a better person or do we dwell on them and let those incidents haunt us for the rest of our life? For me, I learn from my mistakes and then look forward. Constantly reliving the past does nothing but cause torment and pain." Adiva sat next to Raghba and held her hand.

"Don't punish yourself, but instead celebrate the peace, freedom, and friendships that are staring you in your face."

"I don't mean to change the subject, but does Marcus know?" Eowyn inquired as she looked to Adiva for an answer.

"Yes, it was so difficult to tell him. He was devastated. I mean I could see the life being drawn from him when I told him. They had to give him a sedative to settle him down."

"That girl was his life. Yes, he loved Maria, but Janey was the light of his life. She was the only constant in his life after the death of his mother. All I know is that we have to be there for him. He is going to need all of us to recover from this loss."

"No doubt, Eowyn."

"I know Marcus's story is relatively new to both of you but think about this—and I am in no way discounting the many losses we have experienced—Marcus has lost his mother, father, brother, first girlfriend, Ileana, his second girlfriend, Allura, his adopted daughter, Veil, his wife, Maria, and now his daughter, Janey among many others. It amazes me that he can function at all."

The three sat in silence when an unexpected voice interjected.

"I love all of you and don't worry, I'll be fine. I hope you, my friends, will fill the void. We've all lost so much and as soon as it looks like we have found some level of peace, something inevitably disrupts the harmony. I'm starting to wonder if the concept of peace is just an abstract that cannot be achieved."

"By the way, has anyone heard from Ferris?"

"Nothing yet, but I can tell you he went straight to the top." Eowyn looked to Marcus to gauge his reaction.

"You mean he went to see Selima?"

"Yep!"

Marcus was in mid-sentence when two soldiers burst through the door. Alarmed, Eowyn and the others jumped to their feet. The soldiers dressed in crimson red—their uniforms eerily mirrored those of the Liquidators—stood at attention and after a short pause, Selima entered the room.

"Is it true?" Marcus asked immediately as he glared in her direction.

"Well, hello to you too, Marcus. How are you feeling?"

"Selima, I asked you a question. Did you have anything to do with the attack on my home?"

"Please leave the room," she ordered. Her guards stepped outside, and the others followed once Marcus gave them an assuring head nod.

"Now, can you answer my question, Selima? Please tell me you didn't have anything to do with the attack."

"Not like you think." Selima looked to the ground like an ashamed child and brushed the carpet with her foot. "You know I would never hurt you or our friends."

"That isn't what I asked. Are you responsible for the attack on my home? Yes, or no?"

"Nobody was supposed to be hurt. They were simply instructed to arrest Waffa and that's it. I would never harm any of you. You know me."

"Do I? The Selima I know wouldn't have executed a citizen; the Selima I know wouldn't have kept the extermination camps open, and the Selima I know wouldn't have reopened the Coliseum! So, while I thought I knew you, while I thought I loved you, I wonder if I ever knew you at all."

Selima walked to the side of his bed, sat down, and took his hand. "I'm going to explain everything to you, Marcus. Maybe after you understand my motivation and intentions you'll understand."

4

HARROWING DISCOVERY

Leeba cradled Riya in her arms while her children, Gurr and Batya, gathered rocks on the shore of the Bentley River. In the weeks since Marcus's return from the Second Nill War, after days of deliberation, he decided to name his daughter Riya (Short for Maria). With the loss of Maria and Marcus hospitalized, both Leeba and Celeste served as her surrogate mother.

It had been numerous days since Leeba saw anyone when a glimpse of Eowyn sent a bolt of excitement pulsing through her. Raghba also came into view as they emerged from the wood line. Eowyn dropped her backpack, sprinted into Leeba's waiting arms, and ended the reunion with a long passionate kiss.

"You have no idea how much I have missed you!" They held each other for several minutes before Raghba interrupted.

"So, how is the world of motherhood treating both of you?"

"You know me; motherhood is what I do. I wouldn't have it any other way. At the same time, I am due for a major break. Celeste, Raghba, do you mind taking the kids to Marcus's place, so I can have some time with Eowyn?"

"Sure! Let's go kids." Raghba scooped Riya from Leeba's arms while Celeste corralled the others and headed towards Bentley's Fishery.

Leeba and Eowyn had just stepped into the wood line when Eowyn pressed her against an oak, slid her hands to the small of Leeba's back, and softly touched her lips to hers. "You have no idea how much I missed you! I couldn't get to sleep last night because all I could think about was holding you."

"Funny, I didn't get too much sleep myself. In fact, I have a surprise for you. Come with me!" She grabbed Eowyn's hand and guided her into the forest until they emerged in a clearing surrounded by trees and shrubs. A blanket was laid out with a picnic basket and a bottle of wine placed at the center.

"I knew you were going to be here sometime today, and I wanted to be ready."

"Ready for what is the question?" Eowyn flashed a devious smile, walked Leeba to the blanket, and sat down. Eowyn took off her boots, moved to her knees, unbuttoned her flannel shirt, and threw it to the ground. Leeba watched in awe, cupping a breast in each hand while she softly kneaded Eowyn's hardened nipples.

"I almost forgot how beautiful you are," Leeba attempted to lean forward but was pushed gently to her back.

"And I almost forgot how good your soft hands feel against my skin," Eowyn straddled Leeba's waist, leaned forward, and hovered over her. Her taut nipples lightly brushed against Leeba's while she nibbled on her lower lip spawning a spontaneous moan. Eowyn wiggled out of her jeans, while Leeba hurriedly undressed, slipped in behind Eowyn, and peppered her neck with playful kisses. Her hands stroked and prodded the length of Eowyn's lean thighs, over her well-developed abs, and finally, adventured to her hairy mound.

"Is this what you were dreaming about, baby?" She didn't answer but instead, let out a modest whimper as Leeba maneuvered her fingers, and opened her with one hand, while the other explored the steamy depths. She slowly stroked and hastened her efforts in response to Eowyn's whimpers until to Leeba's surprise, she felt her mons quake and her body shudder as she cried out.

Eowyn's legs were still shaky from the torrential release. Even several seconds after the first, many mini waves continued to rock her shores. "That was incredible! Now, let's see if I can do for you what you so magnificently did for me!"

Leeba laid back on the blanket. Eowyn pinned her hands above her head while she peppered her body with gentle kisses starting at the small of her neck, and slowly descending until contentedly saddled between her breasts.

"I'm so confused. Should I scale the peaks of Everest or venture south to the wilds of the down under?"

"I'm fine with either or if you're feeling adventurous, why not try both?"

Eowyn lightly ran her tongue up the side of her breast until she hovered over her beaded nipple. Leeba purred in reaction, but to her dismay, Eowyn's lips never made contact, instead, her hot breath careened over her sensitized skin adding to the anticipation.

Eowyn sensually nibbled and caressed until just above her sex. Again, her lips lightly grazed, this time just above her dark bush while her steamy breath toyed with and frustrated her lover even further. In frustration, Leeba took Eowyn's hand and tried to coax her to where she desired. "Please Eowyn! I need you to just touch me!"

She laughed and once again, moved so that she loomed over Leeba. "Be patient. I promise the anticipation won't hurt you. The anticipation will only serve to heighten your senses, so patience, please. I promise that you will be glad you were!"

Eowyn playfully kissed her nose, followed by her cheeks, and her forehead, and finally, their lips came together. Their tongues poked, prodded, and massaged as if involved in an elaborate dance while their breasts pressed together, nipple to nipple. When Eowyn finally worked her way between Leeba's sweltering thighs, she lightly probed which sent Leeba into an instantaneous climax. Too modest to cry out, Leeba discreetly whimpered as her body quaked then slowly transformed into a series of modest aftershocks.

They lay, their bodies entwined, staring at the stars as night set in.

"I love you, Leeba! I don't know what I would do without you."

"Ditto!" Leeba replied as the two dressed and reluctantly set off for Bentley's Fishery. "Do you think Marcus is going to be all right?" Leeba asked.

"He'll be fine. I mean, of course, he is going to have to grieve, but he hasn't much time for that since, if I know him right, he will be focused on finding Waffa. Now, if something happens to her, I don't know if he'll ever recover."

"And you? How are you holding up?" Leeba looked to Eowyn for a response, but she didn't answer.

"Are you all right, baby? I know how close you were with Janey."

"I loved her as my sister and would gladly have given my life for hers. I'll be okay though. As long as you are by my side, I can survive anything."

"Same here. I just worry about what's going to happen next. Someone kidnapped Waffa and is responsible for the death of Janey. Once Marcus finds out who, there will be hell to pay, and I don't want you trapped in the middle of a conflict."

Eowyn took a seat on the steps to Bentley's as Leeba scooted in behind her and started braiding her hair. "You know tomorrow is the funeral. Are you going to be, okay?"

"It'll be difficult, but I'll be all right. Just please be there. I'm going to need you every step of the way, especially since Pastor Neufeld wants me to give a eulogy."

"Do you know what you're going to say?"

"Whatever happens to come to mind. I could share a million stories about her; I just need to narrow them down to two or three of the most memorable, that's the hard part."

Tiny and Champ bee-bopped from the forest, ran to the girls, and took a seat next to them. Leeba scooped up Tiny and placed him in her lap.

"Leeba, what's that? Are you bleeding?" Alarmed, Eowyn jumped to her feet. "Where's that blood coming from?"

"That's not from me. Tiny's feet are covered in blood!"

Champ ran to the edge of the woods and looked back as if enticing them to follow. The two of them trotted off behind them and disappeared into the wood line in search of the source of the blood.

5

HORRIFYING REVELATION

"You've got to stop the madness, Selima! This isn't you! You are not a murderer, and you are not a tyrant. I know you better than that. I love you because of your kind heart, and I admire you for your wisdom and patience. Kidnapping, murdering—that's not you! So, please tell me you had nothing to do with the raid."

"I've never hidden my love for you, and I've openly solicited your love on many occasions. Of course, I had to come to terms with your marriage to Maria, but once she died, I anticipated that you and I would be together. You have told me on many occasions that you loved me and that you wanted to be with me, but instead, you married an enemy. You know Waffa is responsible for the murder of hundreds, probably thousands, of our fellow citizens and yet, you choose her over me. I have been patient, suppressed my emotions, and saved myself for you if a time were to arise for us to be together. Instead, you return home married to a murderous Stegapo agent. How do you think that made me feel? I can't believe you discarded me like a piece of garbage and aligned yourself with a person who is everything you have hated in the past. I just don't understand it, Marcus."

"And we will talk about that, but again, you are avoiding my question. Did you have anything to do with what happened at my house?"

You understand that your wife is guilty of heinous war crimes. As the leader of the Stegapo, she is responsible for thousands of deaths. She must be held responsible for her transgressions. So, yes, I did order my men to take her into custody, but nothing more."

"Are you aware of what your men did as a result of your orders?"

"They took Waffa into custody as I requested."

Marcus chuckled. "You mean to tell me you are unaware of what occurred as your people invaded our house? Right! How the hell do you think I got here, Selima?"

"I assumed you were here for your cancer treatments."

"No more beating around the bush, Selima. Because of your orders, Fila was murdered, Janey just died in the operating room, and I nearly died as a result of your orders. I thought we were your family, and I put my trust in you. Do you know how hard that is for me?"

Selima flushed, her face turned from a healthy pink to a whitewashed hue, and she froze as if she were surprised by the news.

"You put out an open contract on my family and are responsible for their deaths. Two people who loved you without reservation and you murdered them! You killed my little girl! So, whatever love I ever felt for you is gone. I loved a version of you that no longer exists. You are as evil as Abbas, Stanks, and the lengthy list of tyrants that proceeded them."

"I...Marcus...no! I distinctly told them nobody was to be harmed. Janey, Fila dead; that can't be!"

"I wish it weren't true, but they're gone. And what of Waffa? Have you killed her too?"

"No...I...Janey's dead? They killed her! Not my Janey. It can't be true. Nobody was to be harmed; I said that...Fila too?" Tears streamed as she tried to process the apparently, shocking news. Marcus simply assumed she had to know but from her reaction, he was convinced that she had no idea.

Selima stood and walked towards the door.

"What about Waffa, Selima?"

"I will set here free today. You can meet her at the capital." She stepped into the hallway, stopped, and faced Marcus. "I swear to you I said none of you were to be harmed. I loved Janey as a daughter and Fila was my friend. If you don't believe me that is fine because just like you claimed, I am responsible for the carnage. Your wife will be set free immediately; I will try to make amends. Just know Marcus, I loved you. I...I..uhh, she's really dead?"

Eowyn reentered the room upon Selima's departure. "Wow, she looked upset. Her guards had to assist her out of the hospital. What did you say?"

"I just asked her if she was responsible."

"And?"

"She did order the attack, but I honestly don't think she knew about what happened to Janey and Fila. She was genuinely shocked when I shared the news."

"That's not surprising. She never would've hurt them, especially Janey. You know that as well as I do."

"Nevertheless, she's responsible." Marcus slid to the edge of the bed and winced in pain. I've got to get to the capital. Can you help me?"

"You shouldn't be out of bed, bozo! Why do you need to go there anyway?"

"Selima is setting Waffa free. I need to be there. Now, can you help me get my pants on?"

"All right! Hold your horses, your highness! There, now sit down, and I'll put your shoes on."

"Wait here. I need to talk to one of the doctors. I'll be right back." Marcus hobbled into the hallway, took a left, and moved with conviction until entering one of the trauma rooms. He ravenously dug through the drawers and then pried open a metal cabinet door. "Ahh, there you are!" He slid a handful of syringes into his cargo pocket, opened one, filled it with morphine, and injected it into his arm. He stumbled, nearly falling to the floor but caught the edge of the counter. He grabbed four more vials and stuffed them into his pocket. The immense pain of his wounds eventually morphed into a dull ache.

Marcus peeked into the room. "Let's get on the road," he ordered and the two of them set off for the capital.

6

SURREPTITIOUS GATHERING

Leeba and Eowyn struggled to keep pace with the dogs. Having already traveled a few miles along the banks of the Bentley River, they lost sight of them for a while but each time the dogs circled back and encouraged them to keep moving forward. They traveled for hours until exhausted.

"Maybe this wasn't such a good idea." Leeba rubbed her arms trying to warm up.

"We'll set up camp here. I'll gather some wood while you find a good spot for us to sleep."

"You don't want to go back?"

"Absolutely, not! We traveled all this way, and we need to discover what these dogs are leading us to. So, camp out it is!"

Eowyn vanished into the woods and returned minutes later with an armful of twigs, and branches. "This ought to be enough to get a good fire going. How about getting an armful of pine straw that we can sleep on while I get a fire going?"

By the time Leeba returned, a fire was blazing. "Here, warm up by the fire. I'll finish preparing the bed." Tiny and Champ curled up next to Leeba by the fire just as Eowyn spread the last layer of pine straw and laid down. "The only thing we are missing is marshmallows, chocolate, and graham crackers!"

She glanced towards Leeba when she didn't answer, found her already asleep, and smiled. She gathered some more wood, stoked the fire, and was about to lay down when a sound caught her attention. Not a crisp, nearby sound, but a crackling of twigs and the shuffling of underbrush at a distance. First, she dismissed the noises as the creations of an animal. Perhaps a deer or a raccoon foraging for food, but when the sounds continued in rapid succession, she couldn't help but investigate. The sky was still dark, and she navigated by the light of the moon being careful not to broadcast her position. The closer she got to the intonations, the humming of distant voices, the more alarmed she became. Eowyn stealthily worked her way to just outside the perimeter of the camp taking cover behind a rocky outcrop. A group of soldiers, many surprisingly cloaked in Nill uniforms, stood at a fire. There was an entire encampment; hundreds of soldiers bivouacked as if preparing for an invasion. While a large group gathered near the fire, others roamed the perimeter while others appeared to be beating on a heavy bag. Eowyn maneuvered to a better vantage point. She managed to move an additional five hundred feet or so when realized what she thought to be punching bags were human beings. There were four that she could see, each bound between trees. Two of the victims appeared to be dead while the other two were badly beaten. The thugs seemed to be focused on one individual, who was especially belligerent. Eowyn could tell the person was small by the silhouette, but at the same time spunky.

"You better hope I don't get loose. If I do, I swear you are all dead!" she screamed just before she was kicked in the face and fell silent. Content that they had shut the prisoner up, the soldiers walked away laughing.

Eowyn was about to leave when she realized there was something familiar about the voice. It was a voice she hadn't heard in some time, and she couldn't quite place it. Carefully, she maneuvered along the edge of the perimeter until just behind the detainees. She crawled forward on her hands and knees until next to the unconscious victim. At first, she was unable to discern who it might be through the bloodied and swollen face, but something about her hair, a lone hairpin laced through her disheveled dark black hair sent Eowyn into a panic. She quickly removed a buck knife from her ankle sheath, cut her loose, and dragged her into the woods. She managed to drag her a hundred feet when two soldiers moved towards them. Not sure if detected, she huddled behind a grove of Canadian Hemlock and hoped for the best. The two soldiers stopped just five feet from them and lit a cigarette.

"That traitor bitch isn't my president!" One man boasted while the other shook his head in agreement. "I don't know if I can go on pretending to be loyal to that woman. I'm going to make that whore my wife once she is dethroned and then I'll show her whose boss!"

"Be patient. It's just a matter of time and we will rid ourselves of her. Once we turn her people against her, nobody will care if she is assassinated. The attack on Martyreon and his family is sure to turn many against her. Once she's forced out of office, they will be in turmoil and will be primed for a government takeover."

"Who in their right mind would ever put a woman in a leadership position anyway? The people of this cooperative are idiots. A female president, not on my watch!" The two stubbed their cigarettes out and walked away.

Eowyn slowly backed away until feeling safe, she picked up Sophi, threw her over her shoulder, and trudged back to Leeba.

"Who's that?" Leeba ran to Eowyn and helped her lower the individual to the ground.

"Nil!" Eowyn tried to catch her breath. "Gotta get...out a here...quick!"

"Why? What's going on?"

"No time. Gather your things while I put the fire out." She shoveled handfuls of dirt on the fire, slung Sophi over her shoulder, and they rushed towards home with the dogs trailing behind.

"What happened?"

"Not now! We'll speak once we get to Bentley's. Hurry now!"

After several hours, they arrived safely and went inside just as the first signs of dawn approached. Leeba fell back into a chair exhausted as she tried to catch her breath. "So, who is this?"

Eowyn laid her on the couch and started removing her clothing to check for wounds. Leeba, I need your help. Get me some warm water and rags."

"You didn't answer my question. Who is this?"

"Dam it, Leeba! Just get the water."

Leeba was leaving the room when Eowyn spoke up.

"Sophi, this is Sophi!" Eowyn yelled as she performed triage. Her abdomen was beaten black and blue and at least one rib protruded, a bright white shard poked through just below her left breast.

Leeba kneeled next to Eowyn and placed a basin of warm water with rags next to her. "What happened?"

"Not now, Leeba. Pull her pants off while I try to stop the bleeding from her head." Eowyn sifted through her thick hair and found a deep gash, two inches long at the back of her head. She cleaned the dirt and debris away and applied a pressure bandage. "Shit! This is bad Leeba. We have to get her to the hospital. Her skull is fractured. She wiped the blood from Sophi's face and applied ice to her swollen eyes.

They wrapped her in a sheet and hauled her off. An hour later, they arrived at Mercy General. "We need help here. Hurry, she's got a bad head wound. Nurse Houlihan rolled a gurney to them.

"She's got at least one broken rib, a major head wound, and I think a fracture of the skull." Eowyn finished.

"Anything else?" Houlihan asked as she carted her towards the critical care.

"No," Eowyn answered but she was cut off by Leeba.

"Yes, she's been raped!"

Eowyn took a deep breath, and despite her best effort, tears rained down her face. "Those fucking bastards!"

"Who?" Leeba asked. "Who did this?"

"The Nill and maybe others."

"No, the Nill are gone."

"No, they aren't. They've been right in front of us the whole time. There's a Nill Army just north of us. Hundreds of them, maybe more. I recognized some of them as part of the Nill refugee population that we took in after the war. They did this. There were some of our people working with them!"

"You're sure?"

"Dam it, Leeba! Of course, I saw them!"

"That's the second time you yelled at me. I'm just trying to understand. So, please slow down and tell me what we need to do."

Eowyn took a deep breath. "I have to notify the government, and I need to speak with Selima. You stay with Sophi. I'm heading to the capitol." Eowyn paused. "I'm sorry for yelling, but those degenerates hurt Sophi! Take care of her Leeba. I'll be back soon." She kissed Leeba on the forehead, sprinted out the door, and disappeared into the early morning light enroute to a meeting with the president.

7

FALL OF AN ICON

Eowyn was about to knock when she heard voices inside. She listened intently.

"You told me you would have her for me. Was that a lie too? Is everything you say a lie?"

"I sent my men for her. She should be here any moment, I promise, Marcus. Please be patient!"

"I just don't know what happened to you. What caused you to turn your back on everyone who loved you? You were family and what are you now? A murdering tyrant, that's what you are! I hate you!"

Selima collapsed to the floor sobbing as Eowyn burst through the door. "Stop Marcus! That is enough. Selima would not nor did she order the attack on your house! She loved Janey and Fila. I know this because I've seen how she cared for them over the past couple of years. Stop tormenting her!"

"Her orders are what got them killed Eowyn; that is not up for debate!"

"Shut up and listen. Both of you. Selima, stop the sniveling. Marcus, be quiet and listen. Last night I discovered a band of rebels within the cooperative."

"Who..."

"Zip it, Marcus, until I'm finished. The group is large. At least a few hundred, maybe many more. I overheard a conversation between two insurgents that shed some light on what is happening to Selima."

Selima raised her head suddenly interested in what Eowyn had to say. She secretly planned on stepping down as the Cooperative President as soon as that evening in response to the news that she indirectly was responsible for the murder of Fila and Janey. She planned on disappearing from the Cooperative altogether, a sort of self-imposed excommunication as punishment for her crimes although lately, her mind wandered to taking much more drastic measures.

"I don't remember exactly what was said, but the gist of the conversation revolved around a conspiracy to turn the people against Selima. They spoke specifically about the attack on your home, Marcus, and how the murders would be sure to turn the people against her. This group is intent on destroying the government and putting its leadership in place."

"Anything else?" Marcus asked as he glanced at Selima, ashamed of some of the things he said. Selima continued to sob and wouldn't look in his direction.

"I didn't hear anything else about their plans, but I do have some more bad news. Sophi..." she paused.

"She should be visiting her family."

"Apparently, she never made it. I found her brutally beaten. She's at the hospital and in bad shape. There were others there too; many were already dead. I only managed to free Sophi."

Marcus shot out the door without saying a word while Selima burst into tears. He sat in the lobby trying to gather his thoughts until he heard someone call his name.

"Marcus!"

Waffa was brought into the corridor with a guard holding each arm. He rushed towards her until they motioned for him to stop. One of the guards uncuffed Waffa and shoved her to Marcus.

"Keep your dog on a leash."

Waffa lunged into his arms. "I didn't think I would ever see you again, but you came for me...you saved me."

"Of course, I did! I would walk through the fires of hell for you, my love. Let's get home."

At the same time, Eowyn consoled Selima. "It's okay. Why don't you take the day to get some rest? Come on, I'll walk with you." They crossed the courtyard and entered her home. Eowyn helped her to bed, pulled the curtains shut, and turned out the lights. She grabbed a bottle of water from her fridge and was about to leave when a piece of paper, propped up on the counter, caught her attention.

My Dearest Marcus and Family,

I've become everything I have come to despise. I've murdered others; my family members whom I loved as my own, but please know that I never intended for anyone to be harmed. At the same time, I know my actions led to both the death of Janey and Fila. Their deaths are devastating and unforgivable. No matter what I do, I cannot right this wrong. I am guilty, and I must be punished. If you can find it in your heart, please provide me with a proper burial. I hope one day all of you can forgive me.

I cannot bear to live while knowing I murdered my darling, Janey, and that I killed my dear friend, Fila. I am so sorry for the pain I have caused all of you. I especially regret the pain I caused you, Marcus. I just wanted a chance to love you and the pain of losing you to another was more than I could bear. I hope one day all of you can forgive me.

Selima

Next to the letter was a bottle of Diazepam. Eowyn emptied the contents of the bottle into the sink and washed them down the drain.

"I was hoping you wouldn't find that."

"Were you really going to end it?"

"I have nothing to live for, Eowyn. If my family turned on me and Marcus already has, I have nothing left to live for. I was going to do it tonight. I want to die or at least, I thought I did."

Eowyn took a seat at the counter. "Come here!"

Selima leaned against the counter.

"I said come here, girl." Selima scooted next to her, and Eowyn took her into her arms. "You have a lot to live for. I don't know what I would do without you. You're my sister. Besides, just because one person decides not to love you, doesn't mean that others don't. Your entire family loves you. I love you and believe it or not, Marcus loves you too, and he always will. What kept you two apart was not a lack of love but was simply a result of circumstances. The timing was off and sometimes that is all it takes to extinguish a flame. Not to say the love is no longer there, but it was simply deferred by bad timing. I'm going to throw this letter away, and we will never talk about it again, okay? So, what are you going to do now?"

"I'm going to resign after I appoint a new president. I am not cut out for leadership. I don't have the stomach for it. I think I'm going to retire to my home and go fishing!" She smiled.

"Whatever you decide to do, I will be by your side no matter what. Shoot, I may even take up fishing as a hobby!"

Selima giggled. "Thanks! I hate to do this, but I need to make an announcement and speak with the Vice President."

"You're sure you're, okay?"

"Fine now. I promise."

"I want you to come to my house tonight. I don't want you to be alone. We'll have a sleepover and maybe a bottle of wine or two if you like."

"Sounds marvelous! I'll see you then."

Selima stepped into the bathroom, refreshed her makeup, and slammed the door behind her as she departed.

8

BUSTLING BOUNTY /
MURDEROUS PLAN

Marcus brought Waffa to the hospital for an exam before getting her home. While she was with the doctor, he checked on Sophi. "Hey Angela, any word?"

"She's still in surgery, but it doesn't look good. Her skull is fractured, and she has a brain hemorrhage but worse than that, it appears they strangled her to an inch of death repeatedly. They deprived her of oxygen, and she is showing diminished brain activity. If she lives, Sophi will never be the same again. She will require around-the-clock care. I don't mean to be callous, but she may be better off if she dies. I say this with a great amount of dismay. I love Sophi too, Marcus."

"But there is a chance?"

"Chance of what?"

"That Sophi may live and be somewhat functional?"

"Yes, there is a small chance, but you're not listening. She'll require constant care. Besides, she'll be on life support and according to the doctor, she's more than likely going to die during the night. Dr. Sheperd recommends that we end life support at this time."

"Who decides about life support?"

"Her advanced life directive lists you and Maria as her Guardians. Since Maria is no longer with us, the decision is yours."

"Well, this is one of the easiest choices I'll ever have to make. If there is a chance that she recovers, I decide that she stays on life support. She's a fighter and if anyone can survive, it will be her. I'm not giving up."

"I'll let the doctor know. By the way, I heard Waffa is back."

"Yes, they are checking her out now. She's due in less than a month."

"How is she?"

"She seems to be in good health. Selima saw to it that they didn't hurt her. She regrets what she did."

"And what about murdering Fila and Janey? Does she regret that too?"

"She wasn't responsible, but I'll explain later. Where can I find Sergeant Ballard?"

"He's busy at the capitol."

"Do me a favor. Can you have him stop by my house tomorrow around noon? I'd like you to be there too if possible. Tell Ballard it's important. I'll explain everything tonight. Maybe the two of you can stay for lunch?"

Marcus trudged towards the doorway. "I'm going to check on Waffa. So, I'll see the two of you tomorrow, right?"

"We'll be there."

Marcus was back at the OB-GYN within a couple of minutes. Nurse Houlihan was just completing an ultrasound when he walked in. "Everything is right on schedule. The baby is fully developed and ready when the moment comes. If you go more than two more weeks, the doctor suggests inducing labor."

Waffa smiled at Marcus. "You hear that. We're going to be parents again."

"Is there anything I can do to bring labor on now? I am more than ready to have this child."

"Just be active and on your feet, but don't overdo it! And if that doesn't work, Dr. House always said that sex will do the trick."

"Waffa smiled and looked to Marcus."

"That's what got us into this situation in the first place, sweetheart, but if you're willing, I guess I can tough it out."

Both Waffa and Houlihan giggled. "So, I will see you next week, same time, Waffa. Take care in the meantime."

"We're all finished?"

"Yep! We'll need to see you at the same time next week. Remember to take your prenatal vitamins and no strenuous activities other than...well, you know. Catch you guys later."

Houlihan closed the door behind her leaving Marcus and Waffa alone. It was the first time they had found themselves alone since she was set free. Waffa cupped Marcus's cheeks in her hands. "My darling, I was so desperate without you. I was beginning to lose hope and wondered if I would ever see you again. How did you convince her to set me free?"

"She decided on her own. She felt guilty."

"She regrets what she did." Marcus hesitated for a moment as if he had something else to say.

"What is it, Marcus? I can always tell when you have something on your mind. What aren't you telling me?"

"I want you to stay seated for a minute while I give you some horrendous news. Wait, maybe I should just save this for when we get home." Marcus regretted bringing up something of the magnitude of what he had to tell her before they arrived home.

"You already have me curious. I am prepared. Let me hear the news."

"The night you were kidnapped, others were harmed; in fact, two people died."

"Who Marcus, who?"

"Fila and Janey. They're both gone. Our baby girl is gone!"

Her eyes suddenly welled, and then after a few minutes, the tears were replaced by a ravenous rage. "I'm going to kill her; that woman will pay for her treachery!"

"Wait. It wasn't her fault. She was framed by some new Resistance Army. They wanted us to lose faith in her as a leader. She had no idea that anyone else was going to be harmed."

"Who?"

"All I know is that Eowyn came upon a large force in the western section of the Cooperative and overheard some soldiers talking. She rescued Sophi while she was there."

"Sophi? What happened to Sophi?"

"She was beaten to within an inch of her life. She probably came upon them just like Eowyn did. Anyway, she is on life support."

"Will she be all right?"

"Only time will tell." Marcus purposely kept the rest from her. He had already burdened her with the awful news of Janey and Fila. He wanted to feed her one tidbit of bad news at a time.

The two had traveled a couple of miles when they ran into Private Sakato and Nadia Romonov heading in the opposite direction.

"Where are you headed, ladies?"

"The entire military has been summoned to headquarters for a presidential announcement. Sounded pretty important. Did you happen to see Specialist Acacia? She should be ahead of us."

"No, we must have missed her."

"By the way, Marcus, I was sorry to hear about Janey and Fila. They'll be missed!"

"Thanks. They were amazing people, and I like to think they are here looking over all of us."

"I wouldn't doubt that at all. How are you feeling, Waffa?" Ayase asked as she dug through her backpack for something.

"I'm fine. Should have the baby in the next couple of weeks."

Ayase pulled something from her bag and handed it to Waffa. "These are for the baby. I wasn't sure if you were having a boy or a girl, so I made them in light blue with some yellow striping." Waffa held up a pair of knitted baby booties.

"How sweet of you. They're perfect. I didn't know you knew how to knit."

"I have many hobbies but could never share them due to combat. Knitting doesn't come in handy during battle, but now that I have more time on my hands, I'm returning to some of my old interests. I'm in the middle of making the baby a blanket, but I ran out of supplies. It's difficult to get things like yarn around here."

"I tell you what. The two of you stop by my house tomorrow around noon—I will be meeting with some others—and

I will give you the yarn that Maria left behind. She also left a half-completed blanket behind that you are welcome to complete if you have the time. I can't quite tell what the symbol is that she was incorporating into the Afghan. Anyway, she has quite a bit of yarn if you want it. So, can you two make it?"

"Sure! Can we expect lunch?"

"Of course."

"We'll fill you in. See you tomorrow!" The two continued towards the capitol while Marcus and Waffa arrived home within the hour.

Waffa plopped down on the couch. "So, some traitors are plotting against the capitol?"

"I don't exactly know what their motive is, but I intend to find out. Their primary goal is getting Selima out of the office, which will happen any time now. After that, who knows what motivates them." Marcus put a kettle over the fire and pulled the tea from the cabinet.

"I wonder where Leeba and the kids are?" Waffa looked around at the empty house.

"Probably at her place. Eowyn mentioned she wanted to get some things done at home. Maybe we'll see the kids tomorrow."

"Then we have the night to ourselves?"

"Sure do. What do you think we ought to do?" Marcus smiled at her while he poured two cups of tea.

"You heard what Nurse Houlihan said. As much as I don't want to—she smiled deviously—I guess we should do whatever we can to get this baby into the world. We must do our part!"

"Baby, you know I would like nothing more, but I am still weak and sore from the surgery. You know me, I never say no, but I am hurting."

"All you have to do is sit and relax. I'll do the work. You know how much this pregnancy has my hormones out of control. I need you, and I mean right now. Do you get me?"

"I thought the last thing on your mind would be sex. You just got out of a couple of weeks of confinement."

"That's exactly why I need you. I had nothing to do there except think about you, and I am sure you can imagine where my mind traveled to on those long, lonely nights, right?"

"You're a nymphomaniac. You know that, right?"

"I'm not sure if that tag is applicable. A nympho screws not just their mate, but out of desperation and will often screw random strangers to fulfill their desires. I only crave you."

Marcus sat down and handed her a cup of steaming tea. Waffa grabbed his hand and placed it on her belly. "Do you feel the baby kicking?"

Sure enough, after a few seconds, he felt the baby kick and tumble. "I think the baby is getting as impatient as we are."

"As much as I want to have this baby, I'm scared, Marcus. I've been told childbirth, while amazing, is also very painful. It's scary to think a child, a real human child that weighs anywhere from 6-20 pounds is going to fit out of such a small space."

"I'll be there with you the entire time if that means anything. I swear I would gladly take the pain away from you if I could. You know, if birth were left to the men, the population would be much less than it is. I'm not too proud to say that men claim to be macho and tough but in reality, most are wimps when it comes to pain. Women get a bad rap."

"You speak with a wisdom well beyond your years, sweetheart." Waffa held Marcus's hand and pulled him to his feet. "Come on!"

"I never thought I would see this place again, but my mind was here repeatedly during my captivity. Help me to stage the scene. The bed here and you—she grabbed him by the shoulders and sat him on the bed. All right, scoot up and put your head on the pillow. Good, now take off your shirt."

"Oh, I see what you're up to!" Marcus smiled. "You first then."

"You don't want to see my whale of a body!"

"Oh, yes, I do. You look magnificent. I'm as attracted to you now as I've ever been. That baby bump is a major turn-on and besides that, you're beautiful to me whether you're a hundred or three hundred pounds!"

"Okay then." She removed her shirt and threw it at Marcus. "Your turn!"

"Oh no, you still have on a brassiere. I won't take my shirt off until you remove your bra." Waffa threw it to the side."

"Yowza! You are more beautiful every time I see you."

"Be quiet. You're just trying to make me feel better about myself."

"Honestly! You look amazing."

Marcus stripped off his shirt. "Your move."

Waffa slid her pants off and Marcus did the same. "Now your panties."

"You're going to have to work for that but not too hard, I promise." She crawled into bed and snuggled up next to him.

"You know, you are gorgeous." He swept her hair from her face.

"I don't feel it."

"You're like a flower in a barren field. I could pick you out from a mile away."

"That's kind of cheesy."

She hedged over him. "Does this hurt you?"

"No, not too bad."

"Are you up to a little fun?"

"I'm up for all the fun you can manage. What do you have in mind?"

She unbuttoned his pants, lowered his zipper, and tugged his pants off. "What do you think?"

"Wait! Will you do me a favor?"

"It depends. What?"

Just stand back for a minute and let me take in your beauty. She peeled off her panties.

"You are the most scrumptious pregnant lady I have seen or ever imagined seeing in my lifetime. Come here, baby."

She crawled to him; her breasts hovered over his chest. She whimpered slightly as she lowered herself onto him and began undulating.

"Have I told you that you are incredible?"

"Yes, yes, incredible." She plumbed with a desperation not cognizant of anything other than bringing pleasure to herself. Just days ago, she cried in a cold, dark cell wondering if she would ever see him again, and now she was closer to him than imaginable.

They were joined as one and she intended on making the moment one that Marcus would never forget.

"I'm...not hurt...ing you...am I?" She gathered her hair and flipped it over her shoulder; a bead of sweat slipped from her brow, meandered down her nose, and dripped onto him. Marcus didn't answer, but instead, Waffa felt his body spasm and his warmth fill her.

"You, okay, baby?"

"Better than okay."

She plumbed with purpose trying to douse the fire that bloomed inside her. Her pace hastened. She cried out in a language Marcus didn't recognize and her nails dug into his chest.

"Uhh, Waffa, you're hurting me a little."

He realized that she didn't hear a word he was saying. Instead, she gyrated her hips wildly, back and forth. She felt the storm wash over her, unlike anything she had ever experienced before. Her breathing became choppy, she was unaware of anything, or anyone around her; she completely focused on dousing the fire rising inside her. Moments later, a tsunamic wave inundated her every thought; her body shook uncontrollably, and once spent, she collapsed onto Marcus's chest.

"Now if that didn't cause you to go into labor, nothing will." Marcus slid out from under her and lay next to her.

"I guess..." Waffa took a deep breath, "...we'll just have to keep trying then."

The next morning, Waffa woke to an empty bed, a note left on the pillow. She quickly skimmed what he had written and jumped into the shower. She had just turned the water on when Leeba and the children trounced inside. Leeba stuck her head through the doorway. "We're home, Waffa. I hope you had a nice evening alone with your husband."

"Yes, we had a great night. Thanks!"

"I bet you did! Where's your better half?"

"Went to find Ferris and speak with some people at the capitol. He's hoping to catch up with your wife there as well. Is Eowyn at the capitol?"

"She's been at the hospital with Sophi."

"Any change?"

"No, but she's hanging in there. Her blood pressure has leveled off and her brain activity has increased, which is a great sign. Doctors are optimistic, but at the same time, she isn't out of the woods yet. What we need to keep in mind is that she will never be the Sophi we once knew. Well, nobody can predict how she will recover cognitively, but doctors leave no doubt that she will be handicapped physically. We're all going to have to be there for her."

Marcus navigated the forest and somehow managed to get disoriented. The trip that should have taken an hour evolved into a multi-hour journey. He was growing increasingly frustrated when he came upon a large encampment. At first, he hovered just outside using the foliage to stay concealed, but after careful deliberations, he marched into the perimeter. Three soldiers drew their weapons and took him into custody.

"What business do you have here?" The larger of the three inquired.

"I'm lost and was fortunate enough to come upon your camp. Who's in command?"

"Hang on!" One of the soldiers frisked, cuffed him, then escorted him to what appeared to be a bunker lined with sandbags.

"Are you out here for training purposes?" Marcus asked despite already knowing they were there to create chaos and unrest.

"Yes, training exercises. By the way, are you Martyreon? You look like him."

"Wow, I didn't know I was so popular. Yes, I'm Marcus. Your name?"

"Sanders. Private Sanders. Good to meet you."

"Why the cuffs?"

"He was about to reply when he was summoned inside the tent."

A woman sat in a chair, her feet resting on her desk. Marcus recognized her as one of Sergeant Major King's soldiers. "Acacia, right." The last time I saw you was during the Second Nill War. You were a specialist back then not a captain."

"You have a good memory, Martyreon. Nice to see you again. How did you find us?"

"It's embarrassing. I was taking a shortcut to the capital and got lost. After a couple of hours, I ended up here. Are all of you on a training exercise or something?"

"I'm glad you found us. I've been wanting to talk to you."

"Take the cuffs off him and leave," she ordered. The guard did so and left.

"Here I am. What do we need to discuss?"

"Do you agree with what the president has been doing?"

"Some things, yes, some things, no. I think she made a huge mistake keeping the Coliseum and extermination camps open. I also think she made a horrific error in judgment when she had the citizen executed during her inauguration."

"Well then, we seem to agree that she shouldn't be in power."

"You're making a giant leap there, Acacia. I think Selima has made some mistakes, but underneath, she truly believes she is working to make the Cooperative better."

"I see. Well, our militia believes she has overstepped her authority, and we are intent on removing her from office and electing a new president as soon as possible."

"I hate to be the bearer of bad news, but if your primary function is to usurp her position, you're too late. Selima resigned yesterday. The Vice President is currently in charge until a new election can be held. You could add your candidate to the ballot once the election is announced."

"She resigned?"

"Yes, mam. She will be retiring to her home. She no longer wants anything to do with politics, and I think she made a wise choice."

"Great news, but her resignation does not exonerate her past actions. We are going to see to it that she pays for her murderous ways. As a community, we will bring her to justice. We will not be satisfied until she is held accountable."

"And what do you mean by accountable? What is going to make your people happy?"

"Death!"

"Why can't you just be happy that she resigned? She is trying to make amends for her error in judgment. I for one, wish her my best. Keep in mind, not a single leader has gone through a term in office without making at least one major gaffe."

Acacia looked Marcus up and down. "I am unsure what to think of you, Martyreon. My mentor looked up to you, but I wonder if King was mistaken. He told me that you are willing to see things through to the end, but now you are hesitant to eliminate Selima. What am I to do?"

"What do you mean? Am I your captive?"

"For now. You will be free within the confines of our community, but you will not leave until I decide the proper disposition."

"Can I ask one more question?"

"Proceed!"

"Who are all the people being tortured at the south side of the camp? Is that what your 'community' does with anyone that doesn't agree with you? It seems like your actions are just as destructive if not worse than what Selima did."

"Get him out of here. He is not to leave, so keep him under surveillance."

"Listen, Acacia, I didn't mean to offend you in any way. Sergeant Major King thought very highly of you. What do you think he would do if in your situation?"

"Take him away!" she ordered.

9

FORCED AFFAIR

Ferris fought his way through a wayward throng of Stalkers and arrived at Bentley's to find Eowyn, Leeba, and Waffa sitting on the front porch while the kids and dogs rambled in the yard.

"Hey, wadies! Is Ceweste awound hewe?"

"No, but she's been looking for you. She's probably at your house about now. Where have you been anyway? You've been gone for days."

"Weww, wike I towd aww of you befowe, I went to speak with Sewima. She didn't know about the attack. She just owdewed Waffa to be taken into custody. Anyway, she wesigned. Thewe's going to be anothew ewection next week. Fouw peopwe awweady wegistewed as candidates. By the way, whewe's Mawcus?"

"Should be at the capitol by now. You didn't see him?"

"No. I must have passed wight on by him. When's he supposed to be back?"

"He's supposed to meet with Sergeant Ballard and some other military leaders to discuss the situation in...let's see," she looked at her watch "...in a little over an hour."

"What situation?"

"You need to speak to Eowyn. She discovered some sort of rogue force camped in the forest. By the way, did you hear about Sophi?"

"What about hew?"

"As I said, Eowyn found this force and they had prisoners and were torturing them. Eowyn rescued Sophi, but she was beaten badly. She's at the hospital now."

"Who awe these peopwe?"

"She wasn't too sure other than they were plotting to overthrow Selima. They were responsible for the attack on Marcus's home and were accountable for both Janey's and Fila's death. They were trying to set up Selima."

"Awe they Niww?"

"A mixture of Nill refugees and disheartened citizens of the Cooperative. At least a few hundred according to Eowyn."

"Hewe we go again! We need to addwess this issue head-on. The wonger we wet it festew, the lawgew the gwoup is going to become. I teww you what. I'm going to go see Ceweste, but I'ww be back for the meeting." Ferris set off immediately.

Marcus walked the perimeter several times first, to determine the size of their force, and second, to provide a mental image of the camp set up. After several laps, he determined Acacia's force to be two to three hundred well-equipped rebels. On his third lap, he stopped and spoke with three prisoners, each badly abused. They claimed that approximately three days ago they were simply walking through the forest when they were captured. Sophi was with them.

"She resisted and no matter what we said, she would not stop until the soldiers beat her until she was unconscious. This happened nearly every day until we thought she was dead. Some girl came in late at night and carried her off. Did she survive?" One of the prisoners asked.

"She's hospitalized in serious condition, but I have a feeling she'll recover soon."

"I hope she does. She is one of the most stubborn and yet, one of the bravest people I've ever known. She refused to provide them with any information. She even kicked the ass of one soldier who got too close."

"Yes, my sister can be feisty! Listen, if I can get out of here, remember, I will be back for you one way or another. In the meantime, just be strong and do what you have to survive."

The guard grabbed Marcus by the shoulder and dragged him away. "Enough conferencing with the enemy. Captain Acacia wants to see you. Follow me."

Marcus buttoned his shirt and pulled up his saggy jeans before he entered. He had no idea what she might do, but he hoped that she would release him. In any case, he knew that she was in charge and knew that he was just as close to being beaten and bound as he was to being set free.

"Hey, Acacia! So, what are your plans for me? I'm going to be late for a meeting if you don't let me go. I would like to get home to my family."

"What is it with you and women? I see the way women react to you. You're a bad man and your bad-boy ways for some reason or another seem to draw women like flies. Even as I stand here trying to decide your fate, I'm drawn in by your charm. Normally, I would just brush it off as I've been alone for weeks, and I need to douse my passions, but even back then, during the Nill war, you piqued my interest. The way you strutted around the battlefield like you didn't have a care in the world. I told myself then I knew better than to fall for your cocky self, and I did fine at the time, but now, I'm afraid I haven't been quite as successful repelling your Spanish Fly-like intrigue. So, what am I to do with you?"

Marcus's mind searched for a solution. Life would be so much easier if I were single, but I am married to the woman of my dreams. On the other hand, Waffa always told me to do whatever was necessary to stay alive when my life was in danger. After an extended pause, he stepped towards her.

She held up her hand, palm out. "I didn't give you permission to invade my space."

"If you didn't want me closer, you would have called the guard, right? You can play coy with me, but I see right through your facade. He cocked his hips and looked her in the eye. "What do I need to do for you to set me free?"

"Who said I'm letting you go? Maybe, I'll keep you for myself." She giggled. "What are you looking at anyway?"

"I was just admiring that beauty mark between your cleavage." He stepped closer. So, will I be set free?"

"Only if you earn it!" She placed her hands on his hips. She stood nearly the same height as Marcus and weighed maybe all of a hundred and thirty pounds on a precipitous day. Her long red hair ran down the length of her back and stopped at her firm, round ass. She had to know how good she looked. Her full red lips shimmered mesmerizing Marcus as she nudged into his personal space. Marcus had no idea why she showed any interest in him, but at the same time, he was glad because her attraction was possibly a ticket to freedom.

"I'm waiting for your answer." His lips brushed against her forehead as he spoke.

"Naturally—I'm not a tyrant! You will have to earn it though." She hardly had time to finish her thought. Marcus slid his hand into her camo pants, pushed aside her panties, and slid two fingers into her while he lightly stroked the fleshy knob at the top of her sex with his thumb. Acacia let out an unexpectedly loud moan as she ground against his thigh.

"Captain, is everything okay in there?"

"Yes, fantastic. We are in the middle of some serious negotiations here, so do not interrupt. Understood? I'll call you when you are needed!"

"Yes, mam!"

"Is that what we are doing, negotiating?"

"Of course!" She stepped back, unbuttoned her shirt, and threw it aside, leaving her bare chest open for examination. "You like?"

Marcus wanted to keep the encounter as impersonal as possible. He reminded himself he was only acting in this way to gain his freedom, but, at that moment, he began to feel guilty. He didn't remember ever seeing tits quite as beautiful as hers. They were large, each the size of a well-ripened cantaloupe. Full, round, and accentuated by large areolas that nearly blended with her light pink porcelain skin and pencil eraser nipples that stood erect. She knew she was playing with a full deck and wasn't afraid to show it.

Marcus tried to slow things down. He was beginning to lose faith in himself. "So, Acacia, why?"

"Why what?" She started to unbutton Marcus's pants as she spoke.

"Whoa! Slow it down! I want to know why you are doing what you're doing?"

"That's obvious, silly! I need some attention. I already told you it's been a long time for me, and I need to release some stress."

"I didn't mean that." She hedged his pants down while he spoke. "I mean why are you starting another..." Marcus gasped as she took him into her mouth. "...why another war?"

He didn't want to enjoy it, but she was masterful. She brought him to the edge. Just one more contact, one more touch of her lips, and he wouldn't be able to stop himself, but she sensed he was close, stopped, and lay on the large Persian Rug that lined the floor.

"It's not what I want but what my people want. I was just voted into office not long ago after our previous leader was killed by a Stalker. I truly want peace just like most others. Once Selima is killed, I can raise the idea of peace but not until I present her head on a platter."

She fanned her legs apart. "I don't have all day sailor! Please me." Marcus wanted nothing more than to be inside her, but the guilt would have been too much for him. Instead, without much of a choice, he put a hand on each thigh, spread her legs wide, and delved into her. He knew she was close when she stood and leaned over her desk."

He didn't have to be told twice; he was all in. In one swift motion, he sunk into her.

Marcus emerged from the tent twenty minutes later with Acacia at his side.

"He is to be set free and given unobstructed travel to his home."

"What if she is already dead? What if I discover that Selima is already dead or if she's killed her before you get the chance?"

"Why would you want to kill her in the first place?"

"She invaded my home, killed my daughter and a dear friend, and put me in the hospital for a few days." He knew she wasn't responsible, but he didn't want Acacia to know that he knew of her plan to undermine Selima's leadership. She may be dead already. My friend Ferris was on the job even before I got out of the hospital." Marcus was devising a plan as he spoke. He needed to find a way to appease Acacia while at the same time, keeping Selima safe and unharmed.

Captain Acacia thought for a moment. "We want peace as much as anyone else. Once Selima is confirmed dead, I will negotiate but with you alone."

Marcus was led to the outskirts of the perimeter and set free. He rushed towards home hoping that he was able to meet with the others before they left.

The minute he walked inside, Marcus headed to his room and foraged through his dresser drawer. He removed a Remington .38 special and slid it into his waistband.

"What's that for?" The voice startled him.

"Just in case I run into any trouble. I'm glad you're here. Do you have a minute to talk before I begin the meeting?"

"I always have time for you, my love."

Marcus walked into the living room to find not just Sergeant Ballard, but four or five other soldiers: Private Sakato, Nadia Romonov, and many others gathered inside.

"Good afternoon, everyone. Sorry, I am late, but to be honest, I was out gathering intel on the rogue force that has been the talk of the Cooperative lately. Honestly, my goal this morning wasn't to come into contact with the rather large force, but I got lost. I tried to take a shortcut and ended up being taken prisoner. That's why I am late."

The room was filled with idle chatter.

"What is their objective?"

"Please, indulge me as I try to explain. Their leader is someone you may be familiar with. Her name is Simone Acacia."

"Do you mean Specialist Acacia?" Ballard inquired.

"Exactly! Although she is no longer 'Specialist' Acacia; she claims to be 'Captain' Acacia.'"

Again, the room was filled with persistent chatter. Marcus opened a bottle of water, took a swig, and sat down waiting for a lull in the talking.

Eowyn stood while Selima sat at her side. "Marcus, what are their intentions? Do they plan on attacking our Cooperative or do they simply want to begin a community of their own?"

Acacia shared with me that they simply want the president, or rather, the ex-president, to resign..." He paused to allow for the room to quiet again while he positioned himself next to Selima as a show of support. "The controversial part of their plan is that they not only want her to resign but also demand she be executed for, as they put it, her tyranny. I will not permit them or anyone else to harm her!" He placed his hand assuredly on her shoulder. "Selima is a patriot who has fought at our side through both Nill Wars. Without her, the freedom that we currently share may not have come to fruition. Sure, she may have some sketchy judgment calls as president, but who here isn't without mistakes? I want to repeat myself one last time to be sure all of you know where I am coming from. Selima will not be harmed! I won't allow it!"

"Moving on, I think it would be short-sighted to believe that the only thing this group wants is Selima. There must be something else they desire, but Acacia would not divulge what that might be; however, they do plan on nominating a candidate to run for president."

Private Sakato stood. "What should we be doing in the meantime?"

"For now, keep all people from entering the southeastern section of the Cooperative. I witnessed three prisoners. By now, most of you must have already heard about my sister, Sophi, who Eowyn rescued from the rebels. She is in the hospital and has a 50-50 chance of surviving her injuries. We do not want to provide Acacia's army with more prisoners."

"Again, Marcus, what are we to do in the meantime? What do they expect us to do?"

"They expect us to murder Selima. Once that is accomplished, I am to meet with Acacia— me alone—as she requested, to discuss the reintegration of her army with those of the Cooperative."

Selima motioned for Marcus's attention. "I cannot stand here and let this rebel group threaten the peace of the Cooperative because of me. I don't want a single life to be lost because of my actions, or because of something that I did. If they want me, then that is what I will provide them with. I will gladly sacrifice my life for the safety of my friends and family. I will not let another person lose a life on my behalf!"

Marcus at first started to object but had thought that he chose not to share with the others, but he shared his plan earlier with Selima. "As much as I do not want you harmed, Selima, maybe this is the best thing to avoid war. While I say this, I disagree with you turning yourself into them. You will be subjected to torture and undue pain. May I suggest, and I only make this suggestion since you decided to forfeit your life, that your death be peaceful? Furthermore, your death should occur as an act of your loving family, so that we can see to it that you are treated with dignity and receive a proper burial."

Eowyn couldn't believe what she was hearing. "No, no Marcus! She's our sister. No! If you kill her, I will never speak to you again; you'll be dead to me!"

"It's all right Eowyn," Selima whispered and then shouted. "I choose to be put to death for the good of the Cooperative. I wish my family and friends to be present when my execution takes place, and for them to decide the disposition of my body upon my death."

Selima quickly exited the room with Eowyn on her tail.

"Are you positive, Selima? You don't have to do this. We could run off together and live on our own."

Selima put her finger to Eowyn's lips. "Shhh! Everything will be fine. I must face the consequences of my bad choices. Besides, there is no greater reason to die than to give life to guarantee the well-being of others. I'm at peace with this decision, Eowyn."

"Well, I'm not nor will I ever be. Marcus is dead to me if he follows through with this plan."

"Just take my word, one day our paths will cross again. I promise. Marcus is only doing what he thinks is right, and I am asking you to support him. Please, do not abandon him—for me, Eowyn. He will need you."

Sergeant Ballard stuck his head outside and called for Selima.

"Good, Selima, it's best we don't drag this out. Do you agree?"

"Yes, the sooner the better. I just want it to be over."

"Tomorrow at six pm. Is that suitable for you?"

"Of course."

"This will allow me time to locate Acacia and escort her to witness the act as well as allow time for gathering the necessary medical personnel. The only people in attendance will be Selima's family and friends, the others that she requests, along with Acacia, Sergeant Ballard as our military representative, and government officials. No others will be permitted in the confines of this home."

"And where do you want this to occur, Selima? You choose the place."

"Here. It is only fitting that I die where the people I love reside."

"Then it is decided! I will contact the necessary medical officials tonight and meet with Acacia tomorrow to make arrangements. I will see all of you tomorrow at six."

"Can you stay for a minute? We need to discuss your final directives and arrangements for tomorrow." Marcus addressed Selima as she was exiting.

"You don't have to, Selima. Just come with me." Eowyn pleaded.

"I'll meet up with you at your house, okay? I promise I'll be there soon."

She marched up the steps; Marcus laced his arm through hers and they disappeared inside.

10

DEMISE OF A PRINCESS

The day arrived sooner than anticipated. Waffa woke from an afternoon nap in the midst of what Marcus suspected was active labor. The consistent waves of what Waffa described as stabbing pain occurred every seven minutes. Marcus woke Eowyn and the two rushed her off towards Mercy General Hospital. Nurse Angela and Houlihan performed the initial exam and were surprised to find her nearly fully dilated. They immediately moved her to a birthing room and hooked her up to a series of monitors.

"You're already eight centimeters, Waffa. You're almost there, sweetheart!"

By four, she was dilated to eight centimeters; by five, nine, and five-thirty, she progressed to near full dilation. Marcus glanced at the clock every so often, fully aware that Selima's execution was to take place within the next hour. He promised Selima he would be there. Waffa knew as well and thought his being there was a priority.

"It's okay, honey. I know you have to be there. I am just having a baby, so spend time with Selima before she is gone. The baby will be here by the time you return. Besides, Celeste is here. Now, go on!"

Indeed, the day Selima's execution had arrived. Within the hour, she would be put to death while droves of people observed, mainly select friends and family along with Captain Acacia, her guard detail, and capitol officials. The only room in the house large enough for the gathering was the living room, so the furniture was removed, a gurney and the necessary equipment to conduct the execution were brought inside. Selima lay on the table, she appeared like Jesus on the cross, her arms extended and strapped down. A catheter was already placed in her right arm and a series of three eccentric-tipped syringes were intricately plumbed to one common line that led to her brachial artery.

She lay in isolation—alone—no one was to interact with the condemned.

At 5:55 PM, a doctor entered the room and fiddled with the various contraptions connected to Selima. After a few minutes, he gave the thumbs up to the acting president.

"For crimes against the Cooperative, you have been sentenced to death. Do you have any last words?"

"She shook her head side to side."

The president signaled and the doctor administered the contents of the first syringe; the contents of which contained a sedative to relax her; he then injected the second which contained a muscle paralytic, and he hesitated a few minutes before pressing the plunger of the third providing time for the other chemicals to do their job.

Suddenly a commotion stirred towards the back of the room. Like a battering ram, Marcus pushed through security, rushed to Selima's side, took her hand, and wiped away her tears. She gazed into his eyes and smiled just as the doctor injected the contents of the final syringe of Potassium Chloride. Selima's body went taut for a moment, her face turned a beat red, and every muscle in her body tensed then as if releasing the stresses and difficulties of the world, a smile came to her face, her body softened, and the monitor signaled her death.

Captain Acacia and an accompanying doctor immediately checked for life and once satisfied, they departed.

Marcus, Dr. House, and two other physicians rushed her body to a back room and so ended the life of Princess Selima.

Simultaneously, across the Cooperative, Waffa squeezed Celeste's hand as she made one last push. Seconds later, she heard the cry of a baby boy. Angela wrapped the baby and laid her on Waffa's chest. The time of birth was 6:03 PM which coincidentally matched the time of Selima's death.

"She's beautiful!" Celeste cried as the child grabbed her finger and squeezed. "You did so well, Waffa! I know Marcus is so proud of you. I bet he will be here soon."

"Thanks for being here for me! I couldn't have done it without you!"

"Sure, you could have. I wouldn't have missed this for the world! Maybe one day our roles will be reversed, and you will be here for me."

Waffa smiled, handed the baby back to Celeste, and drifted off to sleep. Marcus arrived within the hour.

"Shhh!" Celeste told Marcus as he barged into the room. "You are the proud father of a bouncing baby boy! He's in the NICU but is fine. Doctors are just being cautious."

Marcus scooted a chair next to the bed. "I love you so much!" he whispered as he held her hand.

"How long was she in labor?"

"About 2-3 hours, but she did so well, Marcus."

"I just wish I could have been there for her."

"You were," Waffa cut in. "Right here." She pointed to her heart. I hope things weren't painful for Selima?"

"She left this earth with dignity. It was so hard to say good-bye—you know I loved her?"

Celeste looked at Waffa with a look of shock expecting her to be upset.

"I know you did. She was your sister or, as you once told me, she was your Princess. Are you all right?"

"Ya know, I'm surprisingly content. I'll miss seeing her and receiving her level-headed advice, but I feel confident that her soul lives on."

"So, have the two of you decided on a name?"

Waffa looked to Marcus, and he motioned for her to share. "Omar Enigma Martyreon."

Eowyn, Leeba, Raghba, and Ferris entered the room just in time to receive the announcement.

"Congwatuwations! You did it Waffa. Youw awe a mom! I'm pwoud of you."

"Thanks, Ferris. Now it's your turn. How about a Ferris Junior?" Ferris blushed. "Maybe one day, but I don't think I wiww be a good fathew"

"I think you'd be an incredible dad. I believe in you and I would love it if you and Celeste would be Omar's Godparents."

"Absowutewy!" Ferris excitedly agreed. "You heaw that, Ceweste! We'we pawents."

Angela peeked inside. "I don't mean to break up the party, but a huge storm is brewing outside. We've lost contact with the neighboring Cooperative and the escort for Captain Acacia has not reported back. Massive flooding has already started, and Hawthorne Village was ravaged by high winds and tornados. Strange weather anomalies have popped up throughout the Cooperative. If you plan on heading home, you better make it soon."

"Thanks, Angela. Is Ballard coming for you?"

"Already here! I'll see you tomorrow."

"Can you excuse me a Minute, Waffa? I need to speak to Eowyn in private. Do you mind?" He wanted to tell her something of great importance, even though he agreed to keep the information under wraps.

"Eowyn, do you mind stepping outside? I have something to tell you."

"Go to hell, Marcus! You and I are finished. The last thing I want to do is speak with you. So, yeah! No fucking way I'm ever going to speak to you again!"

"It's something very important I need to share. It involves Selima and her final message."

Eowyn flipped him off as she marched out the door. Marcus glanced outside. The sky was dark, and the wind had picked up. Marcus kept his eye on Eowyn until she was safe within the confines of the forest.

"Ferris, why don't you get the ladies home? I'm going to stay with Waffa until she's released. You better get out of here quick!"

"Come on wadies! Wet's get home. See you tomowwow, Mawcus."

11

STORM ON THE HORIZON

Torrential rain pelted the area for three days straight and there seemed to be no signs of letting up. Rivers and streams breached their banks and flooded the low-lying plains. Many homes had already been overcome by the rising waters and displaced families moved from one family or friend's house to the next. Likewise, the waters of the Bentley River slowly spread across the acreage in the expanse between Marcus's home and currently was within view just a hundred feet or so from the back porch. Winds picked up to an incredible speed with violent wind shear that toppled trees and ripped roofs off many homes. Marcus had never experienced such destructive weather nor had the wisest of the elderly population ever recalled an apocalyptic event like they were currently experiencing.

Marcus peered into the sky. Grey clouds swirled as the rain spackled his face to the point it was difficult to see. He and Ferris filled sandbags trying to fortify and prepare for the waters that slowly crept towards their home. Leeba, Eowyn, Raghba, and most others in the immediate area retreated to Bentley's Fishery which stood elevated about thirty feet higher than most homes. Waffa convalesced in the bedroom and cared for the children while the others braved the hurricane-force winds to board up windows and secure any outdoor equipment.

"Get inside!" Marcus screamed but his voice was barely audible through the heavy squalls. "Go on! Get dried off and start a fire, Eowyn."

"Ferris, let's do one more layer of sandbags at the back side of the house and get inside." They managed to build a four-foot-high wall around the perimeter of the structure in preparation for the quickly escalating storm.

They had just finished laying the final layer of bags when lightning flashed followed by a horrendous, "Crack." Ferris seemed unaware of the massive oak falling in his direction. Marcus sprinted towards Ferris and pushed him sending him sliding across the muddy setting as the tree crashed to the ground missing him by mere inches, but the barbed branches battered them both. Marcus fought to escape the tentacle-like branches that surrounded him and once free, he frantically searched for Ferris who wasn't immediately visible through the torrential rain. Water quickly crept up bypassing the makeshift wall, pooled where the roots of the great oak once stood then inched forward. Marcus followed the screams for help.

"Mawcus, over hewe; Mawcus, I need hewp." He yelled over and over. The screams guided Marcus, but the savage winds and torrential rain made it impossible to pinpoint exactly where he was. Finally, in frustration, he took a knee to clear his mind of clutter. "Listen, Marcus, block out the noise and hone in on Ferris. Through the chaos, he detected Ferris's faint voice.

"Where are you?" His once fervid screams dissipated in the howling winds. Mud and water quickly rose above Marcus's ankles as he searched; he held his hands above his brow shielding himself from the vertical, blinding rain when he found him. Ferris lay helplessly impaled by a massive branch. In a panic, Marcus attempted to lift the enormous tree while undetectable tears blended with the pelting raindrops. The tree branch had him helplessly pinned to the ground and the merciless waters steadily rose, had already covered from the back of his head to his ears.

"Wooks wike this is it, Mawcus." He coughed up a mouthful of blood. "Cwazy how we wived thwough aww the shit of the wast yeaws and now..." He paused trying to take in a breath of fresh air, but his chest heaved then stalled as blood profusely erupted from his mouth. Marcus desperately fought to keep Ferris's head above the quickly rising water.

"Stay with me, Ferris!" Frantically, he grabbed a branch and tried to pry the tree off him, but the thick branch was no match for the sinewy bough that pinned him to the ground. Ferris grabbed Marcus's hand. "Bwothew...my bwo...thew. Okay... Ceweste goodbye." He smiled, his body convulsed violently, and he fell silent. Marcus sat with Ferris's head cradled in his lap, the water lapped at his cheeks within minutes, despite his best effort. the rapidly rising water completely immersed Ferris. He was already gone. Marcus held onto him until the water lapped at his chin. When he started towards the house to share the tragic news, the swiftly moving current unexpectedly shifted the tree enough to pin his leg. Marcus chuckled.

"You win Lord. It's obvious my time on this earth is at an end, just make it quick, please."

struggled to release himself, but he was hopelessly pinned. He watched as Ferris's body fluttered in the ever-strengthening tide while he waited for the moment, he would join him.

Celeste glanced out the window, but she couldn't see anything beyond the front porch.

"I'm worried about them. They should have been back by now." Eowyn peered out the window with the same result.

"I'm going to help," Eowyn slipped on a raincoat and opened the front door. The wind violently grabbed the unlatched door, ripped it from its hinges and it sailed away in the wind."

"Get everyone upstairs," Eowyn screamed. She stepped outside. Her feet hit the water after scaling the second step, the other three were already totally immersed. She trudged forward frantically fighting the waist-deep current that grabbed at her legs, trying to sweep her away but using tree limbs and shrubs she pulled herself forward until she stood amid the fallen tree. Leaves, branches, and debris of all sorts battered her, but she wasn't about to turn back until she found them.

"Over here. I'm here!" Eowyn followed the weak voice and stopped when she felt someone grab her leg. She crouched behind the trunk of the tree shielding her from the immediate onslaught and only then did she see Marcus for the first time.

"Come on Marcus, we have to get inside!" She clutched his hand and pulled.

"I'm pinned. Can't move." He fought to stay afloat, but the water had already reached his neck. "Get out of here while you can, Eowyn. Save yourself!"

"Where's Ferris?"

"He's gone. Marcus pointed and through the dark water, she spotted the silhouette of a body fluttering in the current.

"Just let me be. I don't want you hurt. Go inside and help the others. There's nothing you can do for me."

Eowyn desperately looked around for anything that might help, but she knew that Marcus was right. He was tightly pinned and there was no escape short of amputating his leg. She kneeled and propped Marcus against her chest.

"Go, Eowyn. I'm okay with this."

"No, I'm going to stay with you. I'm not leaving you alone."

"What happened to not ever wanting to talk to me again? Remember your 'fuck you' speech? I deserved it!"

Eowyn squeaked out a giggle between desperate sobs. "You really can be a jackass!"

"What I wanted to tell you that day is that..." The tree shifted and rolled up onto Marcus's hip. "...Selima's..." His head was jerked beneath the water, but Eowyn momentarily lifted his face from the water. "Selima's ali..." The brisk current swept the tree away before he could finish. A dispirited Eowyn could only watch as the tree ornamented with Ferris and Marcus' bodies vanished into the darkness.

Eowyn pulled herself safely onto the porch and clung to the railing. She felt as if her heart had been torn from her chest and considered letting the waters take her as well, but the sound of Leeba's voice snapped her out of her misery.

"What is it, baby? Where are the boys?" She asked as they made their way upstairs and into the bedroom where everyone was gathered.

"Well, where are they?" Celeste inquired. Eowyn didn't answer but instead, stared blankly. "Where are they, Eowyn?"

"Washed away—they're gone."

"What do you mean? Are they all right?"

Still staring straight ahead, "They are gone. They're dead. A tree fell then the water swallowed them up. I couldn't do anything to save them."

"No, Marcus and Ferris are good swimmers. I'm sure they'll return after the storm. There's no way a little water hurt them," Celeste went on. "They'll be back; you'll see!"

Eowyn didn't want to mention that she was sure Ferris was dead nor did she share that the tree had pulled Marcus under. She didn't want to erase their hope, but in her heart, she knew they were dead.

"I expect them to return any time now. They are strong swimmers. I'm sure they are fine." Waffa agreed with Celeste.

"We've got another problem to deal with. The water is making its way up the steps. We need to get out of here, but how?" Raghba looked around the room trying to identify anything that might help with an evacuation.

She gazed out the window and caught a glimpse of what appeared to be a small fishing boat lodged in the branches of a tree fifty yards or so from the house. Digging through the pile of supplies they had gathered earlier, she pulled out a static, repelling rope.

"Eowyn, tie this to my waist." She held up her arms while Eowyn complied.

"What's your plan?"

"Does that look like a boat to you?" She pointed into the calamitous flood. "What do you think?"

"Yes, I think you're right."

"I'm going to swim to the boat and tether it to the rope. I'll yank on the rope twice to signal when I'm ready to be pulled in. Help me out the window."

She climbed out and plunged into the frigid water which had risen to a few feet from reaching the windowsill. Raghba took a deep breath, pushed off the side of the house with all her might, and began swimming. Eowyn and Celeste slowly fed the rope as she was swallowed by the murkiness. Even though it was late afternoon, the sun had no chance of piercing the dark gray skies. It had been several minutes since they last saw Raghba when Eowyn sensed a tug on the line. She pulled the line taut and yanked the rope once. Sure enough, she felt two tugs from the other end. She immediately started reeling in the line which was no easy task in the swiftly moving current.

"Celeste, please give me a hand. They worked in tandem and after several minutes the boat came into sight, but to everyone's surprise, Raghba wasn't there.

"My God, do you see her?" Leeba asked just as water started flowing into the room from under the door.

"No time now, we have to get out of here before the home is ripped from its foundation," Eowyn assessed the situation.

The boat was designed to hold up to four individuals, but the group trapped inside consisted of Leeba, her two children, Waffa, and baby Omar, Celeste, and Eowyn. A total of seven individuals, but weight-wise, with the children probably equal to the weight of two adults, the boat could accommodate them all.

"Put on raincoats and bring only the essentials!" Eowyn ordered. Waffa, I'm going to help you first; Leeba you're next and then we will hand you the children. Waffa and Leeba, get in after." The boat careened about slamming into the house while listing side to side. Eowyn steadied it as much as possible. Once the children were all loaded Eowyn helped Celeste and the others into the boat and then jumped in herself.

The wind and rain relentlessly battered them as they fought to keep the boat upright.

"Once I untie the boat, we will be at the mercy of the current. Use the paddles to keep us from careening into any obstacles. I want Waffa and Leeba to focus on the children, while Celeste and I worry about keeping the boat upright. Everyone, sit as low as possible for stability; the lower we sit the more likely we won't capsize. Is everyone ready?"

As soon as she untethered the boat, the current sent them swiftly sailing into the darkness. Like a pinball, the boat collided with one obstacle after another. They had sailed about a hundred feet when the sound of insidious groaning and the cracking of wood preceded the home being ripped from its moorings and it was swallowed by the waters. The current hopelessly carried them, at one point, lodging the boat in the branches of a massive pine until the vicious waters uprooted it like a blade of grass propelling the boat deeper into the darkness. Leeba frantically used a bucket to bail out the rainwater that quickly filled the bottom of the boat. The Children cried and screamed in fear, but most went unheard blotted out by the mighty sound of grinding rocks and splintering timber. Their tiny ship flailed in the turbulent waters; waves hammered the hull and battered the passengers while the whole time a hellish rain, one experienced by only the most ex-perienced of sailors, continuously assaulted them. The wind-pro-pelled drops stung the bare skin and the cold was all-consuming. Waffa did whatever she could to shield the babies while all the others, except Eowyn, had been beaten into submission. They huddled together with shirts and blankets over their heads not just to deflect the rain but to muffle the sounds of the horrendous wails of the storm.

"I could use some help here!" Eowyn hollered while bailing water from the boat. But the others more than likely were unable to hear her cries through the bellowing winds. She had just raised her head to see what was ahead when she was violently struck in the head and sent plunging into the choppy waters. Dazed and disoriented, she struggled to find her way to the surface. Frenzied-ly, she fought to stay afloat but was hopelessly thrashed by the current and battered by debris. The chilled water quickly sapped her energy and just when she went under fully expecting to die, she slammed into a tree and immediately began climbing until her head popped above the surface. Clinging to the tree, she searched for the boat, but could only see a few feet in any direction. The tree wildly swayed from side to side with Eowyn in tow, while her friends remained oblivious to her peril. For hours, she clashed with the frigid cold but with her muscles atrophied her icy fingers failed her and she disappeared into the oceanic expanse.

12

REBORN

The boat drifted for hours with everyone huddled inside doing whatever they could to protect the children. The unprecedented rainfall mercilessly continued. Spirits were low and what little hope that remained was dashed when they discovered Eowyn must have fallen overboard. Leeba was inconsolable while the others clung to hope that they would be reunited with their loved ones once the storm concluded.

The boat was tossed for seemingly days when in reality, it had only been fourteen hours. In that time, the women managed to fasten an all-weather tarp to the cleats of the boat which provided them a reprieve from the inexorable downpour. Working as a team, they took turns bailing the water from the hull, but currently, they all lay on the verge of collapse.

Miles away, unbeknownst to the small boat of castaways, a person feebly clung to the remains of a roof. Too weak to pull herself completely out of the water, she tethered herself to the drifting debris. Bruised and battered, she floated along drifting between a semi-conscious to an oblivious state. The bulky fragment of roofing bobbed in the rough waters but stopped abruptly when it struck land jostling the wayward waif to consciousness.

Using every bit of remaining energy, her nails dug into the muddy soil. She determinedly inched, scratched, and carved her way forward until her body completely shut down.

Hours later, a stranger scrounging along the shores stumbled upon her, slung her limp body over his shoulder, and carried her to a makeshift shelter; he hung his clothing from the tendrils that projected from an overhead outcrop. He removed her wet clothing, laid her on a bed of pine straw next to the fire, then drifted off to sleep.

Sometime later, hard to tell if day or night through the ominously black skies, she emerged from her slumber, rolled to her knees, heaved up a few ounces of water, and laid back down. Across the room, a man lay sleeping. She scooted towards the back wall and observed from a distance. She wrapped herself in a blanket and peeked outside to see that the heavy rain persisted while lightning peppered the visible surroundings. From her viewpoint, it appeared as if she were marooned on a tiny island in the middle of an ocean.

"Has it let up at all?" an unfamiliar voice asked as she gazed outside.

"No. I wonder if it ever will."

It's almost as if God were purging humans from the earth. I've never seen anything like this. I imagine this is how Noah felt."

"At least he was smart enough to build an ark!" She laughed. "By the way, how did I get here?"

"I found you lying on the shore. I thought you were dead at first, but I grabbed you anyway. Luckily, I did since after a few minutes of laying by the fire you started to stir."

"Is anyone else here with you?"

"No, just myself. Until I saw you, I thought the rains had washed everyone away. I was beginning to think I was the last person on earth until I discovered you."

"What's your name?"

"I'm Dimitry and yours?"

"Raghba."

"You hungry?"

"Starved. I haven't had anything to eat in what seems like ages."

He threw a package of jerky in her direction. "How about some wine? I found a case floating in the water the other day. That's all I have to drink other than, the bazillion gallons of water outside!"

"Wine sounds great. So, how did you get here?"

"I happened to be out hunting when the rain started. I had just started my journey home when the flooding began, so I went to high ground, and I've been here ever since—and you?"

"I was separated from my friends when the water washed me away, and somehow, I ended up here. I don't remember too much other than struggling to stay afloat for what seemed like days. Is your family, okay?"

"I'm it. No wife, no kids, no girlfriend, just me. I've never been too successful with the opposite sex if you know what I mean. I get tongue-tied and have trouble getting a word out whenever I am around a pretty girl."

Raghba finished her glass of wine and refilled her cup. "So, what you are indirectly implying is that I am not pretty. I mean you're not tongue-twisted around me. Wow, I never considered myself gorgeous, but I don't think I am unattractive. Am I?"

"No, I didn't mean that at all. I'm just comfortable talking to you. You're easy to talk to and yes, I think you're very attractive."

Raghba emptied her cup for a third time and this time Dimitry filled it to the rim.

"What's your story?"

"I'm also single but have a large extended family. That is who I was trying to help when the waters yanked me away. I'm hoping they are all right."

"They probably are." A large gust of wind sent a chill down Raghba's back.

"Come closer to the fire. I don't bite---promise."

Raghba attempted to stand, stumbled, and nearly fell. "This wine went right to my head. I guess I should have eaten a little more first. She walked to the entrance. The rain and darkness made it impossible to see much but she sensed the cold wind had picked up.

Dimitry stood next to her and handed her another glass of wine. "It doesn't look like it's going to end any time soon."

"I'm worried about my family. I just need to know they are okay." A tear streaked her cheek. She chugged the wine and walked back to the fire. Dimitry sat next to her.

"It'll be fine. You'll see. Once this rain is over, you'll find your family." Raghba studied him closely when he stood to stroke the fire. He too was naked underneath a blanket while his clothes dried. He leaned forward exposing his hairy chest and well-developed pecs. He stood around 5'8," the perfect height for her, with long dark hair that flowed to his shoulders. She examined his full lips when he spoke and for a moment, lost track of anything he said. She was mesmerized and not sure if the alcohol or just a result of her loneliness, she wanted to pin him to the ground and have her way with him. It had been over a year since she could remember being intimate with a man and the flame centered between her legs was formidable. While Raghba prided herself on her ability to control her urges, she was struggling now. She emptied the bottle into her glass and chugged it. Tears still spackled her face when he leaned in and wiped them away.

"It'll be okay!" he consoled. When he reached to embrace her, his blanket opened slightly exposing his substantial member. Raghba gasped and he quickly covered up. "I apologize." He looked embarrassed as he started to stand, but she pulled him back to the ground.

"You don't have to leave. We're both adults and we're alone, right? Besides that, I owe you, my life. She placed her hand on his leg. I don't know if it's the wine, but..." She didn't get the chance to complete her thought when he kissed her. Raghba dropped the blanket that covered her and pushed him flat on his back. She was in no mood for foreplay and desired immediate satisfaction. The room was spinning as she hedged over and slowly lowered onto him. She took it slowly. First, an inch then paused, invited a little more followed by another pause, until she took him to the hilt. She swayed her hips forward and back, at first, slowly, but gradually, increasing the tempo until she quickly felt the tsunami rising. Raghba had forgotten how good it felt to make love and was glad she rediscovered the euphoric practice. All she knew now was that she couldn't get there quick enough and when Dimitriy took one of her rock-hard nipples into her mouth, she erupted into a series of seismic waves that lapped at her loins repeatedly.

Raghba rolled onto the blanket next to him. "I'm sorry—did you?"

"God, yes! You are magnificent."

Raghba laughed and spooned up next to him. "Like I said, we are two consenting adults alone and willing." With that said, in conjunction with the heat from the fire on one side and the warmth of his body on her back, she contentedly fell asleep.

13

SAVED BY AN ANGEL

At first, the tree shuddered grinding deep into Marcus's thighs, rolled onto him, and pulled him under then a wall of water hoisted the tree and whisked it away with Marcus hopelessly entangled in the myriad of branches. Ferris's body remained fastened to the large branch that impaled him like a kebab. Marcus freed himself from one entanglement and shot towards the surface, but his shirt snagged another branch preventing his emancipation. He kicked and fought to free himself as the last of the oxygen abandoned his lungs.

"Crack!" was the last sound he heard as he blacked out.

Like a piece of driftwood, the tree careened off rocks, other trees, and even segments of land until hours later coming to rest on the shore of a hillside. He woke shivering in the night. Rain still fell but had slowed considerably while a cold wind had picked up. He crawled onto the shore. Bodies floated in the water nearby as he scaled the hillside and searched for shelter. Exhausted, he finally settled on constructing a pallet made of pine straw and leaves. He burrowed into the foliage until completely covered and pondered his situation.

He was unsure of where to start. "I need to recover Ferris's body and give him a proper burial," he said to himself as he strategized. "Must find shelter and food...yes, and only then can I consider any future moves. He thought about Waffa, his babies, and his family to keep his mind occupied through the cold, soggy night as he drifted in and out of a restless sleep filled with horrific nightmares of his family floating dead in an endless sea. In one dream, Waffa struggled to tread water in what appeared to be an ocean. Marcus swam towards her, but no matter how hard he tried, she kept getting farther and farther away until she eventually disappeared below the surface. He woke to his screams and emerged from his shelter like a newborn climbing from the womb. The ravenous rains remained persistent, but the sun managed to provide a defused light signaling daytime had arrived. The water rose another couple of feet during the night, but the tree that ensnared Ferris's body remained firmly anchored to the shore. Marcus waded into the water and swam to the body of his brother. He rested his head on the same branch that skewered Ferris and held Ferris's frigid hand while tears steadily dripped into the water. He didn't know how long he had been there when a voice snapped him back to reality.

"Are you, all right? Do you need some help?"

A person stood on the shore, a man or woman he was unsure through the murky rain. He thought he recognized the voice, but the sound of the teeming rain was deafening.

"I'm just recovering the body of a friend." Marcus tugged until Ferris's body was free and pulled him to shore.

"Is that you, Marcus?" Hearing her voice left no question. Eowyn pulled Ferris onto land and then helped Marcus from the murky waters. Neither of them said a word, but instead, they held one another and sobbed. After several minutes, they carried Ferris's body, and she led them to a tattered ranch-style home.

"Are you the only one here?"

"No others until you showed up. I haven't had a chance to explore too much though. I've been nursing a head injury. I found this house empty yesterday evening; it was the only shelter I could find. I patched up the roof the best I could, and the fireplace works. Eowyn took a seat next to Marcus. Any word on the others?"

"I know they got out of the house safely. We were able to get to your old fishing boat, but I was knocked overboard by a tree branch. They were all fine to that point but no sign of them since. They could have drifted hundreds of miles by now. There's just no telling."

"The babies?"

"Fine. With Waffa and Leeba while Celeste navigated. Raghba was with us but I'm afraid she might be dead. She swam to the boat and tied a rope to it, but when we hoisted the boat back to us, she was gone, probably washed away by the current. Eowyn glanced at Ferris's body on the steps and erupted into tears.

"I can't believe Ferris is gone. I loved him, Marcus! I thought he was indestructible, immortal. I don't know if I want to live in a world without him." Her tears streamed onto his shoulder.

"Ferris would want us to go on, right? He lived an adventurous life; a hardy life and he would want us to do the same. He never gave up even when faced with seemingly insurmountable odds, and we must do the same. He wouldn't tolerate us quitting and besides, we have to keep his memory alive."

"I guess you're right."

"I know I'm right. Besides that, I need you. I can hold it together if you are here; knowing you're alive provides me with a reason to go on. You must know how much I love you. At least I hope you do."

"Ditto, Marcus!" They sat in silence holding one another until Eowyn nodded off. Marcus laid her on the couch and looked around the home for a blanket. One bedroom was empty, but the other had a twin bed still nicely made as if untouched by the storm. Marcus peeled back the blankets, removed Eowyn's saturated clothes, and covered her with the blankets. Unsure what to do next, he explored the house. It appeared whoever lived there quickly evacuated perhaps anticipating the floodwaters and moving to higher ground.

In the kitchen, he found a few canned goods, a box of saltines, and some bottled water in the pantry, which was promising. He was able to salvage a block of cheddar cheese from the many spoiled foods in the refrigerator. He laid the food out on the counter and then stepped outside. He hoisted Ferris onto his shoulder, carried him to the empty bedroom, and covered him with a sheet.

Once back in the living room, he removed his wet clothes, hung them near the fire alongside Eowyn's, and covered himself with a blanket but as exhausted as he was, his mind would not let him rest. He thought about Waffa and what she might be going through. He just sat down after stoking the fire and stirring some chili cooking over the flames when Eowyn, wrapped in a sheet, plopped down next to him and rested her head on his shoulder.

"I'm so glad you are here. I'll never repeat this in front of others, but I am terrified of being alone. I felt like I was the only one left on earth, but then you appeared like an angel. I truly thought you were dead, Marcus! I've been mourning you since."

"To be honest, I thought I was a goner too but here I am. God must have more in the plans for me. Anyway, you're the angel. I don't know if I would have had the energy to crawl from the waters on my own." He smiled. "Since you shared a secret, I'll share one with you and just like you if ever asked, I'll deny I ever said it, I admired you, even looked up to you. You're one of the most incredible people I've ever met and being around you has made me a better person. You know family goes beyond biology. I couldn't have been provided with a better sister. Like I said earlier, I love you so much. Now, let's get to something more important. Are you ready for some chili? I was able to scrape together a can, some saltines, and even some cheese."

"Well, well, Marcus, I didn't know you had formal chef training. I'm excited to try your cuisine. Is that how you say it? Maybe taste the cuisine? I don't know, but yes, I'm starved."

Marcus found a couple of bowls in the cupboard, wiped them clean, and filled them with piping hot chili. "Enjoy!"

He took a seat next to Eowyn and they ate in silence. After a second bowl, Eowyn walked to the front door. "Where's Ferris? I mean, where's his body?" she asked a bit alarmed.

"I moved him to the empty room in the back until we got the chance to bury him. We ought to do it soon even if it is raining. What do you think? Come to think of it, why don't you work on seeing what supplies you can find around here while I bury him? You and I can hold a small service later. What do you think?"

"Normally, you know I would be right there beside you, but my head is killing me."

"Here, let me take a look." Marcus parted her thick hair and gasped.

"What is it? Is it that bad?"

"It's not good. The laceration was about three inches long and to the skull. The tissue around the wound was infected with fragments of bark speckled throughout. We need to clean this up. I tell you what, I saw a sewing machine in the master bedroom. Grab a needle and thread. Also, see if you can find any antibiotics. When I'm finished outside, we'll fix you right up! Sound good?"

"I can't wait to have Dr. Frankenstein operating on my head!" she laughed as she walked to the back room. Wait a minute, Marcus. What was it you tried to tell me after Selima's execution? You said it was a message."

"Do you think I would let anyone kill Selima?"

"Well, you may not have done it yourself, but you saw her die just like I did."

"That's the thing, Eowyn, what I was trying to tell you. She's alive. We faked her death to appease Acacia. I tried to tell you, but you were too busy wishing me dead or at least said I was dead to you."

"You should have let me in on the plan."

"The fewer people that knew, the better. We needed true emotion when she died to convince Acacia and her doctor that she was dead."

"Where is she?"

I left her in a cabin about four miles from Bentley. There's no telling where she is now if she is alive at all."

"Marcus, I'm sor..."

He didn't let her finish, quickly grabbed Ferris's body, and stepped outside. He carried Ferris's body to some higher ground, grabbed a shovel from a backyard shed, and commenced digging. The job was arduous. While easy to dig in the saturated soil, the rain transformed the area into a muddy bog that grabbed at his feet and at times sent him slipping to the ground. By the time he had dug a deep enough hole, it was filled with water, and like a series of mini mudslides, the sides of the large hole continually caved in upon themselves. Marcus gently laid Ferris in the grave, heaved the last shovel of dirt, and took a seat in the mud. He couldn't recall a time without him being in his life. He sat for over an hour replaying the more memorable moments in his mind and realized, that while he knew Ferris had impacted everyone's life, most of his immediate family including himself, would not be living today if it wasn't for his heroics.

"I love you, Ferris, and will make sure your accomplishments are never forgotten. Memories of you will be forever etched in my heart, brother." Marcus stood and trudged towards the house. He found Eowyn leaning back on the couch wrapped in a blanket; her eyes closed. A spool of thread, a needle, and a first aid kit sitting on the end table next to her.

Marcus kicked off his mud-covered shoes, stripped off his saturated clothing, and walked to the back room. When he returned, he had a towel wrapped around his waist. He hung his clothes in front of the fireplace and took a seat on the hearth. He gazed out the window wondering if Waffa and the others were okay. Winds had picked up and rain traveled horizontally full of all types of debris. Various things pitter-pattered against the side of the house playing a hypnotic cacophony that almost put him to sleep. His eyes had just closed when he was jarred awake by a deafening 'Crack' from the backside of the house. Sprinting to the back room, he discovered a large maple tree had crashed through the awning of the back porch shattering the glass of the sliding entry door to the dining room.

"What was that?" Eowyn peaked around the corner.

"It's okay. A tree hit the house. "Could you help me push this China Cabinet?" They moved a large oak cabinet in front of the gaping hole in an attempt to block some of the wind.

"That scared the hell out of me!"

"Yeah, I nearly jumped out of my skin. Hey, let's take a minute to take care of your head before something else happens. Take a seat." Marcus pulled out a syringe, filled it, and jabbed it into her arm without warning.

"What the hell, Marcus! What was that?"

"Put it this way, you shouldn't be feeling any pain in about—let's say—a minute or two."

"What did you inject me with? I found some morphine tucked away in one of the dresser drawers in the bedroom while you were sleeping." He couldn't let her know that he had a stash of his own that he used regularly. "You should feel it right about—now!"

His timing was nearly perfect. A rush of heat pulsed through her body followed by a desensitization that crept from the top of her head to her toes. "Wow, this is incredible."

"Good, then you are ready. Stay still while I work."

Marcus used a pair of surgical scissors from the first aid kit to cut away the infected flesh and the surrounding hair. It looks like you're going to have a bald spot to match the scar from your last head injury. Everything always seems to happen in pairs, huh? And get this, your scars are perfectly placed. You just have to grow a set of matching horns."

"Hopefully this is the last scar. I can't afford to lose any more hair and I don't need a set of horns!" She chuckled. I seriously can't feel my body. I'm in heaven."

"Give me a moment, I have to get some water to flush the dirt out." Marcus returned with a bowl of water and a rag. "Let's try this again."

He wrapped a towel around her shoulder and commenced irrigating the wound. "Looks good now. By the way, you have a shiny white dome to protect that tiny brain of yours."

"My brain may not be so big, but I bet it's much larger than yours, doctor!"

"That's a possibility! What color stitches do you want? You have a choice of orange, gray, or blue, your choice."

"How about sticking with the more traditional gray."

"You got it, sweet cheeks."

"Did you just call me sweet cheeks? Why Marcus, I believe you're objectifying me!" She followed every sentence with a kooky laugh.

"Me, never! I'm not a misogynist. I simply meant the cheeks on your face are plump and rosy. Oh, you thought I was speaking about your derriere?"

"So, I have a fat face and my butt isn't worth mentioning? I always wondered why you never seemed interested in me and now I know, why? You think I'm a chubby girl with no figure."

"Exactly! I think you are ugly, downright unsightly and these stitches aren't going to help. You're beginning to look like Frankenstein." He chuckled.

After a lengthy effort, Marcus tied off the last stitch and applied some antibacterial gel. "There. You're all set!"

"Do you really think I'm starting to look like Frankenstein? Am I ugwy to yoo?" She started to slur her words. Marcus walked to the sink and dumped out the water.

Discretely, he filled the syringe and stuck it in his arm as he was speaking and stumbled toward the couch. The morphine hit him all at once. He plopped down next to Eowyn.

"How do you feel?"

"Not a concern in the vorld. No pain." She laid her head on Marcus's shoulder. "Do you thiwk I'm unsighted or, I mean, uglee?" She dragged out each word unnecessarily.

"I was being a 100% misogynist, and I objectified you. Of course, I was talking about your butt. Sweeter than any I've ever seen. Wait, did I just say that?"

"You like my beaut, my butt? So, you are attracted to me or at least my ass, right?" She stood with her butt in his face. "You like this?" She grabbed her butt cheeks and laughed. Do you want to touch it?" She unbuttoned her pants and dropped them to the floor. "Go ahead. I don't care. Just grab hold."

"So, tempting, but you know I'm married, and you are under the influence of drugs."

"I'm not inviting you to sleep with me. I just asked you to feel." She grabbed his hands and placed one on each of her ass cheeks. "That's not so bad, right?"

"Sit down, weirdo!" Marcus pulled her towards the couch, but she landed in his lap.

"Well, this is awkward." They sat face-to-face. Eowyn lightly kissed him on his forehead. Not sure if it was morphine or simply his need to feel something positive, Marcus didn't object. He did nothing to stop her at first, but the innocent kiss turned into something much more provocative.

"Wait. Is this really what we want to be doing? What about Leeba and Waffa? We love them."

"We don't even know if they are alive. I just want to feel safe if only for this moment. I need this, Marcus. We never have to talk about it again—ever."

Marcus lifted Eowyn in his arms, carried her to the bedroom, and kicked the door closed behind them. The storm intensified; large waves battered the shore, ebbing and flowing, rhythmically cresting, and descending; the swell of water rising and falling vigorously seeking a torrential release. The relentless thrusting inevitably broke down barriers sending a flood of liquid splashing deep into the expanse. The walls of the house shuddered, convulsed repeatedly, and finally, moaned under the salvo of soaking rains that eased following the rapturous onslaught.

An hour later, the two emerged from the bedroom wrapped in nothing but sheets, laughing while holding one another's hand. Eowyn sat while Marcus stoked the fire and added a log.

"Remember, this goes no further than this room. No one can ever know."

"Yes. I know. Do you regret it?"

"Not for a second, you?"

"Never. I forgot what it is like to be with a man and damn, you were fantastic. I didn't want it to end."

"You are the first lesbian I've ever been with, and you represented your gender, lesbian or not, in an exemplary fashion!"

"My head is starting to pound again after that. Do you have anything else for the pain?"

"More morphine, but are you sure? You see what it did to us the last time—super fun, but not good!"

"I'm not asking for sex, Marcus! I need to get rid of this pain. Can you help me or not?"

"Of course, I can. Give me a minute." He walked to the backroom and returned with the vial and syringe."

"Where did you get that? You didn't find something like that in a medicine cabinet or some poor Joe's drawers. That's hospital-grade."

"I'll tell you, but don't judge. I already know I'm screwing up. I stole it from the hospital when I was visiting Waffa. I've been using it for the last year. I'm having trouble stopping."

"How? Why? You're better than that."

"It started while I was held prisoner by the Nill. I used it to help me tolerate cancer treatments. I only meant to use it a few times, but soon I couldn't stop. I'm going to though—one day; I'm going to stop, but I'm not in the position to do that right now."

"I'll help you when the time comes, but right now, I need some." Marcus stuck the needle in the vial and pulled the plunger back. "You're sure?"

She extended her arm towards him. "Do it!"

She felt the drug coursing through her veins, her eyes rolled to the back of her head, and the sheet that covered her dropped to the floor. "I can see how you became addicted. This stuff is amazing."

Marcus injected himself and fell next to her. "Yes. Amazing."

"There's only one thing that would feel better right now." Eowyn grabbed his hand and guided him towards the bedroom.

14

FIGHT FOR SURVIVAL

Massive waves lifted and tossed the boat about. All they could do was stay low and hope that it didn't capsize. Celeste worked bailing water until exhausted and Leeba took over after. She had been laboring for nearly two hours when, through the heavy rain, she noticed the swiftly moving water funneling towards a large valley full of rocky outcrops. Leeba grabbed a paddle. "Stay down! We're about to go through a rough stretch. Celeste, help Waffa with the babies."

The boat entered a virtual gauntlet and at first, Leeba was able to guide the boat safely using the paddle to dodge one rock formation after another, but the speed of the rapids eventually increased to the point she was unable to react quickly enough. The boat careened off one jagged projection after another. Massive swells splashed over the rim of the boat while the frigid waters gradually gathered in the bow.

"What do we do? "Celeste screamed.

"Hand me Omar, Waffa. I'll take care of him." She had just reached out to hand him over when the boat violently crashed into something in the darkness launching everyone overboard. The boat crumpled and was sucked into the abyss in seconds.

Waffa quickly grabbed Omar and bobbed along trying to keep the baby's head above water. However, not fully recovered from the birth of her baby, she hadn't the energy to fight for long. First, her head slipped below the surface, and seconds later, the child she miraculously conceived was swallowed up, their lives forever silenced.

Celeste, once a member of the state champion Alexander High School swim team, frantically clung to a large piece of driftwood but was having difficulty maintaining her grip. She witnessed Waffa and the baby get sucked under, but there was nothing she could do. She managed to salvage a length of rope from the boat as it sank, fastened herself to a large log, and moments later, utterly fatigued, passed out.

Unconscious, she drifted through the frigid water for over an hour before the frenzied current smashed her into something in the darkness. She woke to find herself pinned in a debris torrent that jostled, squeezed, and battered her. Pinned between two large tree trunks, the rushing current slowly pressed against her torso making it difficult to breathe. She blindly searched for anything to pry her pinned body free but with no luck. Making things worse, the churning debris slowly began pulling her under. She had given up all hope when something or someone snatched her under the armpits and furiously tugged. Her body so battered, Celeste was at the mercy of whatever or whoever attempted to free her from the logjam. Soon, her upper torso was pulled free of the logs, but her hips were tightly pinched until a final tug freed them; not before the massive logs clamped on her leg. "Snap." The sound of her breaking tibia was audible through the smothering rain.

"Hurry now. We must get off this gridlock quickly before it shifts, and we are both pulled under. Celeste drifted in and out of consciousness as she was carried to shore.

"Celeste...Celeste, it's me, Selima. Where are the others? Celeste, the others?"

"They're gone!" She squeaked out right before she blacked out a second time.

Selima partly carried and at times dragged her until arriving at a makeshift shelter built against the base of a hillside. She dragged Celeste inside, stoked the fire, and covered her with a tarp and some pine straw. After gathering a supply of wood, she laid down and reflected on the past few hours that so profoundly impacted the lives of her loved ones.

Only four people knew about the cover-up which had to remain confidential. Captain Acacia wanted Selima dead and Marcus decided to make it happen or at least, appear that way. The night before her execution, Marcus, Doctor House, Angela, and Selima all sat and plotted into the night. After hours of brainstorming, the risky plan came together. The first two drugs would remain the traditional drugs used in an execution, but the third, normally sodium pentathlon was replaced with a rarely known Amazonian drug called ayahuasca. In all reality, the drug did stop her heart and was enough to fool Acacia and her doctor into thinking that she was dead, but the drug permitted time for Dr. House to rush in and use reverberation shock to bring her back to life. Afterward, Marcus escorted her home leaving Joanna with her while he left to check on the others. She was packing her things when, without warning, a flash flood hit the house. The tempestuous flood dragged Selima helplessly through the waters while she battled to keep Joanna from going under. By the grace of God, Selima was propelled to land by the same water that claimed the lives of so many of her friends. She quickly scrambled to higher ground and built a shelter. Later, when out gathering wood, she discovered and rescued Celeste.

As she relaxed, sitting between Celeste and Joanna, across the great expanse of water, Sophi sat awake in bed. All patients were moved to the upper floors of the hospital to avoid the water that breached the first floor and most recently began flooding the second. Most patients were maintained on the fourth floor while the hundreds of refugees, those who had to relocate because of the flooding, were housed on the third.

When Sophi first emerged from the coma, she didn't remember anything to include her name, but as of recently, she started to recall some details. Nurse Angela spent every free moment working with her on pronunciation and quizzing her to help reboot her memory.

"Time for physical therapy, Sophi." She tried to help her scoot to the edge of the bed and into a wheelchair, but she waved her off.

"I got this!"

She maneuvered her legs to the side of the bed while Angela wheeled the chair next to her. Sophi lowered herself into the chair. Doctors were skeptical that she would ever acquire the use of her legs again, but she resolutely disagreed. The truth was that the beating she took at the hands of the rebels damaged her spinal column irreparably. Doctors explained to Angela early on that CT scans showed a series of cervical fractures beginning at the C2 Axis to her C4 vertebra with severe trauma to the spinal cord at the C3 junction. Her injuries were neurologically incomplete which meant she maintained some sensory function. From her waist down, she was unable to feel anything while everything above functioned normally. To make things worse, brain swelling caused memory issues. Doctors were ambivalent concerning her overall prognosis, but in Sophi's eyes, she was positive she would fully recover, and Angela did everything she could to assist her.

Every day since waking, she asked the same questions. "Where is everyone? Have you seen Marcus? Where's Janey?" Angela patiently gave the same answer repeatedly. "They are busy but will come to see you once they get the chance."

After a long therapy session, Angela helped Sophi into the hydro-therapy tub and was reading a magazine when Sergeant Ballard arrived.

He snuck up behind her and relished her neck with a kiss. "Now that's what I'm talking about. Please don't stop; I need as much attention as you can give me." Angela stood and pressed her lips to his. "Where have you been?"

"We've been devising a plan to get to the emergency generators. We have to get power to the emergency room and life-saving equipment."

"How in the world are you going to do that? The generators are on the ground floor."

"Nobody said it would be easy, but a few of our better swimmers are going to navigate to the generator room. They can gain access through the ventilation system and activate the bilge system to pump the water out. From there, we just need to restart the generators. A piece of cake, right!"

"As long as you aren't going into that water, I'm fine."

"So far just Private Sakato and Nadia Romonov are involved but they will need help. If they do, you know I must assist."

"And just when is this going to happen?"

Within the next hour or two. We have to act quickly."

Angela stood on her tiptoes and whispered in his ear. "Can we meet in the nurses' quarters before then? I need to spend some time with you. It's been a while."

"When?"

"In about fifteen. Once I get Sophi back to her room, I'll meet you there. Sound good?"

Ballard smiled and pulled her around the corner to be out of Sophi's line of sight. He nibbled on her earlobe, grabbed her ass, and pulled her tight against him. I'm going to eat you up!"

"Oh, you are? And what if I object?"

"Believe me, you won't want to!" His hands wandered up to her chest.

"Save it for later, stud! I'll see you shortly." Angela pushed the wheelchair to Sophi, helped her out of the tub, and wrapped her in a towel. "Nice job today, Soph. Are you up for another session tonight?"

"More the bet...ter."

Angela helped her into her bed and quickly departed to meet Ballard. She opened the door to the pitch-black room and stepped inside.

"Are you here yet?" she whispered but the room remained silent. She felt her way through the room until coming to her bunk at the far side of the room and sat down. A minute later, she heard the door open and close. "Is that you?" she asked but received no response. She could hear some light shuffling and movement in the dark, but each time she inquired, no one replied. Finally, a voice broke the silence.

"Did you miss me?" Ballard asked from across the room.

"You scared the shit out of me. Where have you been?"

"I'm here now and that's what counts." By the sound of his voice, she could tell he was directly in front of her. She reached for him and was surprised to find nothing but bare skin.

"Why Sergeant Ballard, where are your fatigues?" she chuckled. She tried to pull him to her, but he resisted.

"I'm not that easy. Take off your clothes." He ordered.

"Could you unzip me?" Angela turned to him, and he unzipped her nursing gown, and let it drop to the floor. He took a breast into each hand while kissing the nook of her neck.

"Wait a minute. I like to see what I'm working with." She lit a candle across the room which provided a faint light revealing Ballard's broad chest and washboard abs.

"Damn, you look delicious. Come here!" She sauntered to a nearby counter, leaned over, and presented herself to him. "I need something to take my mind off the hell going on around us. Can you help me with that?"

Ballard moved behind her, and together they worked vigorously to temporarily put their troubles behind them.

15

GAME OF EPIC PROPORTIONS

The rain relentlessly fell for the next three days, but on the fourth, the clouds broke up momentarily and sunshine revealed itself for the first time in nearly two weeks. Marcus woke with Eowyn spooned up against him. He tried to quietly peel himself from her arms, but she woke as he rolled to a sitting position.

"And where do you think you're going, young man?"

"I wanted to go check on the weather...take a look outside."

"I'll go with you. A few moments later, they stood on the front porch and gazed into the hazy, rain-filled setting. I know I heard the rain stop last night, and I saw a glimmer of the sun through the window, then again, I may have been dreaming." Eowyn clung to Marcus's arm.

"I wonder if this rain is ever going to stop."

"I'm starting to wonder if we should build an arc. Noah had the right idea." He let out a nervous laugh. Let's get dressed and check the shore for any survivors. I also want to check the water level."

"Go and get dressed while I get the fire going." Marcus stoked the fire, piled on some twigs and small branches, and lightly blew on the embers until flames appeared. By the time

Eowyn stepped into the room, the fire was blazing. "Come on, let's get this over with." They had only trudged about twenty feet, and they were completely saturated. They clutched one another tightly to battle the powerful gusts of wind that at times nearly knocked them to the ground. Despite the treacherous weather, they plodded forward until arriving at the banks of what appeared to be an ocean. The water had risen another few feet and large waves lapped at the land as they ambled along the shore searching for any signs of life. After nearly two hours of searching, they walked back into the house, stripped off their wet clothing, and sat by the fire.

"Marcus, do you think God is punishing us for the violence and killing of the past couple of years? This is an Armageddon-level event here. All we were able to find were bodies. Not another living being! Do you think we are the only survivors?"

"I can't imagine that to be true. I have to believe Waffa and our family are out there somewhere alive and well. Celeste is probably warm and dry with the rest of the family—I'm hopeful—we can't give up hope."

"Being realistic, there's a good chance they are all gone, Marcus. We need to face reality; everyone we love is probably dead! We're all gonna' die."

"What's going on with you? You're usually so optimistic."

"I don't feel so well, Marcus." Despite the cold, he noticed beads of sweat forming on her forehead and she turned unusually pale.

"Are you okay?"

"I'm dizzy and feel numb all over!"

Marcus was well aware of what she was going through. His mom was prone to having panic attacks when he was younger. At times, she swore she was going to die and as a youngster, he believed her, but her dad was always able to talk her through them. That's exactly what Marcus was trying to do now.

"It's okay! Take some deep breaths. Focus on something positive and slow your breathing."

Eowyn stared at Marcus and concentrated on slowing her breathing until she finally calmed.

"I'm so embarrassed! I can normally hold things together, but this was just too much to process. So much death and loss. It's overwhelming." She wiped away her tears. As much as I miss the others, I am glad it's you that I am stranded with. I feel safe with you."

"Same here! You are the most grounded person I know, and your strengths, which are many, nicely complement my weaknesses. We're going to get through this and when we do, our family will be reunited."

"I know." Eowyn stood and walked towards the back room. "Be right back; I have to go to the bathroom."

Marcus sat for the longest and at one point started to doze but woke when the fire iron clanged to the floor. Eowyn still hadn't returned.

I wonder?" he asked himself. He knocked on the bathroom door, but she didn't answer, so he peeked inside and discovered her sitting on the floor with the liquid morphine and a syringe hanging from her arm.

"You're right. It's hard to say no to this stuff," she said with a half-baked smile on her face. "No more panic attacks for me," she chuckled.

"I don't blame you. Things are looking pretty grim." He picked up the vial and moved to the living room. Eowyn fell back onto the couch beside him, plucked the syringe from his hand, filled it, carefully inserted the needle into his arm, and pressed the plunger.

The comforting feel of the drug coursing through him delivered an immediate sense of peace and a well-needed interlude to his anxiety.

"What should we do? I mean I'm a bit bored." Marcus searched the kitchen, found some canned beef stew, and handed it to her. Do you mind warming this up?"

"Oh, I see how it is. You're one of those misogynist pigs who think women should be barefoot, pregnant, and in the kitchen!"

"You know me so well. Get to work, old hag while I do some man work in my office!" He walked down the hall and stopped at the one room they were unable to open. Marcus smashed the door open with one firm kick and walked inside. The office was undisturbed and was filled with expensive mahogany furniture including a large corporate-style desk. The far wall included a massive wall unit full of law books and materials while the opposite donned many framed degrees and certifications. Marcus took a seat and placed his feet up on the desk.

"Honey, dinner is almost ready." Eowyn stepped inside and began massaging Marcus's shoulders. "Rough day at work, hon?" She slid her hands from his shoulders to his chest.

"Yes, but I sense the day is going to get better." He pointed to a shelf of liquor in one of the cubbies. Eowyn grabbed a bottle of vodka and two shot glasses while Marcus was more interested in a door in the lower section of the wall unit. He pried the door open and inside found a mini-fridge full of beer, canned Pina Coladas, and an assortment of fruity alcohol fusions.

"Now this is more like it!" He grabbed a handful of drinks and carried them to the living room.

He poured two shots of vodka and slid one to Eowyn. "Let's play a game of truth or dare. If one of us fails to complete a task, the other takes a shot but if you complete it, the other player drinks. Use the beer as a chaser."

"Sounds fun!"

"You start then."

"Truth or dare?" Eowyn asked in a devious voice.

"Truth."

"Have you ever fantasized about me? I mean before being stranded here together." She gazed into his eyes eager to hear his answer.

"That's super personal. Can I request an alternate question?"

"No, answer my question or take the shot!"

Marcus thought for a moment then slammed the shot.

"Party pooper! You took the easy way out."

"Yeah, yeah, yeah! My turn now. "Truth or dare?"

"Truth."

"Have you ever thought about me in an intimate way?" She immediately picked up the shot and finished it.

"So, I'm the party pooper, huh?"

"I wasn't finished!" The morphine suddenly hit stronger than ever perhaps the effect amplified by the alcohol. "Often."

"Often what? Expand on your answer."

"I have thought about you sexually very often." She blushed slightly but the effects of the morphine eliminated much of her normal inhibitions. Now, you have my answer, but you still haven't answered mine! I was honest with you—be honest with me?"

"All right already! Yes, I have thought about what it would be like to sleep with you many times. I mean what man wouldn't? Have you looked in a mirror lately?" Eowyn poured two more shots.

"Truth or dare?" Marcus asked as they downed their shots and refilled.

"Truth." Eowyn fidgeted in her seat nervously.

"How is it that you are a proclaimed lesbian, yet you find pleasure in men? I thought the last thing a lesbian wanted was being with a man?"

"Technically, yes. I am a lesbian, but a better explanation of my sexual persuasion would be polysexual. I am attracted to who I'm attracted to regardless of gender, so yes, I do prefer intimacy with women, but I also desire men, and sometimes people of other sexual orientations. Is that clear enough for you?"

"Yes. I didn't mean to pry."

"Yes, you did, and I don't blame you. I live a very complicated life. I would be curious if I were you too."

"My turn. Truth or dare?"

"Truth."

"You're so predictable. You should try to be more adventurous instead of picking the 'truth' every time. Anyway, let's see.

When you told me I was amazing, did you really mean that or were you just trying to make me feel good about myself?"

Marcus remained silent for a minute. "Don't let this go to your head. I've been with my share of women, and I can honestly say, that sex with you was without a doubt the best I've ever had. To be honest, I can't stop thinking about it since it happened. Sure, I've enjoyed myself with others, but regarding overall satisfaction, and again, don't let this go to your head, when I said amazing, I was probably understating the extent of your sexual prowess. You could be just as addictive as this morphine in my pocket. I find you dangerous."

"Dangerous! Now that's going a little overboard. I am not a threat to you."

"I don't mean it that way. I trust you with my life, but I mean dangerous in that I literally find myself drawn to you like a drug. You're masterful."

"Wow, what a glowing review! Let's continue with the game. Whose turn is it anyway?"

"Mine. Truth or dare?"

"Dare."

"Hmm, let's see. I dare you to kiss me with as much passion as you would a lover." Marcus couldn't believe the words left his lips. Yes, he was thinking it, but he didn't intend to dare her to do it. "Wait, I didn't mean to say that I was just thinking it."

"Just thinking it, huh?" Eowyn emptied her shot glass finished off Marcus's and sashayed to him.

"You don't have to. I was just thinking out loud."

"Shh! She ordered as she straddled his hips, and ran her tongue down his neck, then worked her way to his lips. Her kiss was gentle and sensuous but methodically morphed into a more urgent, unimpeded act. Her tongue skillfully probed, massaged, and stroked until she nibbled on his lower lip. Just as quickly as the kiss began, she jumped back to her feet. "My turn! Truth or dare?"

"I want to say dare, but I'll go with truth since that's safe." She took another shot and downed her beer. "Remember back when you and I were captured by the Nill. I was naked and being whipped while you watched. Eventually, I woke up alone, left to die. You have never talked about that time. You must have made some sort of deal with the Nill. What was the deal you made?"

"You're right! I don't like to talk about that. I'm surprised you want to revisit that horrible time at all."

"I'm waiting for your answer."

"Okay then. If you remember, that is when we were first introduced to Waffa. After you were beaten, they whipped me as well. Afterward, Waffa and her men drank until they passed out, but I had a brief conversation with Waffa before she went to sleep or rather, fell unconscious. She explained how she could never be with a Nill man because it would project her as a weak leader. She explained she was very lonely, nearly desperate for love. Knowing this, I made a pact with her. I agreed to go with her, to be her concubine if she would see to it that you were set free. I swapped my life for yours. That's all."

"I knew you made some sort of pact. You saved my life!"

"You would have done the same for me. I'm still amazed at how tough you were. I mean, I always knew you were tough, but that day you were a beast! When we departed, I looked back and saw you unconscious on the forest floor beaten to a pulp, but I knew you would rebound, and survive, and knowing that, I was perfectly fine with dying at that moment."

Eowyn kneeled in front of him and took his face into her hands. I know we talked about this not happening again, but we're two adults stranded alone on this hilltop. As far as we know, we could be the last two people on earth. We could be living our last days on this planet. I want to make sure we live these days to the max and if we happen to survive, what happens between us will remain our secret."

"What are you suggesting?"

"I think you already know. Since we are stranded here, we should live like these are our last moments on earth. We need to forget about our reservations and live for the moment, whatever happens—happens. No regrets. Besides that, the size of that bulge in your jeans is turning me on"

Marcus ignored the comment and made his way to the door. "Let's complete another sweep of the shore and then we'll see what fate has in store for us."

"We can put that off until later. Besides, I started the game, so you have to be the one to finish it. Those are the rules so go ahead and ask."

"Fine! Truth or dare?"

"Dare."

"I dare you to kiss me like you did a few minutes ago but don't stop there. I want to feel you over and over, and over again." Marcus was no longer sure if it was the drug that was under control or if he truly bought into Eowyn's suggestion. "Maybe this is our last few days on earth and if that's true, I fully intend to fill the days with happiness and pleasure until our dying hour."

16

CHARADE UNVEILED

Selima and Celeste with Joanna in tow meandered through the forest in search of a more suitable shelter. For hours they explored the foreign grounds without seeing a single human being or coming upon housing of any type. They were about to give up when off in the distance Selima caught a glimpse of light.

"There's something up ahead. Do you see that light?"

Celeste shielded her eyes from the rain. "Yes, yes, I do!" she excitedly replied, and they quickly trudged in that direction. They arrived at the front door of a small ranch-style home. "Should we just knock?" Celeste asked while she peered into a window.

"They're military. I can tell by their uniforms. There are three or four of them. What do you want to do, Selima?"

"I guess we should knock. I'm waterlogged already, and Joanna could use a reprieve from the rain. Anyway, the worst thing that could happen would be they tell us to go away." Celeste rapped on the door and stood back. Soon a soldier opened the door. He looked over his shoulder. "Check this out. We're not the only survivors, Cap!"

"Come on in and dry off." They huddled around the fireplace while a woman handed them a cup of warm coffee. Her nametag read, "Raley."

"Where did the two of you come from?" A young woman no more than twenty years old, standing about five feet tall, with shoulder-length brown hair, and a to-die-for smile, asked.

"We were flooded out of the valley. There were originally eight of us, but when our boat was pulled under, we were all separated. As far as we know, all the others died. We were lucky enough to wash up on shore. Well, at least Selima was washed up. I was trapped in a debris flow, and she rescued me.

"Did you say, Selima?"

"Yes. Do you know her?"

"Hey, cap, you might want to get out here!"

"What is it?" Selima asked as Captain Acacia walked into the room.

"Well, well, look who fell into our laps. It's hard to believe you are alive since I witnessed your execution not long ago. Sergeant Bauers, PFC Dawkins, placed her under arrest!"

"Wait! She didn't do anything. We're just trying to find shelter. We'll leave if you want us to." Celeste stood in front of Selima and scooted her towards the doorway.

The soldiers sauntered towards them while Acacia continued. "For crimes against the state, including the murder of capitol police and civilians, you are under arrest and are sentenced to death. Dawkins trudged closer, but before he had a chance to put his hands on Selima, Celeste lunged and sent him plummeting into his partner and they tumbled over a coffee table.

"Run, Selima, run!" Celeste screamed as they bolted out the door and towards the forest. Selima and Joanna took cover and waited on the outskirts for Celeste; she was within ten feet of them when the gunfire erupted. Celeste took two more steps and collapsed. The bullet ripped through her chest and her body slid to Selima's feet. Bullets continued to riddle the area as Selima dragged her to cover. With no time, she hoisted her body over her shoulder, Joanna in her arms, and scampered back to the shelter. An hour later, she laid Celeste on the floor. She was barely conscious with blood percolated from her mouth each time she tried to speak. Selima did all she could to stop the bleeding, but the internal damage was extensive. Dark blackish blood steadily oozed from the exit wound no matter how much pressure she applied.

"Please Celeste, stay with me! You didn't have to do that baby. You didn't have to." Her tears spackled Celeste's face as she spoke.

"It's okay," she coughed up a mouth full of blood. Ferris is gone. I can be with him now." She smiled and lightly touched Selima's cheek. Her face morphed from a beat red suddenly to a pale gray. Moments later, she stopped breathing. Selima lay next to her lifeless body contemplating ending her own life, but soon her grief turned to anger.

She buried Celeste that evening and marked her grave with a large marble boulder. The grave was not deep enough. The rain made it near impossible to dig so she placed her in a shallow grave fully intending to one day unite her with the rest of the family once they were reunited.

"They'll pay for taking you, Celeste. I promise you that I will seek vengeance on those who murdered you. My mission in life will be to murder every single one of them; I will kill them all!"

Joanna wailed in the falling rain, drawing Selima back to her less-than-optimal situation. A crying baby, no shelter, and her best friend dead. "Shelter, I must find shelter first," she scooped up Joanna and set off being sure to focus her search south of Acacia's forces. Late into the night she searched and was intent on building a makeshift lean-to and resumed the search in the morning when she spotted a cabin nicely concealed in a thicket of trees and mulberry bushes.

She found the door ajar and likewise the home empty. The entire house was furnished, and the kitchen cabinets held some canned goods. After drying Joanna off, she fed her some fruit cocktail and soon the baby was fast asleep. Selima capitalized on the time and searched the remaining rooms and while pleased that she discovered a warm bed with linens, she was frustrated she couldn't locate any sort of weapon. As she was covering the windows, she noticed a small shed at the rear of the house. She quickly checked on Joanna and found her sound asleep, so she ventured to the shed. Inside she found a myriad of tools but what caught her attention was two hand-held scythes. She swung them wildly with a gleam in her eye.

"This will do. Oh yes, this will do!" That evening she sat in front of a fire sharpening the blades possessed with thoughts of murdering Acacia and all her people. She went to sleep and woke up in the early morning hours. Joanna lay cooing on the bed, but after a quick change and breakfast, Selima tucked her in and not long after, she fell into a deep sleep.

Selima set off without delay with only one thing on her mind, a well-designed plan of vengeance. Selima worked through the night putting her master plan into action. She cut down a bushel of immature bamboo trees, cut a series of two-foot-long lengths, and sharpened the tip of each; later she dug a series of holes along the path that led away from the home and set up a series of tripwires in every conceivable way she imagined one might try to escape. She plotted through the night, gathering, placing, and envisioning revenge. After many hours, at what normally would have been daybreak, she struck the match setting strategically placed piles of pine straw tucked away at the crawl space of the home on fire. The fire quickly spread through the dry rotted floor joists, and it didn't take long for the flames to become visible through the windows.

Selima positioned herself against the wall outside the front door and waited patiently. Soon she heard frantic screams and footsteps breaking for the door. The razor-sharp scythes slashed as the first person stepped outside. He never knew what hit him. The blade impacted just below his jaw perfectly excising his lower mandible. Selima pried the scythe loose and swung the other as the second person exited. He screamed, writhing in pain, his leg excised from the knee down as he bounced down the steps. Selima sprinted towards the woods as two others exited and pursued her. She sprinted to be sure to avoid the booby traps. A smile came to her face when she heard the first body tumble followed by a garbled grunt; the booby-traps were working. Then the sound of footsteps suddenly stopped altogether, but she knew at least one more individual was out there.

She was glad that she had at least evened the odds but knew she was outgunned and probably out of her league militarily. Captain Acacia had years of military training to her advantage while Selima was trained in being a princess. She felt confident if it came down to hand-to-hand combat that she could hold her own since she had martial arts training, but tactically, she was outclassed. Selima dashed down the open trail and quickly jumped into a thick hedgerow when bullets started riddling the ground around her. One round grazed her knee enough so that she was having difficulty running. The wet ground and mud didn't make things any easier. She could hear Acacia getting closer as she hobbled along trying to find some sort of cover, but no matter which way she turned, the muddy footprints she left behind telegraphed her movements. Frustrated, she huddled in some thick brush hoping to ambush Acacia, but the captain wasn't having any of that. Again, bullets ripped through the ground around her.

"Come out or I swear I'll kill you right now!" Acacia ordered.

With no other alternative, Selima emerged from hiding with her hands raised. "Answer me one question before you shoot. Why are you so intent on killing me? I don't even know you."

"It's nothing personal but you are responsible for the deaths of many of my colleagues. You ordered the attack on the Martyreons and the Cooperative. You must be held accountable. Now, I have answered your question. Any last words?"

Selima dropped to her knees. "Please just make it quick. I fear those that I love are all dead anyway, so do what you must. You'll be doing me a favor."

"Turn around!" Selima turned her back to Acacia. She pressed the gun to the back of Selima's head. "For the murder of innocent citizens and crimes against the cooperative, you are sentenced to..."

Peculiarly, two shots were fired nearly simultaneously. Selima fell face first onto the muddy ground, but not before Acacia's body jerked and dropped next to her. The sound of the shots echoed through the countryside.

"For the crime of killing my friends, you have been sentenced to death." Raghba emerged from the wood line, the barrel of her gun still smoking. She ran to Selima fearing that she acted a fraction of a second too late.

"She kicked Acacia's body over. The hole in the middle of her forehead left no doubt she was dead. She gently rolled Selima onto her back expecting the worst, but almost immediately, she coughed up some murky water while gasping for air.

"Selima don't move. It's me, Raghba. I don't understand what I'm seeing since I saw you die." She took a deep breath and accessed Selima's wound. Acacia's shot managed to nearly blow off Selima's entire left ear; what remained was hanging by a thread of skin and her cheek was forever scarred by gunpowder burns. "Everything is all right now, Selima. Come with me."

Apparently in shock, she was unable to process anything. Raghba assisted her through a heavily wooded area, up and down a series of dark trails, and stopped when they arrived at what appeared to be an abandoned fast-food restaurant. The windows were boarded over, and the doors appeared to be dead-bolted, but she pried the back door open wide enough for the two to squeeze inside. A propane heater burned in the back corner next to a sleeping bag and some provisions.

"You're all right, Selima. It's over. Are you hurt?"

She didn't answer. Raghba applied a pressure bandage to the side of her head and tied it off then dried her off with a towel. Looks like these might fit you. Get out of those wet clothes." She changed into some dry clothing. "It's safe here, Selima. You can rest!"

A little over an hour later, Selima snapped out of her reverie. "How did you find me?"

"I heard the gunshots and arrived just in time. I admired your handiwork first and then..."

"What handiwork? I don't know what you mean." She interrupted before Raghba was able to finish.

"The other soldiers you killed. I stumbled across a few of their bodies—nearly stepped into one of the booby traps. Why were they after you anyway?"

"It was Acacia and once she discovered I wasn't dead, she was intent on finishing me off."

They never had the right to act as the judge, jury, and executioner. They got what they deserved. As for you, there should be no looking back—simply look forward from this point on. I believe if God wanted you dead, he wouldn't have sent me to save you. God has a plan for you; just make sure you are listening when he tries to tell you what that might be."

"Let me check your wound." She peeled the bandage. "I hate to say this Selima, but your ear is only hanging by a thread. I'm going to remove it. This might hurt a little. She grabbed some gauze, squeezed it around the hanging flesh, and ripped it loose. "Apply pressure with this." She handed her another stack of gauze.

"Thank you, Raghba! I know we haven't always been the best of friends, in fact, we weren't friends at all, but no matter how you feel, I will consider you a friend going forward. You saved my life, and I'm indebted to you."

"I believe you would have done the same for me. Besides, I can't have tyrants going around killing my family. Honestly, I fear this hurricane has taken many of them already."

"How did you end up here anyway?"

"The house was being flooded, so I volunteered to get Marcus's old fishing boat. I barely made the swim, fastened a rope to the boat and as they were pulling me in, the water whisked me away. The rushing waters were too much; I lost my grip and was washed away. I eventually washed up a few miles from here and discovered this place shortly after. I've been here for the best I can tell, four to five days. You're only the second person I have run into since.

"My turn now. How is it that you are still alive?"

"Marcus staged the whole execution. We had to convince Captain Acacia that I was dead."

"Of course, he did. Who else knew about it?"

"Beside Marcus, the doctor, and nurse. The whole incident had to be believable. I'm sorry if I caused you any undo pain."

"No, I get it. The plan was flawless. You have my compliments."

"By the way, where is this other person you mentioned, you know, the one that found you?"

"Dimitry. We found each other the other day. He's out looking for some food and gathering supplies right now. He should be back soon."

Raghba noticed Selima's eyes slowly fluttering shut. "Over here, Selima. You can sleep on my pallet. I'll try to set up another one while you're resting."

The torrential rains beat on the tin roof while winds slammed into the walls through the night and continued into the next day. Selima slept restlessly dreaming of better times. She and Marcus fishing the shores of the Bentley River, the moment when she declared her love for him and kissed him for the first time. "He's gone—he's gone—he's gone!" Eowyn's words reverberated through her head. She couldn't escape the pain of the loss in her dreams. Several hours later, she was awakened by something dripping on her forehead. Water slowly gathered on the ceiling joist, ran the length of the steel beam, and every so often sent a drop cascading onto her. Raghba slept at her side and Abbas across the room. A loose wooden panel slapped against the side of the building keeping pace with the swirling winds. Selima wiped the dirt from a small section of an exposed window and peered outside. Not sure if the blinding rain was responsible or if a result of her tears, everything outside appeared distorted, bland, and dying. Her tears continued as her mind went back to the man she loved. She gazed into the sky hoping God might show his mercy. Instead, the rain suppressed any hopes and drowned out any possibility of a heavenly reply. For the first time since the shooting, her wits returned and in a moment of sheer panic, she screamed, "Joanna!"

Somewhere, nearly thirty miles away, Marcus Martyreon climbed out of bed, pulled a blanket just under Eowyn's chin, and stepped onto the front porch. He stared out into the rain-filled world wondering if Waffa was alive or if perhaps Eowyn was correct when she said they were most likely dead. He looked to the heavens for answers, but other than the sound of the teeming rain, there was no response.

Eowyn startled him when she slid her hands around his waist and pressed her bare breasts to his back. "Come back to bed. I don't want to be alone, and if we die tonight, I want to be in your arms when it happens."

17

A DEADLY MISSION

Plans were made and it was time for action. Sergeant Ballard, Private Sakato, and Nadia Romonov stood at the top of the steps that led to the basement of the hospital. If everything went well, they would swim down the two flights, access the generator room, and switch the bilge system on. They each held a small bottle of medical-grade oxygen attached to a series of translucent lines that led to a poorly manufactured oxygen mask. They worked for hours assembling the makeshift SCUBA gear and hoped it would provide the oxygen they needed to accomplish the task.

Angela clutched Ballard tightly in her arms. "You better come back to me. I'll be waiting for you."

"We'll be fine, Angie. Are you girls ready?" he asked as he slowly descended one step at a time until the water lapped at his shoulders. "Remember, you two are to follow me. If for any reason you feel like something is wrong, do not hesitate to return to safety."

Nadia and Sakato plunged into the water. "Let's get this over with, Sarge," Nadia cranked the valve to the oxygen canister and disappeared underwater; Ballard and Ayase Sakato were right behind her. The water was murky and filled with all kinds of debris floating through the darkness. To Nadia, the scene appeared like something straight out of the Matrix. Boxes, papers, chairs, and various materials seemingly levitated spinning this way and that in slow motion. They quickly swam down the steps and located the generator room. Ballard pried the ventilation grate from the wall and wiggled through the tight space while Nadia followed. Sakato had just maneuvered through the vent unaware that her oxygen line had snagged on some flashing. The sharp edge easily lanced the line sending her into a panic. Bubbles streamed from the severed oxygen line and the oxygen tank dropped to the ground outside of the generator room. Ballard and Romonov worked unaware as she struggled for her life. In one last desperate effort, she shot towards the vent to retrieve the oxygen tank, and in her haste, slammed her head into the iron framework. Her body floated unconscious and began to jerk ever so slightly followed by a stream of melodious bubbles streaming from her mouth, then all was calm.

Unaware, Ballard and Nadia continued to work. They located the bilge pumps but had to reinstall the ventilation shaft cover before switching them on. Romonov swam towards the cover when she spotted Sakato's lifeless body. She quickly placed her oxygen mask on Sakato while laboring to install the vent cover. She installed the first two mounting bolts, quickly placed the mask to her mouth, took a deep breath, placed the mask back on Sakato, and completed the task. Ballard switched on the bilge pumps and the water rapidly drained from the room leaving Sakato's lifeless body on the floor. He started chest compressions while Nadia held the oxygen mask to her face. Puddles of water on the floor sloshed back and forth with every compression until just as he was about to give up, water shot from her mouth, and she gasped for air.

"Thank God you're back with us! What happened?"

"My oxygen line got snagged and broke. My tank fell."

"So, we're here Ballard. Now, what do we do?" Nadia asked as she studied the room. "Our oxygen is about out and everything around us is flooded with water. How do we get out? If we open the vent, the water rushes in and we'll be in the same situation we were before."

"It appears we didn't adequately prepare for what to do after the generator room was clear. Any ideas?"

"We definitely can't stay here, or we'll starve or eventually run out of air whichever happens first." Nadia scratched her head as she thought.

For several minutes they remained silent until Sakato spoke up. "The bilge pumps. We can plumb them to evacuate the water from the rest of the basement. Is there any way we can feed a drain line out of the generator room and into the adjacent room to drain it? I mean, the bilge pumps emptied this room in a matter of minutes. Are they capable of doing the same for the remainder of the basement?"

"We don't have the materials to pipe to the outside nor do we have the tools. Good idea though." Ballard began studying the piping to the bilge pumps. "But you know what? The pipes to the pumps go right through the basement. If we could manage to get to the pipe outside this room and then open the pipe up somehow, your idea would work Private Sakato. The pipes run along the floor against the front wall. The problem would be getting the pipe open and to make things worse, the person who tries to accomplish this would be in grave danger. Once out, there would be no coming back. You'd have to wait until the water level started to drop, and I don't know how quickly that would be. I think I can do it," Ballard professed."

"No, if anyone does this, it should be me. I was top of my drown-proofing class in Basic Training," Nadia boasted.

"You're making that up! Drown-proofing class...yeah, right!" Sakato objected.

"It's a real class. I went through the same training myself. If you were top of the class how long were you able to hold your breath during certification?" Ballard questioned.

"Four minutes and twenty-three seconds. I think I still hold the record for the academy."

"Impressive!"

"If we're going to be sharing information, how long for you?"

"I'm ashamed to say, I'm not at my best in water. Two minutes and thirty-eight seconds."

"See, I'm the obvious one to choose for this task. What will I need to do?"

"First, we need to identify something that you can use to break the pipe open." They searched the room and pulled an ax from the firefighting cabinet.

"Now, the question is how we are going to get you out without flooding the room again."

"Just open the access panel, stuff me out, and seal it up again. That shouldn't be too hard!"

"Yes, but the incoming pressure is going to be immense."

"The panel is hinged and between the two of us, I think we should be able to get it closed." Ballard looked at Sakato.

"Are you sure you're up to this?"

"I am more than willing. I was made for this! Let's get it over with!"

"You're sure? We have time." Ayase wanted to be positive that Nadia knew what she was getting into.

"No, I want to get this over with. How do you want to do this Ballard?"

"Once I get the ventilation cover open, we will push you out and then seal up from the inside. You'll have to work quickly. The pipe will be towards the floor right where this line goes through the wall. Get to work immediately. These are old iron pipes and while they are very durable, they should be somewhat brittle due to age. With a strong enough blow, the pipe will break. I will switch the bilge on once you signal the pipe is open by tapping on the wall three times."

"Okay, let's cook this cat!" Sakato gave her a reassuring hug. "Be careful, Romonov. I'll see you on the other side."

"I'm sure I will see both of you again. Let's do this!"

Ballard backed out the screws and the pressure did the rest. Water poured into the generator room at a much faster rate than expected, but after a Herculean effort, they managed to get Nadia through the opening, and they latched the vent cover back in place. The water hovered just around their knees by the time they resealed the room.

"If everything goes as planned, we should hear a tap on the wall in the next minute or two." Ballard sat with his ear to the wall.

Nadia switched on her flashlight and located the pipe of interest. She planted her feet the best she could and began hacking away at the old pipe; however, the water slowed her motions, and the ax impacted with much less force than she anticipated. Time and time again, she swung but the blade ineffectually recoiled barely scratching the steel pipe. She could feel the air in her lungs quickly being depleted. In a panic, she shoved the handle of the ax underneath the pipe at a junction point with another and pried. The pipes went taut and began to flex. Finally, on what she knew to be her last attempt before she bolted from the room, the two pipes split. She slammed the ax against the wall and the bilges turned on. With her last reserve of energy, she swam to the highest point in the room while the water level started to drop providing her a fresh supply of oxygen. Within thirty minutes, the water level dropped to two feet and the others exited the generator room to find Nadia, shirtless, propped up against a toppled desk.

"What took you guys so long?" she asked while wringing out her shirt.

"You might want to put your shirt on Romonov before we run into any others," Ballard said as he headed towards the steps. "Let's get up there and make sure the power is back on."

Sakato patted Nadia on the back. "Nice work! You saved the day for all of us. Oh yeah, as Ballard said, you might want to get dressed before we head upstairs."

"Why can't people just be comfortable with the human body. Why do we have to cover ourselves with clothing?"

"Hey, whatever floats your boat? I feel more comfortable in my clothes."

To the delight of all, operations had been restored at the hospital while the unabated rain fell outside. Beyond the walls of Mercy General, the devastating flooding claimed one life after another as countless others struggled for survival.

18

LOVE AMIDST OF
AN APOCALYPSE

Marcus woke to the booming thunder. The winds whistled through the cracks of the front door and the windows rattled under the onslaught. He quietly, as if not to wake Eowyn, exited the room and peered out the front window. He suspected it must be morning, but it was hard to tell by the darkness outside. The rain battered the home and two more leaks sprung up in the living room forming large puddles that at first pooled and then erupted into mini rivers that slithered like a snake throughout the expanse of the home. He filled a metal pot with water, placed it over the fire, and after a few minutes, poured two cups of steaming hot coffee.

"Yo, sleepy! How about a warm drink?"

"Eowyn pried her eyes open and slid up against the headboard. "You're a sight for sore eyes. How long have you been up?"

"About a half-hour. I wanted to see what the weather was like and make sure the water level hadn't risen too much." He took a seat on the bed.

"Well?"

"From what I can see, we are fine, but I don't know how much longer the walls of this house are going to hold up. I've never witnessed winds so strong and listen to that thunder! The lightning is putting on quite a show too."

She set her cup on the end table and laid her head in Marcus's lap. "So, what are we going to do?"

"There isn't anything we can do. Besides, we don't need to be out in that lightning. It looks like another day of relaxation."

She looked at him with a devious smile. "I have an idea." She clutched his hand and placed it firmly between her breasts while she kicked off the blankets and wiggled out of her panties.

Accepting her invitation, Marcus lightly kissed her and moved to her breast while his hand enveloped the other. Eowyn purred in anticipation. She reached over her head still lying, the back of her head in his lap, and unfastened the button to his jeans. Then turned, her elbows resting on his thighs. Marcus traced the scars on her back that unexpectedly unleashed a flood of memories; thoughts of Maria and Waffa who both had similar patterns etched on their backs.

"What are you thinking about?" Eowyn inquired.

"Do they hurt? Do you still feel pain?" He ran his finger along an especially deep scar that meandered nearly the entire length of her back and stopped at the middle of her left butt cheek. He lightly kissed where the blemish ended. As he leaned over, Eowyn unzipped his pants. Her feet fluttered back and forth excitedly when he stood and let his pants fall to the ground.

"Well, look at you! Aren't you the eager beaver standing at attention? Come over here and we'll fill this dreary day with something worthwhile, something to outdo the frenzy of these ravishing storms!"

Miles away, Selima and Raghba trudged through the raging storm. The cutting winds whipped at their face while the biting rain pelted them with fury. The wind gusts at times sent them sliding across the mud-covered ground. They clung to one another and traipsed forward at a snail's pace determined to get back to Joanna. The same trip that took Selima a half hour the day before, now elapsed into an hour. After an additional hour, the home came into view. Raghba pulled Selima onto the porch and inside. The door slammed shut behind them. Selima collapsed onto the floor while Raghba rushed to a frantic Joanna.

"I'm so sorry! I'm feeling a little faint," Selima leaned against the wall.

"You just rest. I'll take care of Joanna." She peeled her soaked clothing off, wrapped herself in a blanket, and picked up Joanna. "It's okay baby, we're here now!" Raghba shuffled through the food on the counter, located a container of powdered milk, added two scoops to a cup, and mixed. She dug through the various drawers until she located a straw, then propped Joanna up on the couch and let her sip away at her meal.

"Come here, Selima. We need to get you into some dry clothing." She helped her to the couch next to Joanna and disappeared into the back room. After a few minutes, she returned with some Jeans and a sweatshirt. "Here, put these on," she ordered as she headed towards the kitchen, returned, and handed her a warm cup of tea. "Let me take a look at that ear."

Selima winced as she peeled the gauze from her bloodied head. "Hang on a minute. We need to clean this up. I'm going to see if I can find anything." Raghba once again ducked into the back room and returned with a bowl of warm water, some rags, gauze, and a bottle of peroxide." She carefully dabbed the area cleaning away any blood then applied some peroxide with a rag and covered the wound.

"There. Now, go get some rest. I'll take care of the baby."

Selima walked down the hallway and into one of the bedrooms while Raghba sat Joanna on her lap. "And how are you today?" While she played with Joanna, unbeknownst to her, a water-soaked creature crawled from the tempestuous river, took a few steps, and collapsed on the shore. The animal sat hunched, shivering, and breathing heavily while the gusting winds sent the stinging rains pelting his body. After a concerted effort, he fought his way back to his feet and trudged forward unsure where he was going but driven by a primal sense that informed him, he was close to shelter. His short furry legs feebly pushed through the storm and the muddy soil that adhered to his feet. The journey was agonizing. Earlier his sibling succumbed to the turbulent waters, but there was no quiet in this animal. His legs burned, his body numb, but reaching land restored his will to survive. He began to walk faster on paws that he could no longer feel. A dull gray shadow emerged from the darkness in the distance and his pace evolved into a desperate trot, but he didn't make it far before he stumbled falling face-first sliding in the frigid mud. What he perceived to be a home seemed so far away, but he had no choice but to continue. He stumbled up a set of weather-dried steps. Using his final drop of energy, the creature stumbled to the entrance, scratched at the wooden door a few times, and collapsed.

Inside, Raghba had just laid Joanna down for a nap next to Selima when she, through the panging rain against the home, thought she heard an unusual sound at the door. She glanced out the window but quickly jumped back since the panes of glass pulsed like a pair of heaving lungs that might burst at any moment. Slowly, she unlatched the door, and the wind vaulted the door open sending Raghba to the floor. The noise startled Selima enough that she rushed to the room and attempted to latch the door.

"Wait! Raghba crawled through the cutting wind, grabbed the curled-up ball of fur lying at the entrance chucked it inside then helped to push the door closed. Selima locked the door and turned the leaver of the deadbolt. They sat with their backs to the door and took a deep breath. The animal lay motionless, but every so often, Raghba sensed its chest rise and fall.

"Where did that come from?" Selima inquired as she plopped down on the couch.

"I heard it scratch at the door." Raghba scooped the mud-covered dog off the floor and carried it to the sink. The more she scrubbed the dog, the more familiar he became. You're not going to believe this!"

"What?"

"This is one of Marcus's dogs."

"It's Tiny?" Selima excitedly scampered next to her.

"It sure is. It's Tiny—it's his dog!" Selima wrapped him in a towel and pulled him to her chest secretly wishing it was Marcus. At this point, holding something of great significance to him was enough to provide a well-needed purpose. She held Tiny tightly doing what she could to warm his frigid body and as she did so, her mind naturally wandered to Marcus. She wondered what it would be like to hold him at her breast. Her mind ambled to fantasies of her staring into his eyes as he passionately molded her into every possible position until they lay in one another's arms satisfied.

Across the watery expanse, nearly simultaneously, beads of sweat cascaded from Eowyn's brow ran the length of her neck, meandered to her breasts, and cascaded onto Marcus's chest each time she plunged taking him into her. Outside, thunder rumbled and echoed. The walls of the house shuddered in unison with the waves of orgasm that pulsed repeatedly. She collapsed next to him, her head resting on his chest, her legs laced between his, as she wiped the sweat from her brow.

As Marcus lay, his eyes fluttered as he traveled to the fringes of consciousness, sleepiness started to overtake him. Out of the relative peace, he thought he perceived a faint voice, "I love you." Unsure if dreaming or if the words quietly glided from her lips, a smile came to his face, and he pulled Eowyn tight.

19

MIND UNDER ATTACK

She entered the lodge, dropped a bag of provisions on the floor, and stoked the fire. A young girl slept on a nearby pallet of straw and leaves. She removed two cans of Progresso Chicken Noodle Soup from the bag and poured them into a stew pot that hung over the fire from a pot crane. Humming a soothing song, she took a seat, picked up a half-completed knitted blanket, and went to work. Every so often, she would stand, mix the soup, then continue working. The girl stirred after a half-hour, sat up, and looked around the room.

"Mommy, when are we going to see the others? I miss Janey and Gurr."

Leeba realized for the first time that Batya wasn't aware of Janey's death or what happened to Gurr and as for the others, she had no idea if they were living or dead.

"We'll see them soon, honey. Once this storm passes, we'll find them." She didn't have the heart to tell her the truth and at the same time, doubted herself as the words peeled from her lips. She saw the boat go under and her friends swept away by the current as she desperately struggled to save her children. Eventually, she was able to lift Batya onto a large piece of driftwood while she hoisted Gurr onto her back. For hours, they drifted.

"Just hold on Leeba; this will all be over with soon. Just hold on a little longer," she told herself repeatedly. Time and time again, Batya was knocked from the log by the turbulent waters only to be pulled to safety by her mother while Gurr held firmly to her neck. Exhausted, not sure, if a result of the frigid waters or fatigue, Leeba drifted from consciousness only to be awakened by water lapping at her face or she was jarred back to the present by the cry of her children. Her body battered from colliding with debris and impacting jutting outcrops, she considered simply letting go, ending all their lives. Each time the thought surfaced, she looked at the children and that was enough to motivate her to go on. The thrashing rain assaulted them on the surface while the cutting cold attacked from beneath. The last thing she remembered about their daunting journey was being swept into a series of violent rapids. Gurr slipped from her arms. She tried to save her but just before their hands joined, the monstrous waters consumed her. One minute she was screaming for her mother and the next, she was silenced. As Leeba labored to get back to Batya, overwhelmed by the loss of her loved one, the undercurrent pulled her into the darkness and slammed her into a rocky offshoot. Her head smashed against a finely honed edge, and all went dark.

Batya's cry snapped her back to reality. She stirred the soup and pulled Batya into her lap.

"Mommy's here, baby. Are you hungry?" She didn't wait for an answer, scooped some into a bowl, and sat Batya next to the bowl on the floor.

For a couple of days, they went without food and viable shelter. Leeba woke, her head resting on the shore with Batya lying a few feet from her. Not sure if she was dead or alive, she crawled to her daughter and was relieved to find a pulse. She searched the shore for Gurr until she couldn't go any further, and forced by the heavy winds and rain, she sought shelter. Eventually, without option, they took shelter underneath a portion of a roof that the storm had ripped from a home. She climbed beneath and curled up with her daughter while she considered her next move. Hours later she woke with Batya's head resting between her breasts, snuggly tucked away under her shirt. Starved and desperate for warmth, she made her daughter as comfortable as possible and ventured out to find shelter and food. She returned an hour later with a backpack full of supplies. Batya slept comfortably which provided Leeba time to begin building a shelter. She searched the forest until she located four trees positioned where one sat at each corner of a square. Using lengths of rope, she tethered small pine trunks from tree to tree; one positioned vertically at the bottom of each and then one parallel four feet from the ground and the other at eight. Once positioned at all four walls, she weaved large branches and a series of fallen saplings until all four sides, minus a small entrance, completely covered each wall. She then cut pine branches and lined the walls. Finally, she laid more pine timbers across the roof and lined them with evergreen branches. After a couple of days, working whenever Batya was sleeping, the structure stood approximately ten by ten feet and stood eight feet tall. Constructing the shelter would have been difficult for a single person to do during good weather but completing the project during the violent weather proved Leeba's strength and dedication to her child.

"I'll never question my physical prowess again!" She chuckled as she huddled inside.

After a week, she managed to gather some furniture, some canned goods, clothing, and blankets that she found strewn throughout the milieu. They hunkered down and lived day to day never discovering another human being other than an occasional body that washed up onshore. After scrounging through several leveled homes, Leeba accumulated plenty of supplies to keep them well-fed and comfortable. Batya remained the focus of her life, but during the downtime, she began to lose hope. She lacked any human contact other than brief conversations with her infant daughter. As of lately, she resorted to talking to herself but that didn't satisfy her need to be in contact with others. At one point, she remembered a movie she saw many years ago where a man was stranded on a deserted island, drew a face on a volleyball, and befriended the makeshift human. On one of her journeys, she found a basketball and after a little work with a marker, she created her new companion, Spalding. After a couple of weeks, she added Rawlings, Viceroy, and Mizuno. She had them each arranged in a semi-circle that surrounded the table. While knitting, she held long conversations, held tea parties, and provided free advice while they had tea together. Even with her newfound friends, she yearned for companionship, and love for Eowyn but her longing could not be satisfied.

To keep herself occupied, she regularly patrolled the shore of the river and collected bodies. Currently, her collection consists of thirteen, but after today's efforts, she hopes to surpass fifteen. She was disappointed when she only located one.

Following weeks of effort, collecting and gathering dead bodies, her mind would always wander to thoughts of her family. She feared they were dead. Even when sleeping there was no relief from the horrifying recollections. One nightmare after another tormented her; the terrified look on Gurr's face as the water pulled her under, images of Eowyn consumed by the waters, and various portrayals of her family in one level or another of rigor mortis. At night, she contemplated suicide, and yet, Batya's cries in the night provided her a reason to live. Without her, Leeba did not doubt that she would take her own life. And so, the days passed into weeks and weeks into a second month as Leeba maniacally existed—the oppressive showers systematically pelted her psyche, and thoughts of her dead family tormented her—until she lost touch with sanity.

20

NO QUIT IN THIS ONE

Only recently regaining consciousness, Sophi was becoming increasingly frustrated. Thoughts were clear in her mind, but she couldn't express herself verbally and physically; she felt a persistent numbness in her legs. Over the past few weeks, she learned to consider her legs a burden, two anchors meticulously tethered to her body that served no purpose. If she had her way, she would have dissected them, simply lopped them from her body, but she was incapable of even pouring a cup of water let alone cutting her legs off. But Doctor House felt the latest procedure would be a success. For three hours Sophi laid, her back filleted exposing the spine from her tailbone to the 5th lumbar fully exposing the thoracic extension to the T12 vertebra. The swelling of her brain had long since diminished and with it, doctors expected her mobility would return, but that never occurred. Little did doctors know, nor did they detect that her spinal column was compromised due to numerous vertebral protrusions most likely incurred during the brutal beating incurred over two months ago.

House ordered the nurses to check in often and inform him of any changes following the surgery. Currently, Sophi tried to relax, to breathe evenly, but while she demonstrated no hope to the attending physician, underneath she secretly prayed to every known deity asking for a reprieve from her paralysis. The room was entirely silent as Sophi concentrated on moving her toes, but again, her efforts were futile. A tear meandered along the border of her nose, slid to the slope of her cheek, and dripped onto her pillow. She lifted her arm to scratch her nose, but her hand awkwardly dangled as she tried to extend her fingers unsuccessfully. Instead, she rubbed her entire hand against her nose. Her hands felt as if they were asleep like she had laid on them in her sleep cutting off circulation only this time, she never regained feeling. Her fingers were numb much like her legs and no matter how hard she tried, she could not control them.

"And how are you today, Soph?" A male nurse entered. "I asked you a question and I expect an answer."

"I...I'm pissed." She vocalized after an immense effort.

"So, you say you're pissed?" He knew exactly what she was saying but was trying to get her to speak even if he had to make her angry to persuade her to do so. Doctors explained the more she attempted to speak, the sooner her speech would return.

"Did you say you're pissed?" He asked again when she ignored him.

"F..fuk oo."

"Could you repeat yourself? I didn't understand you."

"Ass—hoe!"

"Good. Sophi. Way to pronunciate, but it's not ass hoe, it's asshole." Try again.

Instead, she clammed up while he removed the blanket and carefully sponged her body from head to toe. "You know, Soph. I know you are frustrated, and you probably just want to give up.

I can only imagine how scared you are, but while what happened to you is tragic, you are lucky in many ways. You have no way to know what has been happening around us, but hundreds, possibly thousands, have died. Torrential rains have been falling for weeks, homes destroyed; families have been literally washed away. You probably wonder why your family hasn't visited. The truth is they may be one of the casualties or if fortunate, they are stranded unable to get to you. Your condition is temporary. You will speak again, and you will eventually walk. My point is that if you are waiting for loved ones to come to your rescue...that's not going to happen. Honestly, you may be the only member of your family still alive." He lightly dabbed a towel soaking up the tears that coursed down her face. "I'm not trying to upset you. It's important that you know that only you can heal yourself and some of the very family members you hope are going to visit may need your help once is all said and done. You're going to have to work hard, but I am confident that you can do this, Soph."

Adiva waltzed into the room and took a seat next to Sophi. "How's the patient doing today, Tony?"

Before he answered, Sophi, replied, "Fine."

"I see that! Are you about ready for some physical therapy?" She asked. "First, let's get you in a clean gown."

"Mar...us, o...k?"

"We don't know. We're not sure about anyone at this point. Before the flooding, he visited you a couple of times, but of course, you were unconscious. He was very worried about you. Let's see, Eowyn visited, Leeba and even Ferris stopped by. You have many friends!"

"Fam..ly."

"Yes, sorry, your family! Listen. Since you just had your surgery, we will only be doing some stretching exercises today. No walking."

"I'm all finished for the day, Soph. Do you need me for anything else, good-looking?" Nurse Tony asked.

She shook her head, no.

Later that evening, while lying in bed, she became aware of an entirely new sensation; a prickly feeling followed by a tingling that started at her toes and slowly traveled to her knees, proceeded up her thighs until her body began to feel whole. Though unable to kick off her sheets, she sensed her toes were moving underneath, and her legs shifted slightly when she attempted to move them.

"Tomorrow begins my journey. I will walk and talk again!" she thought to herself as she drifted to sleep with a smile on her face.

21

WANTED DEAD OR ALIVE

Hauling herself from the muddy ground. Lieutenant Raley trudged through a field of heather and tumbled into a pool of water. About six feet deep, it only took a few strokes to traverse. The water was unusually warm and clear. She considered soaking for a while hut after spotting a body hopelessly entangled in vines of submerged kudzu below, she worked her way to the shore. Crimson-tainted water trailed behind her as she waded. She hoped the waters might wash away her sins before she died and on a more practical note, she hoped the warm water might cleanse her wounds and help slow infection. She looked to the heavens as the rain bombarded from above. Several times she slipped below the surface until she pulled herself ashore. The bodies of her comrades littered around the remains of their smoldering home. The corpse of her commander, Captain Acacia lay in a puddle of blood, a bullet hole in her forehead.

The patrol came upon the smoldering home and the bodies hours later. Dispatched the previous night, they hoped to meet up with Acacia and guide them back to the main force that had taken refuge in the caves of a nearby mountain range. They were about to head back to base when they found Raley lying partially on shore her lower body still resting in the water. The medic detected a faint pulse, applied a tourniquet, and rushed her toward headquarters. They followed the forest up an elongated draw, along the cover of a snakelike ridgeline, then clamored up the hillside until coming to a large cave opening.

"Quick, the lieutenant needs the doctor."

"Where are the others? Did you find the captain?"

A large group of soldiers gathered around awaiting answers. Out of the original force of 300 plus, approximately 200 survived the catastrophic storm.

"So, where's Acacia?"

"Dead. We found her body and the bodies of most of her men. The only survivor is Lieutenant Raley, and she may not make it. Looks like they were ambushed."

"Any idea who's responsible, Sergeant Petry?"

"No, but once the Lieutenant is conscious, we will. For now, we need to double the guard."

"Sergeant Petry, Lt. Raley wants to see you."

A smile crossed his face hearing she was okay. He tried to conceal his feelings for her around others and composing himself, he, as if in no hurry, dallied to the medic's station.

"Everyone out! I need to speak with Sergeant Petry alone," she ordered.

"Thank God you're all right, Sage." He leaned in, took her face between his hands, and their lips fused. She hummed with pleasure as his tongue pressed deep and he would have continued kissing her, but she cooled things down when she pulled away. "We have some things to talk about. Selima is alive. She and another woman are responsible for Captain Acacia's death."

"That can't be. We witnessed Selima's death. She had no pulse."

"Then they figured out a way to bring her back to life or she has a twin. She nearly killed me, Ned. She nearly lopped off my leg. I know the weather isn't optimal, but she is in the area, or at least was. We need to locate her and make a preemptive move. She believes she killed all of us and if we can locate her, we have the element of surprise. I want a patrol sent out to check the immediate area where I was found. Tell them to begin at the burned-down house and sweep in 360-degree concentric circles, every 50 yards. They are not to return until she is found."

"And what if they do find her?"

"They are not to engage. Once found, they are to notify me, and I will see to it that she is exterminated for good this time! We also need to add Marcus Martyreon to the list of traitors. Selima and Martyreon are now top of our list for extermination. I want them dead!"

"Let me see that leg of yours," Petry pulled the blanket from her leg. "How many stitches?" He ran his hand from her calf to the thigh of her good leg. "Oh, the things I would do if you were only healthy."

"To answer your question, forty-one stitches, and regarding us, our day will come again soon." She leaned in and touched her lips to his. "Can you come and see me tonight? I might be open to some physical therapy." She smiled and slid her hand onto his butt. "I could use some attention to help me get to sleep."

"Of course! One quick question before I leave." He took her hand and sat next to her on the bed. "Why don't we just pack up and run away together? Who cares if Selima is alive and as for

Marcus Martyreon, I have no beef with him." He looked for an acknowledgment.

"Who cares if Selima is alive? She killed Acacia, our friends, and nearly killed me, so, I intend to avenge their deaths. Do you have a problem with my orders?"

"You know I would follow you into the fires of hell, Sage, but I want a life with you and that won't be possible if you're dead. You barely escaped death from your last encounter with her and now you want to go after Martyreon? Contrary to your opinion, you only have one life, and you aren't indestructible. Maybe we should just let government officials manage her while you and I live happily ever after. What about our discussions of children, family, and making love from dusk until dawn?"

"None of that's changed, Ned. I do want to have a family with you, but I require justice before I can think of a family and settle down. I need closure, and I won't have that unless Selima is gone. You know that's how I work. I must have closure."

"And what about Martyreon? What has he done to deserve being murdered?"

"He lied! He fooled us into believing Selima was dead and because of that, Acacia is dead, and I am in the hospital. It's not personal that I want them dead, it's simply making amends for their treachery. Some people don't deserve mercy!"

"Okay then. I'll put together a squad to begin the search. I'll have them begin in the morning. I'll stop by afterward if you still want me to." He looked at her with puppy dog eyes wondering if she was angry with him.

"Of course, I do! Not only do I want to see you, but I need you."

Sergeant Petry grinned as he left the room ready to assemble the team Lt. Raley requested. While he supported Raley's decision, he hoped that they would never locate Selima or Martyreon. As far as he was concerned, the past was the past while he also believed that everyone would eventually account for their sins.

As he gathered a squad of his best men, Selima and Raghba sat comfortably in front of the fireplace. The light of the flames illuminated the area directly in front of them but was unable to cut through the eerie Cimmerian gloom that surrounded them; the rumble of thunder rattled the house from the rafters to the foundation. After a worrisome night, Tiny finally pulled out of a coma-like state and regained his vitality. Currently, he lay tightly wedged between the two.

"Who is this man with you?" Selima asked. How in the world did you manage to meet a man with all this going on?"

"He saved me; found me washed up on shore. He brought me to his shelter and nursed me back to life."

"The day I came upon you, we were out scrounging for supplies. Now, of course, you are here with us. I'll introduce you to home once he wakes."

"I sense a smile on your face when you mention his name. Tell me more about him and if you dare, fill me in on how the two of you kept yourselves busy during the long and lonely days and nights."

Raghba blushed. "We sat by the fire and talked about things, about each other. He was a very good cook, was attentive, and made sure I was taken care of."

"Taken care of, huh? What exactly do you mean by that? I mean, if I summarize your own words, you said he was attentive, and caring, and he took care of you. Hmm. What needs did he take care of?"

"Stop, Selima."

"I'm just trying to understand the depths of your relationship. How familiar did you and your man friend become on those lonesome, desolate days?"

She glanced at Selima with a grin and quickly looked away. "First, he has a name, it's Dimitry. As for your question, do you mean were we intimate?"

"Exactly, let me hear the good stuff."

"All I can say is that it was magnificent. At least I believe it was. After going more than a year without, I don't have much to compare our encounter to. I will say that I was totally satisfied, and I crave more. I forgot how good sex can be."

"Sadly, I can relate to that. This may sound pitiful but I'm still a virgin at the age of twenty-six."

"Really? How could that be? You are so beautiful. You must have men throwing themselves at you."

"I'm not all that, Raghba, but I have had my chances. The problem is that I was in a position while Princess where I was waiting for a man to be selected for me. I had no choice, but my father was very scrupulous and never found my mate before he died during the Nihilistic War. Once I became a citizen of the Cooperative, I was already in love with the man I hoped to marry but things never worked out. Just when I thought I might have a chance, he got married and then was tragically killed by this same tempest that has haunted us for weeks now.

"Wait! Do you mean to tell me you have never had sex? No way! I'm one to speak, but after a year I was desperate but twenty-six. Incredible!"

"More like tragic! I don't know what it is like to experience the company of a man. I mean I did kiss him a couple of times but that's the entirety of my sexual experience."

"Do you mind if I ask who you were saving yourself for?"

"Marcus Martyreon. We fought side by side through the first Nihilistic War and even during the second. I would have made him a happy man if given the chance, but God had other plans I guess." She fought back tears.

"I have no doubt you will one day meet the man of your dreams. If I can meet a man amid a prophetic storm such as we are experiencing now, there is no doubt a beauty queen like you can easily do the same."

"'Beauty queen,' far from it. Anyway, perhaps I will one day find my Dimitriy, but at the present, I am still grieving and wondering if I will ever be able to put him out of my mind. Right now, everything I do, many things I see, even smells, draw my mind back to him."

"I'm a pretty good prognosticator, and I see happiness in your future. Good things are headed your way."

22

STEALTHY ASSAULT

The minute she reached into the water, the fast-moving current plucked her from the shore. Marcus had only turned his back for a minute and when he turned back, she was gone. It was difficult to see anything through the cutting rain, but he quickly realized, the only explanation could be that she had fallen in the tumultuous sea. He reacted quickly and sprinted downstream. Every so often, he would get a glimpse of a gray figure bobbing from the depths then disappear just as quickly.

"No, God! You will not expropriate another loved one from me! No, not another!" He darted along the shore, not looking for Eowyn nor focused on anything except the water and land to his front; like an eagle searching for prey, he fully concentrated on locating a suitable projection that would allow him to snatch her from the raging sea. He ran nearly a quarter mile before he located what he was looking for. A large, uprooted pine lay, the top of the tree hanging precariously, extended over the water only inches from the surface of the rushing waters. Marcus climbed to the top of the tree and carefully inched his way over the water, nearly falling in himself several times as he cautiously advanced. He wrapped his legs tightly around the trunk and with one arm looped around a branch with the other he hovered just above the water in wait. He knew he would only have one chance and if his effort was unsuccessful, Eowyn would be ripped from his life forever. For a moment, he wondered if he miscalculated and she had already passed by, but just as he began to despair, her body floated into view. He stretched as far as humanly possible and latched to her frigid hand. The swift current nearly wrenched him from his perch as her body fluttered in the water below, the undercurrent plotting to rip her from his life. Despite an immense effort, her hand slipped from his. Instinctually and in desperation, he scooped at the water with both hands; his legs still moored to the tree trunk, and he managed to snatch her hair. Slowly, with his one free hand, he inched towards shore alternating from one branch to the next, until he fell to the ground. Marcus slowly reeled Eowyn in by her long black locks.

The struggle had drained his energy. Raindrops pelted his face as he took a moment to catch his breath. Eowyn lay next to him with all color drained from her alabaster skin causing him to panic.

Springing into action, he kneeled at her side, desperately placed his lips over hers, and gave her two rescue breaths until water percolated from her mouth. Still unconscious, he hoisted her over his shoulder and trudged towards home. Wet and exhausted, he stepped into the house and placed her on the couch. Her body was ice-cold, her lips a mysterious shade of periwinkle; he knew he had to get her warmed up. At the same time, his body was also beginning to shut down perhaps a bit hypothermic himself. The past hours took their toll. The frigid waters were made exponentially colder by the whipping winds, and the oppressive rain in combination with the emotional toll the day took on him, sapped his body of all energy. He crawled to Eowyn, stripped off her wet clothing, and covered her with a blanket. After adding some wood to the fire, he pulled a vial from his pocket, filled the syringe, and sunk the needle into his arm. A familiar warmth trickled through his body, the room began spinning, and he blacked out.

Miles away, a squad of Lieutenant Raley's men led by Sergeant Perez continued their grid search. They had been at it for two days when they came upon a house. Smoke billowed from the chimney and the light of a candle flickered through the window.

"Corporal Henderson and Private Abdul, go to the back of the house and see what you can see inside," Sergeant Perez ordered. "Make sure you're not detected. Private Masterson and I will reconnoiter the front. We'll meet back here in five minutes. Got it? Now, move out!"

Perez lingered in front of the home for several minutes discreetly peering in the windows before he retreated to the rally point. Henderson and Abdul were waiting.

"She's definitely in there. Should we head back and inform, the Lieutenant?" Corporal Henderson asked as he stuffed a granola bar into his mouth.

"That is what she said, but why don't we just put an end to this now? Sergeant Petry said to eliminate the target if we get the opportunity. There are only two of them and there are four of us. Private Abdul, you're still carrying C-4, right?"

"Yes. Sergeant."

"How much?"

"Four blocks."

"That's plenty to level the house. Here's what I want. Abdul, plant one brick at the left front part of the house; Henderson and Masterson arm the others while I plant the explosives on the opposite side. I want all timers set for ten minutes. Make sure the digital trigger is active, so we can be at a safe distance from the explosion. This will be our rallying point once the munitions are in place. Go on! We rally back here in five minutes."

Perez peered into a side window. Selima sat on a couch in the living room. He pried a ventilation screen from the side of the house and carefully planted a block of C-4, inserted the blasting cap, and wired the digital timer. He peeked in the window one more time before heading to the rally point.

Raghba had just stretched out on her lumpy mattress when she thought she detected a shuffling outside. With the deafening rain, she was unable to detect the source, but she worried the flooding waters might have been wrenching the home from its foundation. She pulled the curtain to the side and was about to end her search when she saw a dark figure sprint into the wood line. Adrenaline replaced her languish and her eyes flew wide-open. "Selima!"

Raghba scurried to the living room. "Get your things together. I'll get Janey. We have company outside, and I believe that they are some of Acacia's men. They were fooling around by the house, and I fear they are up to no good or they are planning an imminent attack. Hurry, Selima! We need to move now!"

Selima grabbed what little she could, and slipped on her boots and jacket while Raghba emerged from the back room with Janey in tow. She grabbed Selima's hand, led her to the back door, and threw the door open. Her foot had just hit the first step when the ground erupted. The immense explosion engulfed Selima in flames sending her hurdling through the air. She slammed into the muddied ground, slid several feet, and came to rest at the base of a tree. The skin of her hands and face glowed a bright red and much of her clothing smoldered.

At the same time, the entire world seemed to be spinning uncontrollably. Raghba surveyed the remains of the house as she searched for Selima. She tucked Janey into her shirt, and marched forward, the entire time stumbling and at times falling to the ground. In her dazed state, the ground seemed to be moving underneath her, shifting, and rising to make it exceptionally difficult to find her way. She dug her nails into the saturated soil and pulled herself forward until protected from the rain underneath a large chunk of what remained of the smoldering roof. While the ground was frigid, waves of heat from the blazing fire warmed them from a distance; Raghba curled into a fetal position nuzzling Janey at her breast, and promptly passed out.

23

LOVER FROM THE PAST

Eowyn woke tucked under layers of warm blankets. The last thing she remembered was falling into the water and fighting for her life. For a moment, she speculated if it was all a bad dream but discovering her tattered wet clothes hanging across the room informed her otherwise. She pondered her situation for a long time before sighing and rolling out of bed.

"Marcus," she yelled and was surprised when she didn't receive a reply. She slipped into some dry panties, pulled an oversized t-shirt over her head, and walked into the living room. A note rested on the mantle over a blazing fire and a pot of hot pork and beans simmering over the flames.

Eowyn

I hope you are feeling better and have had a bite to eat by now. I stepped out to investigate an explosion that I witnessed earlier. It occurred far from here, but I hope to see if there may be others out there and if they require assistance. If I don't reach the area by dark; I will return. Please stay put and keep warm. I already miss you—strange, huh? You gave me quite a scare the other day. I couldn't imagine life without you. Keeping in mind that we are both in love with our significant others, I am still inclined to say, "I love you—I think you tried to tell me the same a few days ago. Life can be so complicated, but yes, I do love you and hope to see you soon.

Marcus

Eowyn kissed the letter and held it tightly to her chest while a smile spread across her face. "I love you too, Marcus. More than you'll ever know." She slipped the letter into the waistline of her panties, picked up a bowl, and filled it with steaming beans.

Marcus had trudged a good ten miles when he became disoriented. He was unable to find the site of the explosion and was now having difficulty finding his way back to Eowyn. Making things worse, the torrential rain morphed into what he could only describe as a monsoon. Winds picked up and uprooted many trees while visibility was nearly nonexistent. Darkness set in, but he trudged on using the ever-growing sea as his compass. He knew if he followed along the shores he would eventually recognize something that would signal he was near home. The downside of the plan was that he was being strafed by an endless barrage of raindrops that felt more like pebbles striking him than water. Many times, he contemplated stopping to find shelter as the bitter winds and the associated wind chill battered him, but he feared entering the forest and losing his way, so he continued.

Eowyn traveled in and out of sleep throughout the night. Waking at times thinking she hears Marcus, but is disappointed to discover the house is empty.

The best Marcus could estimate was the evening had ended and it was the next morning when an overwhelming weariness settled into his limbs and invaded the very core of his being, and he could go no further. He flopped onto the ground, leaned against a large bolder, and closed his eyes; just for a second to gather his thoughts. The second turned into minutes and the minutes morphed into forty-five minutes; he was perfectly fine sitting where he was. That's when he first thought he heard the voice.

"Get up little man! You don't have far to go." An arm slipped around his shoulder, and he opened his eyes to discover Allura sitting next to him.

"You're not real. You can't be here." He closed his eyes and opened them a second time expecting her to vanish, but still, she sat.

"My little, Marcus, you're going to have to get up. Your family is counting on you. You can't give up."

He reached out and swore he felt the warmth of her skin as he gently brushed her cheek with the palm of his hand. "How can this be?"

"The question shouldn't be how, but instead, why?"

"Why are you here then?" he asked.

"You silly little man. I'm here to guide you, to spend some time with you while we get you home."

"I love you, Allura, and I promise I saved that special place for you in my heart just like you asked. You are always on my mind. You are the perfection that I gage all others and no matter how hard I try; I haven't been able to find another like you."

She took his hand and pulled him to his feet. "Come, we need to get you out of this weather." Her touch warmed him; he suddenly felt light on his feet and in what seemed like a minute, he walked up the steps to his home. When he turned around to say goodbye, she was gone.

A loud crash woke Eowyn from her slumber. For a minute, she thought another tree had hit the house, but when she opened the front door, Marcus lay unconscious on the threshold. She dragged him into the living room and tried to wake him, but he didn't budge. Despite being soaked, his skin was hot to the touch; she ran to the bedroom, returned with blankets, and laid them out on the floor until she had a neatly arranged pallet for him to lay on. Next, she stripped off his saturated clothes, dried him off, and rolled him into the makeshift bed. His body shook violently as she slid next to him and wrapped herself around his frigid frame. She tended to him throughout the day, into the night, until falling asleep.

"Hey sleepy. I didn't think you'd ever get up!" Marcus laughed.

"I was taking care of you, bonehead! You were out of it. Talking in your sleep and thrashing around. You had me worried. You had a long conversation with Allura and for a second, you started to hump my leg."

"No, I didn't."

"Only kidding, but I heard the word "love" several times. It was like she was in the room with you.'"

"Honestly, I don't remember too much other than just trying to get back to you. I didn't think I was going to make it, but Allura took my hand, and the next thing I know, I'm waking up in your arms, and you felt amazing."

"Aww, look at you. You think I'm beautiful; you want to kiss and hug me and have romantic moments together. Why Marcus, if I didn't know any better, I'd think you were falling in love with me."

"And you're not?"

"So, what happened the other day?" She avoided his question. "One minute we were walking along the river and the next, I'm waking up in bed."

"You so masterfully evaded my question. I guess in this case what you didn't say answers my question. I won't ask again."

"I just meant..."

"It's fine, Eowyn. I don't need an explanation. Anyway, the answer to your question is that you fell into the river and almost died; you're such a klutz! I placed you in bed once we got home. No big deal. I'm going out to gather some more wood for the fire." He was out the door before she could gather her thoughts.

Her mind returned to his initial question. "I do love you, Marcus," she said to herself. She was in a quandary. On one hand, she loved Leeba and wanted to spend the rest of her life with her, but at the same time, there was a good chance she was already dead. On the other, there was no doubt that her time with Marcus grew from a relationship of convenience to a deeply engrained love. While she desperately wanted to be reunited with Leeba, she was perfectly happy loving him. Filled with a sudden level of guilt and fear that she might lose him; she sprinted outside to catch him. "Marcus," she screamed into the all-encompassing darkness but received no response. Disappointedly, she leaned against the doorway and slid to the ground. A cold mist filled the air sending a chill down her spine, but she was determined to wait until he reappeared.

Then, after several minutes, like a specter animating out of thin air, a dark silhouette appeared from the tree line. In anticipation, Eowyn moved to the bottom step and stood, the frigid rain quickly imbued the material of her thin shirt. Her chest heaved in anticipation of the thoughts brewing in her mind. "I do love you, Marcus," she declared as he approached, but her voice didn't carry through the deafening storm. He marched towards the house completely unaware of her presence until just five steps from her; he froze mid-step and dropped the armful of wood to the ground. Soaked from head to toe, he stared into her eyes. Eowyn raced towards him and lunged into his arms. Her legs wrapped around his waist; she embraced him while her lips feverishly met his. Lightning flashed through the sky, the already heavy rains cascaded uncontrollably, and the Siberian winds set upon them as Marcus lowered to his knees; his lips explored her body until coming to rest at her teat. Her nipple projected from her meager cotton shirt, and he took it into his mouth while his hands firmly grasped her ass and pulled her tight. He wanted her closer, to be part of her, to be inside her. The weather spiraled out of control around them, but even the fiercest storm, the coldest of cold couldn't distract them from easing their passions. Eowyn hoisted Marcus's shirt over his head while he grabbed the collar of her shirt with both hands and in one savage motion, tore it from her body. He laid back on the ground admiring her as water flowed from her billowing chest. Goosebumps inundated her body; every feature stood erect anxiously awaiting contact, the touch of soft skin, delicate lips, desperate to become one with the man she loved.

Unclad, they examined one another, rubbing, stroking, and carnally delving. The whole time the rain beat down, the winds howled, and thunderous cracks followed by bright bolts of lightning peppered the terrain, but they were too preoccupied for any intrusions. Instead, they focused on gratifying one another. Their bodies, lubricated by the hydraulic qualities of the rainwater, glided over them. Eowyn leaned forward, her chest sliding against his, at first, at a leisurely pace, vacillating, her arms wrapped around his neck, her lips hovering above his. Thunder rumbled in the distance; the ground quaked, and her pace quickened with each deafening burst. Her long black locks swung wildly sending water droplets showering Marcus each time she thrust bottoming out then quickly rising again, her lips softly brushing over his. For the moment, nothing mattered but expressing their love; no words were exchanged, but they communicated with masterful precision. Tree limbs, leaves, debris, and clothes, rolled around and careened off them, but they remained joined, intent on meeting one another's deepest desires, their bodies like braille-embossed pages waiting for interpretation. The two lay, bodies meshed as one, face to face as they brushed one another's hair from their face; they kissed one more time. Marcus scooped her from the ground and carried her inside; they curled up in bed and slept in one another's arms.

24

DARING RESCUE

Sergeant Perez and his squad, feeling confident that Selima was eliminated, hustled toward base excited to inform Lieutenant Raley and Sergeant Petry what they had accomplished. They knew that they were instructed to simply locate the target and report back, but they couldn't possibly be mad that they took the initiative to finish her off themselves.

As Raley and his men pulled out, Raghba woke to excruciating pain. Many of the burns formed into blisters during the night. Despite the pain, she gently covered Janey, and crawled out of the shelter with one goal in mind; she had to locate Selima. The explosion yanked her from her grasp, and she was unable to locate her that night, but now that the day advanced, a subdued light shined through the gray sky. The fire had long since burned out or was snuffed by the continuous rain. Only part of one wall of the home stood intact. Raghba maneuvered around the border of the home finding many items of use. The bed in the back room, while water-soaked, sat unscathed, the blankets still neatly covered the bed as if awaiting a person to jump in. At the back of the structure, she located a large wooden shed; after hours of work, she emptied the contents and moved Janey inside. Once fed and comfortably tucked away, she resumed her search of the outer edges of the forest. After traveling a short way, she finally came upon Selima's body about ten feet off the ground wedged in the crook of a tree; her body battered. Her burnt and tattered shirt hung loosely from her waist, flapping in the wind like a white flag signaling she had given up. She appeared lifeless; one arm nearly ripped from her shoulder. Blood-tainted water flowed down the length of the trunk and pooled around the root formations.

"Selima," she yelled but received no answer. Raghba desperately tried to scale the tree, but each attempt failed as she simply slid down the slick trunk to the ground. Through the howling rains, she could hear the roar of the ever-growing sea that slowly inched its way closer to them. Suddenly her head rose like a deer alerted to an intruder. She galloped to the materials she earlier pulled from the shed, unburied a stepladder, and set it at the base of the tree. Even with the additional five feet and stretching the entirety of her five-foot-plus frame, she was unable to hoist Selima's tightly wedged body. Finally, in desperation, she utilized a length of two-by-four and lifted her body until it sat precariously teetering on the brink of falling to the ground. Raghba scuttled down the ladder, repositioned, and climbed, but didn't quite make it to the top when Selima tumbled directly on top of her. Raghba wrapped her arms around her, while the momentum flipped the ladder catapulting them roughly to the ground. The merciless storm besieged the women; one was barely alive while the other moaned and groaned trying to catch her breath.

Raghba got to her feet and dragged Selima inside the shed. She had no idea if she was alive but prayed for a miracle as she pressed her ear to her chest. Frustrated, she slammed the door of the shed closed and tried again. For several minutes, she held her ear to her icy skin. She detected no heartbeat. The explosion had killed Selima. With one hand, Raghba grabbed a blanket that dried over the fire, and with the other, she lovingly coaxed Selima's eyelids closed. For a moment, she contemplated wrapping herself in the toasty blanket, but instead, draped it over her deceased friend.

Joanna stirred on the other side of the room and Raghba scooted next to her. She gently rubbed the baby's back, while lying next to her, and escaped to a deep yet disturbing dream.

As Raghba closed her eyes for a well-deserved rest, miles away, Leeba sat lightly running a blade over her wrist leaving fine blood-engorged patterns across each. Every time she resolved to sink the blade deep, she glanced at Batya sleeping across the room and reluctantly etched another shallow gash in her arm, thigh, or both. As each dreary day passed, she lost all will to live, yet wasn't selfish enough to abandon her child and leave her for dead. She raked the razor across her thigh, let the blood dry, and then slipped on her coat. Over the past weeks, she kept busy adding cadavers to her graveyard collection. The count rose to over twenty bodies, and she was excited to see how many washed ashore today. Burying the bodies was the highlight of her day and today would be no different. After discovering three more yesterday, she buried the first two and saved the last for the next day just in case no others washed ashore. She patrolled for a couple of hours when weariness set in. Halfway home, she dropped a lifeless body and commenced exploring the deeper recesses. She discovered what appeared to be a once-traveled path and as she followed it deeper into the forest, located a quaint little cabin tucked away in a thicket of trees and shrubs.

She stepped onto the porch, rapped on the door, and when she didn't receive an answer, peered through the window. The inside appeared as if frozen in time. The table was neatly set for two, while plates of festering food and empty glasses were positioned in an orderly place setting. She knocked again only this time much more sternly, but no one stirred inside, so she turned the handle and the door creaked open. Stepping inside, a foul odor immediately slapped her in the face. While a bit dusty, the inside was nicely arranged with a small kitchen, a dining room combination with shelves of spices, and every imaginable baking ingredient possible on the kitchen counter. Leeba moved to the hallway that branched off from the left of the kitchen. The dark corridor stretched fifteen feet; each side endowed with a polished oak door with a bright gold handle. She switched on a flashlight. The light reflected brightly off the glossy cedar floors.

"Hello, is anyone here?" She opened the first door and glanced inside. A desk sat at the far wall adorned with a bronze lamp, stapler, tape dispenser, hole punch, and a stack of documents. An ancient typewriter was centered perfectly in front of an oak chair with a sheet of loose-leaf paper hanging from the carriage. The two perpendicular walls consisted of built-in bookshelves each neatly lined with volumes of novels and reference books that covered just about every topic. Backing out of the room, she proceeded to the door at the end of the hallway; cautiously advancing, she tiptoed so as not to be discovered but already perceived the inhabitants were deceased. The rancid odor screamed death. She twisted the handle and let the door float open. Slowly, she raised the light and found the first body. A woman lay on the floor next to a king-size oak bed on a large cottage rug, her body well into the decay process.

"She will make a nice addition to my collection," she whispered to herself as she stepped over the body and glanced through a doorway into the bathroom.

"Nice! I'll take it!"

"Oh, if Spalding and Mizuno were here to see this, they would be so excited."

"Yes, of course, we'll move in immediately. No, money is no issue. No, no, don't burden yourself; I will dispose of the body. Yes, if all is right, we'll move in today. Thank you. You are very kind and by the way, the most cooperative real estate agent I've ever worked with. I'll be sure to put a good word in with your supervisor."

She laughed wildly to herself as she trudged towards the shelter to collect Batya and after several minutes, she stepped inside. "Batya baby, I found us a new home. We'll be moving immediately."

She quickly gathered their belongings, dressed Batya for the journey, and set off for their new home with purpose.

25

MATCHMAKER

"Dr. House said your surgery went well, so even though this will be your first physical therapy session since, you should expect big things, Sophi. The results may not be immediate, but I suspect you will regain some feeling which will also lead to more muscle development. Are you ready?"

Reluctantly, Sophi reached for Adiva while she hoisted her to her feet and guided her to the walking rails. Tony held her waist tight, and she smacked his hand away. "I c..ca...can do it."

Across the room, Adiva, Nayla, and Nurse Angela provided their support. They gave her a thumbs-up as she progressed.

"I don't want to hear it if you fall, Mrs. Independent!" Over the past few weeks, she built a muscle tone in her arms that amazed Tony, and he was confident she wouldn't fall.

"Fuck oo, bozo!"

"That's fuck 'you', not 'oo,' Sophi. Try again.'"

She didn't reply but took a few steps and a smile came to her face.

"What is it? Tony asked.

"Toes, feew toes." She said excitedly as she took three more steps, rested, and finished one rotation of the bars for the first time since being injured. Her supporters cheered loudly. "You can do it, Sophi!" She completed three more rotations and was assisted back to her wheelchair.

"Great job, Sophi! You'll be on your feet for good soon," Nayla took the handles to the wheelchair. "I am so proud of you! Are you ready for some speech after you clean up?"

Sophi gave a thumbs-up as Nayla wheeled her away.

"How about some lunch, Angela?" Adiva asked.

"Sorry, got a date. Maybe tomorrow."

"The two of you are getting serious, huh?"

"Unexpectedly, yes. I hoped this would be a casual relationship, one of convenience with benefits, but I'm falling for this guy. By the way, he has a friend, and I was hoping you might want to meet him. Maybe, a double date at the cafeteria tonight? There's nothing more romantic than cafeteria food." she added with a smile.

"Who is he? I mean what's his name?"

"Corporal Ladner. He's cute too!"

"What time tonight?"

"How about eight? We can meet in the cafeteria. I'll get there a little early if you are nervous. We can wait on the guys."

"Make it a date," Adiva seemed excited. "Is there any chance your boyfriend might know a cute girl who would want to meet Nayla? You know Nayla, right? She's cute as a button and needs someone to pull her out of her funk."

"I'll see what I can do. Just tell Nayla to meet us, and I will dig up one of my girlfriends. See you then." Angela walked towards the E.R.

"Hey, Christie, do you have any plans tonight?"

"Right, like there's something to do around here. We're locked down in the hospital, Angie!"

"That doesn't mean we can't have some fun."

"What do you have in mind?"

"Well, I've arranged a double date with some friends and was hoping you could join us. It would be a lot of fun and break up the monotony for you."

"Thanks for asking, but I'm not going to be the fifth wheel. You with Ballard and your friend with their significant other and me by myself? No thanks!"

"Maybe I should have been clearer. I have someone I want you to meet. She's funny, intelligent, and beautiful. You've been telling me that you will never meet the right person, but I have found the one for you. Trust me."

"What's her name?"

"Just show up at the cafeteria at 8:00, okay. You'll learn her name when I introduce you. Your friend Ladner will be there if that makes you more comfortable. He'll be meeting someone too. We're going to have a great time. See you tonight. Don't be late."

"Nayla, oh, Nayla!" Adiva yelled, attempting to gain her attention. "Nayla, I have something to ask you. Wait up!"

"What is it, Adiva? I have to get meds to a patient." Not only was Nayla in a funk, but she also abandoned her normal cheerfulness and was becoming increasingly cynical.

"I wanted to ask if you wanted to meet me at the cafeteria tonight after your shift so we can talk. We never get a chance to sit and relax together anymore, and I thought it would be nice for both of us. I miss you." Adiva avoided mentioning the others since she knew Nayla would never agree to a blind date.

"We speak practically every day while at work and besides, I am exhausted."

"Oh, you can spare a few minutes tonight, say at 8:00 in the cafeteria. "I'll expect to see you. Don't leave me hanging!"

Adiva didn't give her a chance to reply and bolted from the room. It was nearing five when she started the inventory of the controlled substances locker, and she hoped to be finished within the hour. A smile crossed her face as she thought about the possibility of seeing Nayla happy again, but her thought was interrupted by the winds that pounded at the large pane window to her back. She stood on her tiptoes determined to see what was happening outside until finally frustrated; she scooted a box to the wall and stood on top of it. Peering outside, the wind carried everything not nailed down through the air and smashed into the building. The winds squealed as they pushed their way through the finest fissures between the window framing and the block wall. She had just stooped to get a count on the lowest shelf when all hell broke loose. A large branch smashed through the window and toppled the metal shelving on top of Adiva. Glass rained down, some smaller shards driven by the tropical winds were propelled as if fired from a gun, and many pelted her while she grappled trying to free herself from the twisted shelving that pinned her. Security arrived within minutes and with some effort, were able to extract her.

"Are you all right?" the guard asked as he pulled her towards the E.R. You're going to need some stitches; you might want to let them know about the knot on your head too."

Adiva didn't realize the extent of the lacerations that peppered her body nor was she aware of the large bump on her forehead.

"Get her into trauma room four, stat," the on-call doctor ordered as two nurses helped her onto a gurney and wheeled her away.

"What's the big rush? I just have a few bumps and bruises."

"It's a little worse than that but don't worry, we'll get you all fixed up. I'm going to give you something for the pain. Just lay back and relax."

A warmth quickly spread throughout her body and after a minute, she didn't have a care in the world.

"Stay still while the doctor works," the nurse ordered.

"Hee, hee," she giggled. "I'm fine. I don't understand what all the hype is about."

The surgeon worked for over two hours removing over thirty shards of glass. He finished by stitching the worst of the wounds that impaled her right shoulder. The large gash left her tendon severed and once repaired required thirty stitches to close.

She woke in recovery an hour later. Nayla was sitting at her side reading a novel.

"Hey, Nayla. What time is it?"

"Hey, how are you feeling?"

"I told the doctors I didn't understand what all the excitement was about. I'm fine! Now, what time is it?"

"It is almost 7:30. Why?"

"We are supposed to meet Angela in the cafeteria at 8:00. We need to get going."

"Are you sure you're up to it? I don't know if you realize it, but you had surgery. You won't be able to use your right arm for a while, they had to reattach your tendon and besides that, you received over a hundred stitches by the time they removed all the glass. You were in a lot worse shape than you thought."

"Really? It didn't seem that bad at the time. I'm okay now. Help me get dressed." She sat up and quickly figured out that the painkiller was working its way out of her system. One of her arms was immobilized in pain. She peeked under the sling and could see something that looked like ragged flesh nicely stitched back in place. When she glanced into the mirror for the first time, she was shocked. Lacerations covered her face, and nearly every exposed area. Wow, it's amazing how adrenaline can mask pain."

"So, you have come to your senses? You're not going, right?"

"Hardly. Can you help me get dressed? We're going to be late, and I have someone I want you to meet. Besides, Angela has gone through a lot of trouble to arrange this event."

"Oh, what have you gotten us into, Adiva? I told you I'm not ready for another relationship."

"Just slip my shoes on and follow me!"

By the time they arrived at the cafeteria, the whole gang was sitting laughing and joking at a large round table; Angela sat on Ballard's lap while the others gathered around.

"There they are! Where have you two be..?" She stopped mid-sentence. "My God, what happened Adiva?"

"Just a minor accident while performing inventory. I'm fine though."

Ladner jumped to his feet and scooted another chair to the table. "Here, have a seat."

"Seriously, what happened, Adiva?" Angela inquired.

"I was just inventorying the controlled-substances locker when a tree fell through the window sending glass and everything else on top of me. The doctor said my arm was impaled by a large shard of glass that severed my short-head tendon which resulted in surgery and this here sling."

"I'm glad you're okay. Anyway, I have some introductions to make. Ladner this is Adiva, and Christie, this is Nayla and of course, you all know me and Ballard. I thought it would be nice for all of us to get to know one another and have a late dinner at the same time."

"Hello, Nayla. It's nice to meet you. Adiva has told me so many great things about you including how cute you are. I have to admit that her description fell well short of your beauty. You are gorgeous!"

Nayla was unsure how to react, but instead, turned away and blushed. "You are very pretty yourself, but she didn't tell me anything about you. In fact, I had no idea that I would be meeting anyone tonight."

"You're disappointed?"

"No, not at all. I just didn't know—I mean I thought this was just a small gathering for dinner, but it seems like Adiva and Angela are trying to play matchmaker again."

"Not me! I just went along with Angela. She's the one trying to start her own dating agency. But I must say, I am very pleased." Adiva glanced to Ladner."

"Yes, extremely pleased!" Ladner scooted his chair closer as the waiter dropped two baskets of dinner rolls on the table and passed out drinks.

"I took the initiative of ordering everyone a Margarita and a shot of Maker's Mark. Shot's first." Angela held up her shot glass. "A toast to love being in the air despite all of the death and destruction that surrounds us."

Their glasses clanged together, and they drained them. After three pitchers of Margarita's and a dinner of pork chops and baked potatoes, Ballard and Angela departed. "Don't do anything we wouldn't." Ballard quipped.

Minutes later, Adiva and Ladner left to catch a movie at the entertainment services branch leaving Nayla and Christie to be better acquainted.

"It's amazing that I haven't met you before tonight. I am happy that Angela introduced us."

"Me too."

"Tell me a little about yourself."

"There's not much to tell other than I have been fortunate enough to become part of a family that has welcomed me with open arms. I was in love with someone who died months ago, and I am struggling to get over her. I thought she was my soul mate, but it wasn't to be."

"I'm sorry that you had to go through something like that. It must have been hard on you."

"Right now, I just feel empty, drained, and lonely. My family has been there for me, but there's only so much they can do and to be honest, I haven't even considered dating. I guess if the right person were to come into my life, I might be open to another relationship."

"I'm glad to hear that because I find you intriguing, and I'd like to get to know you better; that is if the feeling is mutual."

"There's only one way to find out how we truly feel. Let's go on a date or two and see if things develop."

"I've got a better idea. Why don't we make tonight our first date? This may sound brash, but I mean this in the most innocent and unassuming way possible, but what if we go to my place to catch a movie? There are only so many things we can do here, and wouldn't a movie be fun?" Christie looked to see how she received her question.

"A movie sounds great. Let's go."

Christie took Nayla's hand and walked her to her room. "And this is where the magic happens," she said nervously as they walked inside. Nayla glared letting her know she didn't appreciate the comment.

"I'm sorry. I didn't mean to say that or at least infer anything. Sometimes when I'm nervous, I make dumb comments. Would you like to sit?"

She grabbed a handful of DVDs. Do you like any of these?"

"This looks good." She handed her a copy of "The Sixth Sense" and she slid it into the DVD player.

"So, you like spooky movies?"

"I like all genres, but to be honest, I wasn't too sure what any of these movies were about, so I picked randomly."

"Are you okay? I mean you look very uncomfortable. I can sit in the chair across the room if that makes you feel any better."

"I'm just wondering what I am doing here. I don't normally go to a stranger's place, especially when I don't know anything about them. Therefore, yes, I am nervous, but you don't have to move. We are here to get to know one another after all. What kind of films do you enjoy?" Nayla asked. She felt conflicted. She knew it was wrong to be alone with a stranger, but at the same time, she enjoyed her company. At this point, she would have enjoyed the company of just about anyone, but she was too modest to make that admission. They were halfway through the film when Christie held her hand and by the end of the film, Nayla rested her head comfortably on her shoulder. Christie draped an arm around her and for the first time in many months, Nayla felt safe and without worry.

26

VOLUPTUARY STORM
UNLEASHED

Rain stopped falling from the sky,
and the water thatcovered the earth began to recede;
the floodgates of the heavens closed.

"Do you hear that?" Marcus asked as he spooned behind Eowyn. An empty vial of Morphine lay overturned on the bedside table alongside two empty syringes.

"I don't hear anything."

"That's my point! The rain has stopped and the wind has died down. Maybe we will survive after all."

"It won't last long. Give it a minute and the rain will begin again. For now, I need you." Eowyn could feel him pressed tight against her, his flaccid member holstered between her butt cheeks. She lightly gyrated, massaging him gently until he stood rigid then repositioned herself so that he was nestled at her willing threshold. She pressed against him and shifted her hips slightly until he was tightly sheathed inside her. At first, she rode him much like a carousel horse, rising and ascending gracefully, but once awakened, Marcus assumed control of the reigns. He increased the gait to a trot, then to an all-out gallop. Eowyn took him in cadence, extending herself to the utmost, a broodmare eager to satisfy her rider on the home stretch.

"Oh, Marcus. Give it to me...give it...give it!" Eowyn screamed while their bodies suddenly quaked and after lay in a blissful drug-induced euphoria. It no longer needed to be said; they were well aware that they were in love or at least felt they were, but as of recently they did not decide anything with clarity. The rainy days left them bored. Other than playing board games and cards, they stayed hyped on morphine and made love multiple times a day to pass the time. They lost all hope of ever reuniting with their loved ones but instead, lived for the moment.

The next morning, Marcus woke to the sun shining through the bedroom window. He rolled out of bed and stretched. "Eowyn, check it out; the sun is out." He walked to the front porch and basked in the sunlight. A few minutes later, the storm door closed, and Eowyn's arms wrapped around him.

"Beautiful. I never thought we would witness a day like this ever again. We ought to have a picnic," Marcus suggested. "I'm tired of being cooped up in this house. We can also see if the water has receded." Marcus turned to face Eowyn. The rays of sunshine illuminated her nude body and he gazed in admiration.

"What is it? Why are you staring at me?" She felt a little awkward and began to cover up.

"I apologize. It's just that seeing you in the light for the first time in months, I realized you are even more amazing than I remember."

A smile spread across her face. "I don't know what's going to happen once we unite with our family—that is if they are still alive which I pray they are—but know that I won't stop loving you."

"Likewise. I don't know how I will handle it if, or rather when you are reunited with Leeba. It will be difficult. Is it possible to love two people at the same time because I will always love you? I can't imagine life without the dorky games, our deeply philosophical conversations, our journeys together, and most importantly, I can't fathom not waking next to you in the morning."

"It's kind of scary to think about, isn't it? Can we put off the picnic because all I want to do right now is to be close to you?" She went inside, returned with a blanket, and spread it on the porch but instead of lying down, walked to the railing and stared into the distance.

"You know there probably isn't a single living person within miles of us. We are so very alone and on our own." She leaned over, her elbows on the railing, and purposely presented herself. "Oh, I wonder how we could pass the time."

She was surprised when Marcus went inside and returned minutes later with her clothes. "Put these on and let's go on this picnic." Feeling dejected, she reluctantly dressed.

"Let's get moving. We have the whole day ahead of us, and I don't want to waste a minute of it." Without further word, he descended the steps and slipped into the woods with Eowyn following.

"You know once these waters recede, we could simply disappear, Marcus. The world is our canvas, and we can paint our own story together. At the same time, we have a life we can return to; a life that probably won't include us being together, but that allows us to return to our loved ones—if they are alive

"Yes, you have a wife and children, and I have Leeba. Despite what has happened between us, I still love her, and I am sure you love Waffa. We owe it to them to try to find them, help rebuild, and return to our pre-apocalyptic lives. That doesn't mean we won't be able to see each other and hang out."

"But it does mean that we will no longer be free to hold one another. Sadly, our time together is quickly coming to an end, but I understand it must," Marcus added.

"You're right, but we still have time. I don't know about you, but I intend to continue to cherish our time together. Until we are reunited with our family, I'll strive to love you enough to make up for a lifetime."

Their fingers interlaced, they walked along the banks of the mammoth sea that formed from the months of torrential rain. The watery surface was mirror-like sending bright sun-filled rays over the looking-glass expanse. The water level had already dropped a couple of feet, and Marcus expected the floodwaters to disperse completely over the week to come.

"Over here!" Eowyn discovered a spot just inside the wood line, the forest floor lined with pine straw and leaves. She laid out the blanket and sat down. "So, what type of food did you bring?"

"There wasn't much. I grabbed a couple of granola bars and some of the wild strawberries you found the other day.

Eowyn lay on the blanket. "I can't believe we finally have some good weather." Marcus brushed the hair from her eyes. "You are incredible; you know that, right?"

"Yeah, I'm pretty awesome; maybe one day you will be as magnificent as I am." She laughed. "You're not so bad yourself. Now, come here, silly." She pulled him next to her.

"It's so nice to finally get out of that house and feel the sun on my face again," Marcus began.

"If you don't stop talking and kiss me, I swear I'm going to leave."

He didn't have to be told twice. He gazed into her eyes while he gently caressed her cheek. For several minutes, they tenderly kissed one another oblivious to anything going on around them. Not a single word was exchanged but their bodies communicated perfectly. Marcus peeled his shirt off and shimmied out of his pants. Eowyn slowly swayed her hips, unsnapped her pants, and danced her way out of them. Then just as quickly strolled behind a nearby tree. "I'm feeling mighty lonely over here, handsome."

"How much do you love me?" Marcus inquired. "Seriously, are you just infatuated or is our relationship simply a result of convenience?"

Eowyn laced her arms around his neck. "At first, it was just convenience, but it has morphed into so much more. Other than Leeba, I have never loved anyone more. I feel like a giddy high-school girl when I'm with you and can think of no one else when we are apart. I don't feel whole without you. Does that answer your question?"

He peppered her neck with kisses.

"Are you curious what my answer would be to that same question?" Marcus asked in between nibbling on her earlobe.

Eowyn pressed her lips to his, her tongue caressing his while gently probing, whimsically dancing through his mouth. "Don't say it, show me."

Again, he stippled her neck with kisses and then traced a trail to the warm pocket between her breasts. She moaned faintly when his lips suckled her stiff nipple, and he playfully tweaked the other before dropping to his knees. His hands traveled up and down the back of her thighs while he delved into her. Eowyn laid down and hedged her legs apart. Minutes later, her back arched, every muscle in her body went taut, she ground her pelvis against him taking him over and over until she let out a guttural cry. Her body quivered from head to toe, traveling in tsunamic waves, only providing her enough time to catch her breath in between each cathartic release. From one orgasm to the next, like being helplessly trapped in an undertow, she was powerless, hopelessly trapped in a euphoric bliss. The waves of pleasure were seemingly interminable until he provided her a reprieve, climbed to his knees, positioned himself over her, and swept his lips over hers, as they slowly joined.

"Are you beginning to feel how much I love you," he muttered in her ear, but her mind was inundated with a bottleneck of emotions preventing any coherent reply. Instead, her body reverted to her more primal senses; her nails dug into his backside, and she tried to take as much of him into her as humanly possible. Her legs wrapped around his waist; their hips moved in unison while drops of sweat speckled her body. Still wanting more, she pivoted her hips, and exchanged positions; she rode him gracefully as beads of perspiration cascaded from her forehead onto his chest. Marcus rapidly plumbed while Eowyn worked to keep pace until she felt him tense. The warmth of his release, the gratifying groan was enough to send her body into another coterie of seismic spasms until she collapsed on top of him.

After several minutes, Eowyn broke the silence, "I had no idea anyone could love me that much!" She chuckled.

"I would gladly stay like this all day, but don't we have a picnic to get to?"

"No, thank you. I'm quite full," she replied. Marcus reached into the bag, removed a handful of strawberries, and fed them to her one by one. At the same time, he pulled a vial of morphine from the same bag. Eowyn quickly snatched it up. "What do you say?" she asked while smiling deviously.

Soon their senses dulled, but at the same time, their hearts pumped vigorously; the drug jump-started their libido. Eowyn began slowly undulating and other than an errant moan and the carnal sounds of coital exchange, their bodies labored as one in a melodious rhythm in silence. So, it went day after day and while the floodwaters continued to recede, the two of them strenuously endeavored to fit a lifetime of love into a series of quickly fading days.

27

REUNITED

Raghba gasped. Selima's dead body lay just inside the shed when Raghba cried herself to sleep, too exhausted to bury her the previous evening. She was prepared to memorialize her friend that morning but when she woke, she was gone; the silhouette of Selima's body was still etched like a chalk line into the blankets. The door to the shed stood partially opened. Joanna lay sleeping. Raghba jumped to her feet and peeked outside. Someone had to have moved her body, an uninvited intruder with nefarious intentions. She stood speechless for several minutes and her adrenaline-driven fear transitioned to a hopeful elation.

"Selima, is that you?" She asked, nervously ducked back inside the shelter, and awaited an answer.

"Oh, hey. Yes. Where are we?"

"You don't remember anything?"

"Nothing."

Raghba lunged into her arms and held on for dear life.

"What is it, sweetheart? Why are you crying?"

"You were dead, Selima. I swear you were dead. The explosion—you weren't breathing."

"Explosion? Is that where the burns came from?"

"You honestly don't remember? The house exploded. That's why we're here."

Selima's smile suddenly shifted to alarm. "Joanna? Please tell me she's all right."

"Sleeping inside. She is fine. It appears you and I are the only ones with injuries."

"I think I broke a rib or two and my pinky needs reset." Selima held up her hand to reveal her finger bent at a ninety-degree angle. "I've been trying to build the courage to reset it."

Raghba sniffled and wiped away her tears. "Let me see your finger. You may as well get it over with."

"On three, all right? One...two." She didn't bother going to three and yanked causing Selima to cry out.

"I'm so sorry but look, it's straight." Raghba ripped a strip of material from her tattered shirt and wrapped it tightly around Selima's finger. "There, that should hold it stationary. I'm more worried about those burns, especially the ones on your face."

It doesn't matter. I've already lost an ear and my beauty has long since abandoned me. A few more burns and scars won't make much of a difference."

Raghba glared at Selima. "You are still very beautiful. Anyway, are you up for a walk?"

"I feel fine other than the pain from these burns. Where are we going?"

"Now that the rain has finally come to an end, we can search for some better accommodations and hopefully locate something to treat our burns. If you haven't noticed already, I've got a few of my own."

Raghba packed up their things, mounted Joanna in a carrier, and they set off. They hiked several miles without locating anything of significance and were considering returning when Raghba stopped and signaled for Selima to be quiet. "Shhh, listen!"

After a minute, they heard what sounded like a child's voice cry out. "Where's it coming from?" The voice seemed to echo throughout the valley.

"What do you want to do?" Raghba asked as she listened carefully. "It could be a trap."

"Shhh," said Selima, "Quit being so fidgety. They might hear us."

They cautiously moved forward until spotting two individuals ahead. "I see two of them."

"Yes. Try to be quiet." They cautiously moved forward to within fifty yards of the two individuals when Selima held up her right hand, signaling to stop. For a moment neither stirred. Once sure they weren't detected, they shuffled forward again, this time stopping a mere twenty yards from them. The child was the first to discover their presence. She stood about three feet tall and wore an oversized sweatshirt, a fringed skirt below her knees, and a ruffled red bow flapping in the wind. At first, she was silent but then to their astonishment, the girl called out.

"Sewima, mommy, Sewima's here."

"Oh, how grand! We have visitors. Please make yourself at home."

"Selima immediately recognized Leeba but there was something strange about her. She didn't seem to recognize them and instead of the confident and sure-handed, Leeba everyone was used to, she appeared confused and fidgety.

I am Leeba and this is my daughter, Batya. And your names?"

"Leeba, it's us Raghba and Selima. We've been worried about you."

"No worries. We are quite content living in our cottage. What did you say your names were again? I'm a bit forgetful and honestly don't know how I got here."

Selima grabbed her by the shoulders and stared into her eyes. "Leeba, it's me, your friend, Selima. Do you remember me?"

"Oh no, it's just the two of us and some friends, she replied nonsensically. Haven't had time to make friends. So much work to be done. Would the two of you like to stay for a while? We don't get many visitors."

Raghba glanced at Selima. "Nice to meet you Leeba."

Thank you! Spalding and Mizuno—they are my new friends—they stayed home while Batya and I agreed to get some fresh air. Would you like the grand tour?"

After following her through a winding trail, they came upon her home tucked away in a well-concealed nook.

"Wow, your home is even more beautiful than you said, Leeba."

"Come inside and meet the rest of my friends and you can take a look around while you're here." She rustled them inside. "Selima and Raghba, I'd like to introduce you to Spalding and Mizuno.

Raghba laughed thinking she was joking while Selima scratched her head trying to contain herself. The two balls sat wedged between the table and the back of the chair. Each had a set of eyes, a nose, and a mouth painted onto them.

"Don't be rude! Introduce yourselves." She addressed her child-orbs. "Oh, please excuse them, they are so rude sometimes."

"Of course," Selima replied. I hate to change the subject, but would there be room for us to stay for a while? We just need some shelter until we can get back to civilization."

"Plenty of room here, but one will have to bunk with Spalding, the other with Mizuno, and your baby can sleep can sleep with Batya. So exciting to have guests."

"You must be lonely out here all by yourself."

"Oh, at first, but I met my new friends, and I have my collection. I'm so busy that I don't have time to be bored or lonely."

"What are you collecting?"

"Bodies. I found them along the shore and other places. I have about seventeen right now. I'll take you to see them later. Little ones, full size, skinny, fat, and even decomposed; I have a little of everything and of course, I can't get these children to help me at all. Batya helps sometimes, but Mizuno and Spaulding are lazy as all hell; I love them anyway."

That evening, they moved in and gathered around a cozy fire. For the first time in recent memory, happiness returned and life bordered on a comforting normalcy. While Leeba tucked in her three children, Selima and Raghba considered the future. discussing a return to home and the hopes of rebuilding the Free Zone.

28

NO LOVE, HERE?

Sergeant Perez reported that they killed Selima weeks ago, but Lieutenant Raley continued to receive reports that she was alive and well. Two of her soldiers reported seeing her since the explosion. Raley put a squad together to reconnoiter the area and either confirm or repudiate the claims. With the change in weather, she was able to consolidate most of her force and was prepared to do whatever was necessary to ensure the princess and Marcus were killed.

"Be careful, Raghba. I realize the weather has cleared up but there's no telling who's out there which includes wild animals," Selima handed her a bag of jerky and a bottle of water. "You'll need this for your trip. When should we expect you back?"

"No more than a day or two. I'll be fine. Take care of Leeba; she seems to be the one in need. Maybe give her a break from the kids and let her get some rest. I'm afraid she's had a psychiatric breakdown. I mean, she's adopted balls as her children! She needs some help." With that, she departed.

She had hiked a few miles when she stopped at a stream to wash up. All she could think of was being in Dimitry's arms. Lost in thoughts of him and a smile implanted on her face she was surprised to discover two soldiers had crept up on her. Startled, she stood quickly; her eyes widened when she noticed guns pointed in her direction.

"Who are you and what's your business?" The first soldier asked but the other interjected before she could reply.

"Wait, I recognize her. Yes, you are Selima's friend. You helped her to escape,"

Raghba knew exactly what she was talking about but thought it best to claim no association with Selima or her escape. "While I do admit Selima is a friend, I assure you I haven't seen her for a month or more. You are mistaken."

"I may have been stunned and wounded, but you must realize that I have an excellent memory. When I was a child, my parents noticed I was extremely bright. So much so that they had me tested, and I was identified as having a highly superior auto-biographical memory; the doctors call it hyperthymesia. I assure you, I am not mistaken. Sergeant Petry, take her into custody. Before he got to her, Raghba sprung to her feet and sprinted into the river trying to escape. She was nearly across when someone tackled her.

She woke later, her arms and feet bound, tethered to a tree by a chain. Dozens of tents bordered the open field where they were bivouacked while soldiers scuttled about completing their daily business.

"Mam, the prisoner's awake," he yelled. A few minutes later, Raley stooped in front of Raghba. She took a swig of whiskey from a bottle and laughed. "I've got a couple of questions for you but before I begin my inquiry, I want to lay down some guidelines. I have a built-in bullshit meter and can sense when a person isn't telling the truth. If you answer my questions truthfully, you will be treated with dignity, but if you lie, there will be severe consequences. Do you understand?"

"Understood!" Raghba glared.

"Good! First question. Do you know where Marcus Martyreon is hiding? He is wanted for aiding and abetting the escape of Selima."

She looked confused when Raghba laughed in response. "If you want Martyreon, you might want to bring a shovel once you discover where he is. He died weeks ago when the flooding first devastated the Free Zone."

Raley rubbed her chin perhaps checking the reading on her meter. "How did he die?"

"A tree fell that impaled his friend as the flood waters were rising. Marcus tried to help. The tree rolled on top of him as the waters rose, and then swept them away. They were never seen again."

"You have me curious. Who was it he was trying to rescue?"

"His name was Ferris. To be honest, I never learned his last name."

"Not Ferris!" Raley cradled her face in her hands.

"I take it you knew him?"

"I fought next to him on many occasions during the Second Nill War. He was already a legend after the first war. He was a sight to see in action. I never saw a warrior like him. He saved my life on more than one occasion."

"Are you okay?" Raghba inquired after seeing tears well in her eyes.

"Fine! Martyreon's dead then?"

"I was there when it happened. I didn't witness him being swept away, but my sister Eowyn did, and her reaction was enough to confirm his death. She was devastated—we all were."

"You mention another of my acquaintances. How is Eowyn?"

"I'm unsure of her whereabouts. She disappeared early on in the flood. She was knocked from our boat and hasn't been heard from since."

"I can tell you one thing about her, she is too ornery to be killed by a mere flood. I expect at time goes on, we'll see her again. Anyway, thank you for your honesty, but at the same time, there have been some very serious accusations made against you. I think you would agree that actions have consequences. Now, my trusted soldier unequivocally states that you were with Selima and not only that you helped her, but that you are directly responsible for a soldier's death. I'm going to give you one more opportunity to be truthful and doing so will positively impact your case.

After a considerable pause, Raghba spoke up. "All right, I did help Selima, but I had no idea from whom I was defending her. I just knew that my friend was under attack and I acted in her defense just like any friend would. As far as I was concerned, your men could have been Nill operatives. You probably would have done the same thing if you were in my situation"

"Either way, that doesn't mean you indiscriminately murder others. My people are expecting a swift and severe punishment, and I must give them what they want. Normally, the punishment would be immediate death, but I believe what you are saying. At the same time, I can propose an alternative punishment that may satisfy everyone. Following this meeting, you will be brought to a tribunal where your case will be presented and the panel of three judges, including myself, will decide your fate." She departed without another word, and a few minutes later, two soldiers escorted her to a large outdoor arena. A chair was placed in the center bordered by a large group of Raley's followers. The soldiers shoved her into the chair. Moments later, three judges took a seat to her front. "Will the defendant please rise?"

"For crimes against the state you are sentenced as follows: You will be immediately tethered to the pillory and receive twenty lashes. If you survive, you will be set free; your debt paid. If you do not, you will receive a respectful burial. This sentence is effective immediately and is final. Sergeant of the guard proceed with the flagellation."

They yanked her from the chair, ripped her clothing from her back, and securely fastened her wrists and ankles to each pillar. The first lash cut deep leaving a gaping wound the length of her back; those that followed were no less damaging, but after the sixth lash, she couldn't feel anything other than streams of blood streaking down her thighs. She woke much later in the middle of a forest in immense pain. After a colossal effort, she stood and woefully trudged forward.

"I must find Dimitry!" Raghba pushed forward as she wavered between periods of lucidity and delirium until finally, she collapsed, and promptly lost consciousness.

For several hours, she lay with only brief episodes of consciousness. The third time she woke to something tugging at her leg and through blurred vision, witnessed a large coyote violently ripping at her calf but she had no energy to fight. Accepting her fate, she prayed for the end.

In her mind, she was with her family having dinner at Bentley's Fishery. Marcus and Ferris sat across from her incessantly joking while the children played contentedly outside. Fully immersed in her dream, she chuckled aloud then just as suddenly, was awakened by a piercing "Yelp."

The sound wrenched her from the moment of serenity. She sensed her body being lifted perhaps to what she thought was the start of her spiritual journey to heaven. Every so often, her eyes pried open; the world passed by in a blur. She hadn't the strength to object let alone communicate. Her body was shutting down only focused on the most primitive life functions.

Unsure if a dream or if she had truly moved on, she discovered herself resting on a soft pallet of leaves and pine straw.

As the sun peeked over the horizon, rays of sunshine crept into the shelter. The warm rays of light slowly coaxed her from her slumber.

"Easy, my love. You need to rest." Dimitry appeared from around the corner. "Swallow these," he ordered. "You must be hungry."

She declined. "It's funny because I was starved just the day before."

That's when he knew how sick she was. "Raghba, please eat a little. You need nutrition. Here, try this. I remember how much you love rabbits. She wrinkled her nose and turned away.

"Can't I just get some more sleep, Dimitry?" she asked.

"I need to check your wounds first." This is going to hurt, but I promise you can sleep after."

He peeled the fabric of her shirt from the festering wounds simultaneously husking layers of skin with it. He wasn't prepared for what he discovered. The lacerations were severe the previous evening, but now, a blood-infused puss oozed steadily from her back.

Dimitry dug through his bag of medicine and shook his head. "You need antibiotics. He tried to remain calm but underneath he was in a panic.

"I know where we can get some medication," Raghba declared. "But it's going to take some traveling. I'm just not sure I'm up for the journey."

Dimitry shrugged his shoulders. You don't worry about that; I'll get you to where you need to be. For now, the first thing we need to do is clean you up. There's a stream nearby. She threw her arm around his shoulder, and they set off.

29

A SHAG FOR THE ROAD

The water and winds brought more than just death. Perfectly healthy fish remained trapped in shallow pools of water left by the quickly receding waters. Marcus jabbed at the vagrant fish with an improvised spear and before long had gathered three large trout for dinner.

"You relax. I'll prepare the fish." Eowyn leaned over the back of the chair to give him a quick kiss, but Marcus yanked her over his shoulder and into his lap. She started to object, but before she could get a word out, his tongue pressed between her soft, parted lips. Her body, even on the worst of days, naturally omitted a jasmine scent that kept Marcus continuously aroused. Her lips were artistic; one kiss leading to the next as if each one added to the last, each furnishing a sliver of what would eventually become her Magnum Opus. That's one of the traits he so much admired about her; she approached everything with hopes of perfection while at the same time remaining grounded in the realization that all of creation is flawed in some way. To Marcus, Eowyn had achieved perfection, her kisses each a sensual masterpiece that not just connected them physically, but their spirits allied as they leaned into one another endeavoring to be one with the other. When their lips separated, Eowyn lay staring into his eyes, her heart racing as she brought her fingers up to his hair, butterflies danced in her stomach.

"I love you so much, Eowyn."

"And I you." She had no idea why, but tears started to streaking down her cheeks. She wiped them away. "Let me make some dinner, silly." Minutes later, she handed him a plate of steaming hot trout, placed a glass of red wine in his hand, and took a sip of her own.

"You know the water has receded enough for us to leave; for us to search for our loved ones. I don't think we should wait any longer. It's our responsibility. We need to bring some light to the darkness that has plotted to destroy us."

"Okay, Ms. Philosopher, I get your point. We need to act for the greater good and look beyond ourselves. All right Wonder Woman, we'll set out tomorrow. Now, can we please eat?"

After a bottle of wine and the best meal they had eaten in months, Marcus stoked the fire and curled up next to Eowyn. "I think our best plan will be to first search the surrounding area and see if we can locate any survivors. By then, the water level will have dropped even more, and we can work our way into the valley toward the Free Zone. How's that sound your highness?"

"You're such a meathead sometimes. If I'm royalty, then you're my court jester. Entertain me you bumbling fool!"

After a brief silence, Marcus asked, "What were you like before all of the post-apocalyptic wars?"

"What do you mean, what was I like?"

"What type of teenager were you? Were you preppy, worried about your makeup and clothes, an athlete, or maybe a Goth chick? I'm curious."

"I was just a girl like any other. I liked sports, movies, and even wearing dresses. I guess you could say I was an average girl."

"Did you have a boyfriend?"

"A couple of them but nothing serious. I did go to the prom my senior year. I thought I was in love but later realized he was a jerk."

"Aww, did he break your heart?" Marcus laughed. He had no idea that the boy had hurt her deeply, and it took months for her to recover. After a couple of years, she managed to put him out of her thoughts only for him to appear in the most unusual of places. While watching the Coliseum Games during the second Nill occupation, Thomas Selleck ended up being one of the contestants. He died within minutes. The yellow fog enveloped him and seconds later, only his bright white skeleton remained. Even after so many years, seeing him rekindled some feelings but on the bright side, she no longer had to wonder what he was doing and if he ever thought about her.

"Sorry. Anything else about yourself that you would like to share?"

"Yeah, I was a real slut. I screwed the entire football team and during my more experimental stage, I slept with the girl's field hockey team. I did all of them just days apart. It was quite exhausting," she laughed. "Seriously, I was just an average, boring student."

"I wish I knew you then."

"You know me now; isn't that what counts?"

Marcus laid down and rested his feet on the hearth. Thinking about high school brought back memories of the prom he attended with Ileana. "You know, I had my heart broken too. I thought I was in love with my neighbor, Ileana. We went to the prom and dated for a while, but her family moved away, and we lost touch. We reunited right after the mass deportations and might have fallen in love again, but she died."

"How?"

"A Stalker scratched her, and she died from the infection. Later, I grew closer to her sister, Maria and you know how it went from there."

Eowyn poured another drink and recorked the bottle. She slid a glass in front of Marcus and lay next to him. "The fire feels good on my feet, but you know what would be even better?" She looked at him and smiled.

"We promised to take the day off, remember? We agreed that we would start weening ourselves off the morphine."

"This is our last day together. Can't we start after tonight? It would be so much fun. Come on you old stiff, loosen up." Marcus didn't object. "I just happen to have everything right here."

"How convenient. It's almost as if you had it planned."

"You first?" She looked at him tentatively, and he plopped his arm in her lap. Minutes later, they both lay in a state of bliss. Marcus stroked Eowyn's cheek; she grabbed his hand and kissed it sensually. "What are we going to do once we get back to civilization?"

"Go back to our normal lives. You with Leeba, me with Waffa, and we will be the best of friends with some intimate secrets that we take to the grave."

"It won't be that easy though."

Marcus smiled. He agreed that making the transition from lover to friend would be difficult but knew it would be necessary.

"It will be extremely difficult, but we need to cherish the time we have together."

Eowyn leaned forward and kissed him tentatively then circled his mouth with her tongue. She moved her hands up Marcus's sides and peeled his shirt over his head while he methodically unfastened each button of her flannel shirt. She gathered her long hair and formed it into a ponytail.

"You are scrumptious!" His lips moved to her breast while her fingers slid down his waist, undid the button to his jeans, and slid inside. Marcus duplicated her every movement.

The fire crackled and popped in the background only interrupted by an errant moan, a sensual whimper, and the unmistakable report of flesh meeting flesh. They passionately expressed their love perhaps for the final time.

30

FORCES DIVIDED

On an exceptionally humid evening early in September, Lieutenant Raley emerged from the home in which she lodged along with her fellow officers and walked slowly, as though in deep thought, towards a large formation of soldiers.

"I received some disturbing news from a recent patrol, and I wanted to share that with you today. Somehow, Selima was able to survive our most recent effort to exterminate her; like a roach, she managed to survive the explosion. At the same time, our patrol was able to narrow down within a few square miles of where she might be. We have limited information regarding if she is alone or if she has other forces with her, but we do not have time to hesitate. We will be moving out tonight and will attack immediately once her location is determined."

Chatter erupted in the crowd and Sergeant Petry stepped forward. "Lieutenant, many of us believe we should focus on rebuilding the Cooperative and be less worried about seeking revenge for something that happened so long ago. We rather begin rebuilding on a positive note instead of fighting against ourselves."

Raley stood glaring for several minutes. She couldn't believe the person she trusted most and who she secretly loved would betray her. "For those of you who feel the way that Sergeant Petry does, pack your bags. I want all of you out of here within the hour. Those that remain, we will meet at 2100 hours to finalize the attack plans." She immediately departed with Petry following her into her quarters.

"Sage, listen. I love you, and normally I would follow you into the fires of hell, but what you are doing is wrong. You're better than this!" Petry cupped her cheeks in his hands and looked her in the eye. "Stop all this madness; we can run off and start our new lives together. The canvas is blank, and we can paint a new future. I love you, Sage!"

She jumped into his arms, kissed him then just as suddenly, shoved him away. "No, I'm not going to compromise! A crime was committed and there must be consequences. Selima killed our people, my friends, and for that, she will pay."

"So, you are the judge, jury, and executioner now. Let's kill Selima because she defended herself, why not beat Raghba half to death because she helped her, and oh yeah, let's murder Martyreon, the leader of the Resistance because he lied about executing Selima. It's insanity!"

"Every society is built on a foundation of laws and likewise, consequences for those that do not follow the rules. Each of the people you mention broke the rules. They must be punished."

"Show me where the laws of the Free Zone say someone should be found guilty before they are given a chance to defend themselves. You can't because the law states that all citizens are presumed innocent of a crime until proven guilty."

"And I determined they were guilty!"

"Sage, you are not in a position to judge anyone. Shoot, according to your law, you are guilty of vigilantism as well as treason which is punishable by death. You're more guilty than Selima."

"Get out! Get out before I have you arrested! As the leader of this militia, it is my responsibility to enforce the law. Leave now and take all of the other traitors."

Sergeant Petry didn't say another word. He gathered a large group of followers—many more than he anticipated—and they set off. He led them aimlessly through the forest as he tried to devise a plan.

"Where are we headed, sarge?"

"Towards the Free Zone. We're going to meet up with what remains of the Free Zone forces and join them. We're going to help rebuild."

By the next morning, they managed to make it to the Bentley River only miles from Marcus's old home. While the water level had dropped considerably since the rains stopped, the river still flowed well beyond its normal shores. Emaciated bodies riddled the area; some were wrapped in the branches of trees, some peacefully laid on the ground, and others floated down the rapids of the river.

"Take a break and get something to eat. We'll get back on the road in fifteen."

While Sergeant Petry and his soldiers rested, Lieutenant Raley and her force of a little over one hundred after the mass defection, departed in search of Selima. Patrols had narrowed down the search area to a couple of square miles, but they were having difficulty locating where she was staying.

"Fan out everyone. We are on the south side of the search grid. I want everyone to sweep north in groups of two until she's located. No one is to act without my order. Does everyone understand?"

"Let's Move out!" She ordered.

31

PARTING WAYS

He was standing at the end of a very long, dimly lit corridor bordered by thick spiny shrubs that wrapped around the trunks of unwitting trees as if trying to strangle the life out of them. Unkempt, the bushes grew wildly, higher, and higher until burdened by their weight, they bent over, one side meeting the next forming a dark tunnel. They had followed the overgrown trail a hundred feet when they came upon an obstruction. Tree limbs and foliage were haphazardly stacked preventing any further progress without taking the time to clear the passage.

"Whoever is beyond this wall doesn't want to be discovered. They've gone to great strides to remain hidden. What do you want to do?"

"Let's clear it and see what's up ahead. I don't want to go back. I swear I heard voices and the shuffling of leaves. Someone is out there, and whoever it is wants to remain undetected."

"Give me a hand then, gorgeous."

They replaced the foliage after entering and cautiously trudged forward. "This kind of reminds me of us during the First Nill War. You and I crossing enemy lines, or the time we were in Nill headquarters to rescue Veil. I missed those moments; the rush I used to get knowing danger might be right around the corner. Do you remember that feeling, the shot of adrenaline that keeps you on edge?"

"Sort of like I'm feeling now. Yes, I miss that feeling and you know what else I miss?" Marcus asked as he nudged closer to Eowyn.

"What's that?"

"No matter what type of danger we were in, I always felt safe when I was with you. I knew we had each other's back. The only other person who put me at ease like that was Ferris. Of course, he was so impulsive and at times, reckless, but God was he a warrior."

"Same here. He was one of the greatest people I've ever known." Eowyn took a seat; Marcus plopped down next to her and held her hand. "Are you okay?" He propped her chin up with one hand and wiped a tear from her cheek with the other. "I know it's hard imagining a world without him. Sometimes I half expect to see him come prancing into the room with that shit-eating grin of his."

Eowyn rested her head on his chest listening to his softly beating heart when, like an alarmed deer, her head raised. The voice she heard was a familiar one. Before Marcus knew what was happening, she sprinted into the clearing ahead and dropped to her knees. "Leeba, my God, Leeba it's me!"

Seconds later, Marcus followed behind.

"It's me."

Leeba froze in her tracks, turned, and ran toward her home. "You're dead. Drown. You're a figment of my imagination.

Batya, come with me. Hurry now!" She sprinted into the house and slammed the door.

"What's wrong with her, Marcus?"

"She's in shock...must have thought you died when you fell overboard. See, here she comes now."

The door opened, but instead of Leeba, Selima walked out with Joanna cradled in her arms. "By Allah's grace, Eowyn, I can't believe it's you!" Eowyn accepted her into her arms and when Selima glanced over her shoulder, her knees buckled. The color suddenly drained from her face. Twice she shut her eyes only to open them and discover it was the man she loved in the flesh. Eowyn held Joanna while Selima remained kneeling in disbelief; tears cascading to the ground.

"We thought you were both dead, but I always held hope that you survived the fall from the boat, but you were there when Marcus died. You witnessed his death. How?" She spoke to Eowyn but her inquiry was meant for Marcus.

"You know I have nine lives. And you of all people should know that a mere flood couldn't kill me." Marcus sat next to her and placed his hand on her shoulder.

"I worried about you so much, and I assure you that I am not a figment of your imagination. Please look at me."

He draped his arm around her.

"Eowyn, why don't you go check on Leeba? I'll be right behind you." She stepped inside leaving them alone.

"Selima, please look at me."

Slowly she turned to face him. "I've changed, Marcus. You're not going to like what you see." She covered her face. "I prayed for you every day; I prayed you were still alive, and Allah has answered my prayers."

"Why are you covering your face?"

"Something happened. I was burned in an explosion. I'm ugly."

"You're too beautiful to ever be ugly. Let me see."

She removed her hand and quickly let her long hair fall over her face. Marcus swept it to the side revealing the burn ravished skin. Selima looked everywhere except into his eyes. She expected him to be repulsed.

"You are as beautiful as ever. You remember my axion that all of our cuts, scars, scrapes, and bruises are signs of character. In your case, I couldn't possibly find you any more beautiful."

"You don't find me revolting?" A slight smile surfaced.

"You are perfect! How long have you been here?"

"Me a couple of weeks, but Leeba, months."

"Are there any others here? Nay sign of Waffa?"

The look on her face and sensing her hesitation to answer, he inferred the news wasn't good. "It's okay. Just tell me; I need to know."

"She and your baby are dead. They were swept away when our boat flipped. She went under and never resurfaced. I'm sorry, Marcus, but she's dead."

Marcus quickly stood and walked towards the trail.

"I'm sorry! There was nothing I could do—where are you going?"

"I need some time. Please, give me some time to process."

Eowyn found Leeba sequestered in a back room. She peeked inside and discovered her cuddling with who she first thought to be Joanna but quickly realized she was singing a lullaby to a Volleyball.

"Leeba, it's me. I missed you so much."

Instead of replying, she continued singing."

Selima strolled into the room. "She's not the woman you are in love with."

"What's changed? She sounds the same and looks the same."

"She had some sort of breakdown. She was alone with Batya for months. She must have gone through hell thinking you were dead then Gurr died, and as far as she knew, everyone was dead. When we found her, she was having a tea party with Batya and the three balls she called her children. It's best just to play along. Maybe once it sinks in that you're alive, the Leeba we know might return. To be completely honest though, I think she's too far gone. Raghba and I have worked with her for days with no progress."

"Where's Raghba?" Eowyn abruptly changed the subject.

"She met someone weeks back and went bring him here. I expected her back by now. We'll probably see her soon. Enough about everyone else. What happened to you that night in the boat? One minute you were there and the next you were gone."

"Got clotheslined by a branch and was at the mercy of the water. Later, I washed up on shore and have been surviving since."

"And Marcus?"

"A day after I came ashore, I found him in the water trying to free Ferris's body from the tree that impaled him. We buried him the next day. We've been together ever since."

"Have you come across anyone else?"

"No, just us. By the way, where did Marcus go?"

"He went for a walk. Said he needed some time after I gave him some bad news."

"And the news was?"

"Waffa and his baby are dead. They drown."

For an instant, Eowyn privately celebrated the news thinking they could be together again, but her joy quickly transformed into pain. Waffa was her friend, and she realized how painful the news must have been for Marcus. On one hand, she wanted to run to him; to comfort him, but on the other, she had a responsibility to be there for Leeba.

"He's going to need someone, Selima. Go and be with him. He shouldn't be alone." The words peeled from her lips with trepidation. It wasn't natural to not be there for him, and she found it especially difficult to send Selima in her place, to send another woman to comfort the man she learned to love. Selima set off right after Eowyn's suggestion. For a moment, Eowyn hesitated considering if she should follow the urge to run to Marcus or go to Leeba and try to bring her back to reality. Before she had a chance to decide, Leeba stepped outside with Joanna in her arms and Batya at her side.

"Why are you crying?" Leeba wiped the tears from her eyes. "Don't be sad."

"I missed you, baby! Didn't you miss me?" Eowyn hoped her voice might jar a memory.

"You died. How are you here?"

"I'm alive, Leeba. You may have thought I was dead, but I'm right here. I'm here for you. Please come back to me." She cradled her in her arms. "I'm right here," she whispered.

"Dreams, dreams, dreams. You're here but shouldn't be. But I feel you, I smell you, I'll live this dream. I missed you. She pressed her lips to hers; the kiss was sensual like they once used to be "I've been so lonely, and the kids are driving me crazy! Do you want to fuck?"

"Leeba! You don't talk like that."

"Hurry before the dream ends!" Leeba clutched her hand and dragged her towards the bedroom."

"Mommy."

"Go play, Batya!"

"Leeba! Maybe we should wait."

She slammed the door and unbuttoned her blouse. "Well, what are you waiting for? This fantasy isn't going to last forever. Get undressed."

Eowyn did as she was told. She truly missed Leeba and thought that intimacy might be another opportunity to deliver her back to the corporeal world.

Leeba had a gleam in her eyes that Eowyn didn't recognize, and her normally gentle touch seemed foreign as her kisses roughly, in a state of desperation peppered her body. The attention felt good but at the same time, unnatural, not like the intimacy they once shared.

"Leeba, we should save this for later."

"Would you shut up! We haven't much time." She pinned Eowyn's arms over her head while her lips traced a trail of kisses from her lips to her breasts.

"Ooh, Leeba! Come back to me. I need you to..." Eowyn's body tensed. Leeba hummed as she dropped between her legs. After a few moments, Eowyn let out a planned mechanical moan.

She felt as if she were being assaulted by a stranger but knowing it was Leeba, she didn't want to hurt her feelings.

"So realistic," Leeba declared. "Your turn. We must hurry, so I can get back to the kids." She laid her head on the pillow. "Hurry now before you disappear."

"I'm not going anywhere, Leeba. I'm here to stay."

"If you're real, show me."

She knew it was the woman she loved underneath her, but it was as if an extraneous spirit inhabited her body. She didn't love this version of her at all and as a result, imagined Marcus lying next to her. Only minutes later, Leeba's body quaked followed by a series of pleasurable ripples. Eowyn expeditiously dressed, rushed out of the room, and collided with Marcus.

"Are you okay? I heard about Waffa. I'm sorry."

"We need to talk. We have a situation. Where's Leeba?"

"Don't worry about her. She's not going to be of any help. She's just too far gone. I don't even recognize her anymore."

"Give it time. She'll eventually pull out of it. I'm confident." Selima reassured. "What is it that we need to speak about?"

"There's a military patrol not far from here. I recognized some of them as Captain Acacia's men. I think they may be looking for you, Selima. It won't be long before they discover this place."

"I'm not leaving. I will not run, Marcus. This must come to an end."

"If you stay, I stay, Selima. How about you Eowyn?"

"I have nothing else to live for. Leeba is here, you are here, and I will not abandon you."

"Then I suggest we prepare. Do you have any weapons?"

"We have a .45 and a hunting rifle, but that's about it. Marcus, what about the kids?"

"We'll leave them inside with Leeba and set up defensive positions out here." Marcus ran to the shed to get some supplies but froze in his tracks. Acacia's soldiers were within fifty feet of the home."

32

TAKING A STAND

To Sergeant Ballard's eyes, everything was strange and new. Once the water receded, a whole new world emerged, the terrain forever shifted and remolded by the flood waters. Roads were gone, homes nonexistent, and not a sign of life outside of the hospital. Two squads stood in formation awaiting Ballard's orders.

"Today we will be reconnoitering the local vicinity for any survivors. Doctors and nurses will be on standby to receive any in need of medical attention. We are going to head to high ground where the water may not have reached. Squad One will take the southern ridge while Squad Two will survey the northern range. Any questions?"

"What if the survivors do not want to come back with us? How should we manage that?"

"They cannot be forced but inform them that the hospital is up and running. Additionally, make sure all soldiers have an entrenching tool. Our secondary mission will be to bury any victims but be sure to try to get names so that family can be notified. Any other questions?" Ballard grabbed his backpack and gave the order to move out.

As Ballard and his men spread out through the Cooperative, miles away Marcus sat in silence huddling behind a shed watching as a small group of soldiers filed in. He didn't have a moment to react when a voice startled him.

"You must be Martyreon. Am I correct?"

The soldier stood behind him and could have easily killed him on site.

"Yes, I'm Martyreon."

"That's up to you. We're here to lend a hand. We don't have much time. Lieutenant Raley is nearby. If I found you, she will too."

"I don't know Raley. Why should we fear this Raley person?"

"Is Selima with you?" He asked as he lowered his rifle.

"She's here."

'Lieutenant Raley believes that Selima should be put to death for her crimes. She not only wants Selima executed, but also wants to hold you accountable for your deceit. You know, the whole faking her death scene."

"Selima is..." Marcus began but was abruptly cut off.

"I am right here!" Selima walked around the corner. How close is Raley's force?"

"Very close. We don't have time for any more questions. We need to fortify positions. There's no time to run. I might be able to convince Raley to end the madness if given the chance. Martyreon, is there any other way in besides this entrance?"

"Not that I know of."

"Good, we will set up men on either side of the entrance and catch them in a crossfire. Nobody shoots until I at least try to convince Raley to give up. If talks don't go well, I will give the order to fire. Understood?"

"Yes, Sergeant!"

"We will be greatly outnumbered. Raley has over a hundred men versus our force but we have the advantage of surprise. If it comes down to a shootout, soldiers on the left side concentrate fire on those to the end of the column and the rest of you focus on those to the front. If necessary, we'll pick them off one by one as they scurry for cover. Get to your positions."

"I need a rifle, Ballard. I'm going to take a position at the front of the house. Eowyn and I will protect the children and Selima. If any of Raley's men get through the crossfire, we'll finish them off as they scramble this way."

"I'm not going to let it go that far if I can help it but by all means, take position wherever you want. I heard about you, Martyreon. I wasn't fortunate enough to serve under Sergeant Major King or to fight side by side with you, but it's an honor to serve with you now. Much like you fought for peace and the safety of the Cooperative, I will do whatever is necessary to deliver a newfound peace to the Free Zone. Keep your ass down and if things get ugly, I'll finish this. Godspeed, Martyreon! I wish we had more time to get acquainted."

"Get to your positions men!"

Sergeant Petry stood in the open awaiting Raley's arrival. "Remember, no shooting until I give the order!"

First one, then two soldiers peeked from the cover of the entrance. "Petry is that you?"

"I need to speak with Lieutenant Raley."

The two men disappeared and returned with Raley a few minutes later.

"Ned, what are you doing here? I told you to leave."

"I can't let you do this, Sage. It's insanity. Our people are reeling from the effects of the storm and need help rebuilding. We could assist with the recovery. We don't have time to be warring. This is a time for all of us to unite and work together. We can be together, Sage."

"Ned, the law is the law. Selima is guilty of murder, and Martyreon is complicit in the crime. They must be punished."

"I can't let you do that. You're going to have to kill me to get to them. Think about how many lives will be lost because you believe you are doing the right thing. We could be happy together, Sage; make a life for ourselves."

"This is your last warning, Ned. You're not going to change my mind."

"So be it." Those were his last words. A single shot broke the silence. Sergeant Petry's body fell to the ground.

"Noooo!" Raley screamed, her shriek cut through the volley of gunfire. "Hold your fire! I said hold your fire," she ordered, but it was too late. Once Petry went down, Raley's troops rushed in and as expected were caught in a crossfire. One soldier after another dropped. At the same time, a rogue force managed to flank Petry's militia and maneuvered towards the house.

Eowyn was the first to notice, sprinted from the porch, and positioned herself between the invading force and the house. One minute she was next to Marcus and the next she was gone with Marcus following close behind.

"Hurry, Marcus!" Eowyn yelled as she provided cover fire. He made it a few more steps when his body contorted most peculiarly and dropped to the ground.

Eowyn took out two aggressors and rambled to Marcus. He curled in a ball with a puddle of blood surrounding him while bullets riddled the area. Eowyn grabbed his collar and dragged him towards safety. Time stood still for her as she lugged him towards cover. She had tunnel vision only seeing what was directly in front of her, totally focused on helping Marcus.

She never saw the man rush in from the side other than catching a brief flash of steel gliding towards her. She had no time to react. The six-inch blade entered just above her hip sending paralyzing that sent her tumbling to the ground next to Marcus.

"You, okay? Marcus draped his arm around her.

"It hurts, Marcus." she cried.

"It'll be all right. We're going to be all right," He wiped her tears away.

"How cute! Martyreon looks like he has a crush." Three of Raley's men stood over them with rifles pointed.

"Who would have thought?" Marcus smiled.

"Thought what?" Eowyn inquired a little confused.

"That you and I were going to die today." Marcus held her hand as the soldiers raised their rifles.

"Don't be scared; I'm with you." They stared into one another's eyes waiting the moment. "Don't look at them; stay focused on me. Think about the last time we were together." They clung to one another waiting for the moment the trigger was pulled when from seemingly out of nowhere, a figure dove from the porch, blades slashed, and bodies fell. Marcus opened his eyes to catch a glimpse of Selima swinging her blades a final time. Raley writhed on the ground. Marcus was losing the battle to remain conscious as Selima sprinted to his side and just as quickly, he fell into darkness.

33

LIVES ON THE LINE

Day by day, the injured poured into Mercy General once the waters receded. Most minor injuries, scrapes, cuts, and bruises, but on this particular day, one patient after another arrived—some of their own volition—others with gunshot and stab wounds were carried in.

"What's going on here? We've gone from a few patients to an overflowing E.R. in a matter of hours. Are we at war again? Have any of the patients said anything?" Angela asked while she assessed the condition of yet another gunshot victim.

"I was told by one patient that a rogue force was sent after Selima and Marcus. For what, who knows? Anyway, the current death count is over forty." Nadia Romanov finished and joined Private Sakato in setting up a triage unit just outside the E.R. They performed a quick assessment of each victim and then escorted the most gravely injured to surgery.

"Have you heard anything about Marcus and Selima? Were they wounded?" Nayla asked. She treated a young soldier with a through-and-through in his thigh. Adiva irrigated the wound, administered local anesthesia, and started to stitch up the entrance wound.

"Nobody has been able to say so far."

"I saw him." The soldier interjected.

"You saw who?" Nayla asked as she tied off the last stitch.

"Martyreon. I saw him drop. He was shot."

"Do you know if he survived?" She was suddenly panicked.

"I was evacuated. Sorry. I can tell you that Princess Selima is alive. Many of the wounded you are treating were her victims. She went berserk when she saw them shoot Martyreon and commenced massacring everyone. I've never seen such a perfect killing machine. It took three of her people to stop her."

"Was anyone else with Martyreon?"

"A woman, but I think she was dead. The last thing I saw as I was being evacuated was the two of them, Martyreon and the woman, lying on the ground with medics trying to help them."

"All we can do is pray, Adiva. It wasn't long ago that we thought Marcus was dead, but by some miracle, he might still be alive."

As the day went on, the wounded began to dwindle, but there was still no sign of Martyreon or Selima. Adiva and Nayla were peeling off their bloody scrubs preparing to go home when they suddenly heard a shuffling of footsteps and the emergency room came back to life. Dr. House stuck his head in the locker room. "We need our two best nurses in the E.R. We have two critical patients who require emergency surgery. What do you say?"

Nayla looked at Adiva and smiled. "What do you say to saving a couple of more lives today?"

"Let's do it!" They put on a fresh pair of scrubs and went back to work.

"Nayla, our first patient presents with a serious stab wound to the abdomen. She has lost an immense amount of blood, her liver has been lacerated, and her odds of surviving are less than ten percent. On the table next to her, we have a man in his mid-twenties with a gunshot wound that has ruptured his spleen and compromised his left kidney. He also has little but slightly better odds of surviving."

"Who are they?"

"That doesn't matter, nurse. The question is, which of these two people should we attempt to save first?"

"We must work on the patient with the best chance of survival, so we need to prep the man for the E.R." Nayla answered but was quickly overruled.

"Eowyn first! I can wait. Please save Eowyn."

"My God, Marcus!" Adiva while glad to see him looked confused.

"God damn it, Adiva. Save her!" he screamed. Seconds later, the electrocardiogram shifted from a steady beep rhythm to a shrill tone.

"Get the defibrillator. The patient is in cardiac arrest." Dr. House yelled. "Administer 1mg. of adrenaline, stat! Dr. Casey, take over here. I'm taking the other patient to surgery. Adiva, you're with me. Nayla assist, Dr. Casey," he ordered as he departed for the operating room.

The reception counter of the E.R. finally slowed down providing Angela time to tidy up and catch her breath. She had just taken a seat when a woman covered in blood barged through the double doors with a blade in each hand. "Where's Martyreon? Is he okay?" She asked frantically.

"Mam, please put the knives down. We don't need any more killing today. Angela didn't recognize the person through the blood that covered her from head to toe.

"Put down the knives and calm down! Are you hurt?"

"I don't know, Angela. I just need to see Marcus."

"Do I know you?"

"It's me—it's me, Selima."

"Please drop the knives, and I'll get you to him. He is in surgery. Have you been injured?"

"That doesn't matter. How is Marcus? Please tell me he's alive."

"Both he and Eowyn were alive but in critical condition when they arrived. Unfortunately, things don't look good for either of them, but we have our best doctors working on them as we speak. Now, come with me. I need to examine you."

"I don't know what I'll do if he dies."

"He's in good hands and you are in surprisingly good shape. Why don't you take a shower? Here are some clothes to change into. Clean up and get something to eat at the cafeteria. It will be a while before we know anything about either of them."

Early in the next morning, Angela discovered Selima curled up on the bench seat of a booth in the cafeteria. "Selima, hey Selima, I have some news for you. Marcus is out of surgery. The doctor said the operation went well. He was moved to the ICU."

"Is he going to be, okay?"

"Doctor Casey said that the next few hours will tell us a lot. We just need to keep our fingers crossed."

"And Eowyn?"

"She made it through surgery early this morning but is in a coma and on life support. The odds are against her."

"Can I see him?"

"He's still unconscious but there's a chair in the room, and I'll bring you some blankets and a pillow. Follow me."

"Hey, Angie. Where are you headed?" a fellow nurse inquired.

"Dropping off a guest and then trying to catch up with Ballard. He is leaving with a squad to investigate the battle and make sure that the hostilities have ended.

"You'll have to fill me in later. See you, Christie."

"Okay, Selima, this is his room. I'll check with you in a little bit."

Angela rushed off towards the nursing quarters and was relieved to find Ballard waiting on her. He lay in bed with his hands interlaced behind his head. "What took you so long, beautiful?"

"I do have a job I have to accomplish. So, what is this I hear about you taking a squad to check out the battlefield?"

"Exactly what you heard. It'll be perfectly safe. All the fighting is over, and command wants me to determine what happened. That's it. It shouldn't take longer than a day or two. I leave in an hour and we're wasting precious time."

Angela smiled as though she anticipated his intentions. "You act as if I'm a sure thing. You shouldn't assume."

"I'm not assuming anything, but you invited me here. I'm just following orders."

Angie strutted towards him while her nursing gown dropped to the floor. "You think that you're going to get some just because I invited you to see me?" She kicked her shoes off and wiggled out of her panties. "You're a very confident man, aren't you?"

He sensed an excited hitch in her breathing. She sat and began kissing him with a wild fervor; their lips pressed tightly together. He kneeled at the foot of the bed and peppered her thighs with light kisses until he disappeared underneath her skirt. Seconds later, her entire body bucked wildly, her breathing became erratic, and a familiar storm began at her core and slowly spread throughout her body when, without warning, Ballard abruptly stopped.

"Why, Baby. I was almost there?"

On a floor of the hospital just above them, Selima rested her head on the bed next to Marcus. "Come back to me. God just delivered you back into my arms, and I can't lose you again." She lightly kissed his forehead and was about to go for a cup of coffee when she thought she sensed him squeeze her hand. She ran to the nursing station and excitedly reported her encounter. While the doctor dismissed the incident as a simple misinterpretation of an involuntary bodily movement, Selima was positive that he moved. "He did weakly squeeze my hand," Selima reassured herself as she fervently prayed for a miracle.

34

RAGHBA & DIMITRY REVISITED

After pilfering several homes, Dimitry located some antibiotics in a small shack hidden in a heavily foliated section of the forest. He shook the cushions of the couch outside sending a cloud of dust blanketing the air, put them back on the couch, and carried Raghba inside. "Rest my darling while I find some water. This medication will help you. She developed a high fever during their travels, became physically sick, and was unable to hold down food. Dimitry placed two tablets in her mouth and handed her a glass of water. "Drink! This medicine will help you feel better."

"So cold...I can't stop shaking." Dimitry pulled a blanket over her and worked on starting a fire. Soon the room was illuminated in a bright orange and the heat crept throughout the structure. He stripped off his shirt and slid in next to her using his body to help warm her. In mere minutes, they both drifted to sleep; Dimitry was physically exhausted from carrying Raghba on the long journey, while she fought to remain conscious. The wounds to her back became infected and sepsis set in.

The winds and rain returned late in the night. Everything inside the old shack rattled at pace with Raghba's chattering teeth. At times, Dimitry worried that the wind might peel the roof from its rafters. Each time the boisterous monster yanked at the roof, he clutched Raghba tighter. He wasn't going to let any storm, no matter how ferocious, husk his lover from his arms. He spent the night half-sitting, half-lying next to her until overcome by an overwhelming urge to sleep.

By morning, her fever broke. She woke alone. A light layer of sweat remained on her brow, and droplets of perspiration dappled her forehead, but she felt a boost of energy and was hungry for the first time in days. She struggled to her feet, added a log to the fire, and sat on the hearth wondering where Dimitry might be. Across the room, a steaming teapot sat on a wrought iron stove. She was pouring herself some tea when the door swung open.

"Good you're up, but you shouldn't be on your feet. Sit down. I'll get you a drink." He stripped off his rain-soaked jacket and hung it by the fire. "You are a sight for sore eyes. You had me worried. Are you hungry?"

"Famished. I could eat a horse, but I'd settle for just about anything at this point. First, let me look at your back. He peeled her shirt up to the back of her neck. Looks like the infection is clearing. You're going to need to soak in a hot tub and clean the wounds. Here's your coffee. Give me a minute to warm up some hot water, my sweet querida."

"Thank you, Dimitry."

"For what?"

"You saved me. Thank you!"

"You do owe me big time. For now, just drink your coffee, relax, and let me take care of you."

He filled six, five-gallon steel buckets with water, and placed three on top of the wood stove and the others next to it.

"Should be hot in a few minutes. Here's a couple of towels. I'll let you know as soon as the water is ready."

"Could you slow down and sit for a minute?" Raghba asked. She patted her hand on the floor next to her. "I'm feeling much better, and I want to thank you for caring for me."

We can't get sidetracked. Your health comes first. We need to clean your wounds and get some food in you; only then can we think about some play. I'll prepare the tub while you have some stew. He scooped a ladle full into a bowl and handed it to her. "Eat!"

After soaking in the hot bath for several minutes, Raghba laid chest down while Dimitry hunched over and carefully trimmed away the dead flesh.

"Pretty gross, huh?" Raghba asked as she rolled over.

"Radiant! You are a magnificent piece of art. I am going to take your mind off your pain. Did I tell you I am a therapeutic touch practitioner?"

"What's that?"

"I can manipulate, ease pain, bring joy, and heal by manipulating your energy field."

"Yeah, right! And I can cure injuries telepathically," she laughed.

"I'm not going to debate with you. Instead, I'll demonstrate. Just lay back and relax."

His hands floated over her, inches above her flesh tracing the contours of her body. He basked in the brilliance of her womanhood not once touching her and yet, like an ethereal masseuse, she felt his touch, the feel of his rough skin stroking her abs, his fingertips caressing the peaks and folds of her body. She wondered if her fever had returned because wherever his hands hovered, her skin became balmy and relaxed at the same time. His hands maneuvered over her shoulders, around her neck, and over her abs numerous times, and with each pass, she felt more relaxed like floating in a tub of tepid water infused with Epsom salts. He concentrated on her legs from her calves to her thighs, occasionally skimming her hips, moving up the flanks of her abdomen, and over her chest.

Raghba wasn't sure if it was her imagination or if the therapy had some merit, but she became increasingly aroused with each pass over. When he adjusted her legs, spreading them slightly, and continued, Raghba could hardly contain herself. Her breathing became raspy, she nearly screamed each time he fixated on her chest. Although he never physically touched her, waves of pleasure rippled through her body until she wasn't able to contain herself. When she didn't think things could possibly get better, he ran his hands over her hips concentrating on her thighs. Despite knowing he wasn't touching her, it was as if he were caressing her; she felt his touch, and even his hot breath until without warning waves she climaxed. When she opened her eyes, Dimitry was sitting across the room gazing at her.

"And now do you have any doubts?"

She modestly covered herself with the blanket. Were you sitting there the entire time?"

He sat with a smug smile on his face. "Again, I ask, do you believe in my abilities now?"

"That was amazing therapy. I don't know exactly how you accomplished what you accomplished, but I am a believer.

"I can pleasure you in more ways than you can ever imagine my sweet cherub. For now, I believe we must end our extended retreat and return to civilization. We must begin our lives and blaze our future together."

EXTENDED EPILOGUE

A little over a year passed since the apocalyptic storm that nearly wiped out the people of the Free Zone. The exact number of the dead couldn't be determined but early projections estimated that the storm had killed nearly half of the inhabitants. Not a single family weathered the storm unscathed. Eventually, the Free Zone was on the mend, homes rebuilt, an interim government put in place, and normalcy returned. The only thing missing was any sign of the Martyreon extended family. They decided to abandon the Free Zone and established the community of Harmony. Not that they cut all ties but rather, chose to start fresh and create their own city while maintaining close ties with the people of the Free Zone.

Lieutenant Raley's efforts to usurp the leadership as well as murder Selima and Martyreon fell short with one slash of a sword. The remainder of her army quickly surrendered following her death, and later rejoined forces with those of the Cooperative.

The new president, Sergeant Ned Petry, was elected just weeks after his return to the Free Zone. He gained notoriety and the support of the citizens of the Cooperative for coming to the rescue of Selima and Martyreon despite it nearly costing him his life. He rode the wave of recognition to the highest office in the land.

His primary initiative as president was to rebuild the Free Zone and once that mission was accomplished, he turned his efforts to building a strong military. He knew the Nihilistic State could reemerge and strike at any time and as a result, he focused on building the strongest army assembled since the Nill invasion.

1

PRESIDENT PETRY
& THE FIRST LADY

Pulling back the curtains, President Petry went to the sliding glass door, slid it open, and went outside. Butterflies fluttered in his stomach when he saw Adiva coming up the steps. It was a fluke that they met at all a little over a year ago at Mercy General. Shortly after being mowed down by Lieutenant Raley's troops, he was rushed to the hospital and after an extended stay, including weeks of physical therapy, he was given a clean bill of health. Initially, Nurse Houlihan was assigned to assist in his therapy, but as the head nurse, her abilities were needed elsewhere and that's when Adiva was introduced to Petry. The damage from the gunshot caused trauma to his spinal cord that left him paralyzed from the waist down. After months of one-on-one rehab, the two became well acquainted and romantically involved.

"Hey, Ned! I'm so glad to be home."

"Was it that bad?"

"No, don't get me wrong, I had a great time seeing Nayla, Raghba, Marcus, and the whole gang, but there's nothing like being home. Besides, I haven't seen you in a week, and I've missed you.

"I missed you too."

"How about showing me how much you've progressed while I was gone?"

"Once a nurse, always a nurse, huh, sweetheart?"

"Physical therapy is ongoing and besides, it's been a week since I've seen you walk. I want to see if you practiced while I was gone. So, come on now. If you want a hug, you'll need to come to me."

"Fine!" Petry grasped the armrests of his wheelchair and hoisted himself to his feet. His legs shook; he leaned his weight onto a set of forearm canes and slowly advanced until he stood near Adiva."

She wore a white muslin top with a low v-cut that bisected her breasts placing her plumage on display. Her beige areolas and erect nipples pressed through the sheer bleach-white garment that laid loosely over her curvy body coming to an abrupt stop at the ruffled hemline that struggled to cover her tight round butt.

"I would walk miles if it meant being with you." He dropped both of his arm supports and took Adiva in his arms. "You have got to be the sexiest woman ever."

"Do you think so?"

"No doubt, but I'm just wondering if you wore this outfit in public."

"Of course, I did. If you have the goods, you may as well flaunt them," She laughed. "That is unless you prefer I don't."

"As long as I am the only one who gets the pleasure of partaking in the merchandise, I'm perfectly content. And how is Martyreon coming along?"

"He's doing well. Selima hasn't left his side, and I got the feeling that they are a thing. Selima couldn't stop smiling and Marcus, well Marcus walked around with a hard-on whenever she was in the room. His pants could barely contain him. He thought he was hiding it, but any respectable young woman couldn't help but notice."

"Sort of like me right now. You're like an aphrodisiac."

"I'll tend to that momentarily, Mr. President. Selima wanted to thank you for coming to her rescue, and Marcus wanted to assure you that you had his complete backing and support."

Adiva poured herself a coffee and sat next to Ned on the couch. "And I assure you that you have my complete and utter dedication as well."

She squeezed his forearm lightly. "Do you still think about her?"

"Less and less each day. I loved Sage, and I'm still having trouble reconciling what happened to her, and how her life was ended by my command. I will say this, while my thoughts occasionally revert to her—mainly out of guilt—thoughts of you monopolize my mind."

She tilted her head inquisitively. "What type of thoughts?"

He gazed into her eyes, then softly replied. "Of being with you not just today or tomorrow, but for the rest of my life."

Adiva flashed a wistful smile. She was excited at the prospect of a union with Petry, but at the same time, realized that he still wasn't completely over Sage.

"Until Sage is completely out of your mind, I can't possibly marry you if that's what you are asking. In the meantime, I'm perfectly fine serving as a surrogate; I'm even content that you sometimes call me Sage when we're making love, but marriage isn't the answer. It would be reckless."

He reached out and stroked his fingers across her cheek. "I only love you."

"And yet, you still think of Sage and call her name out at night. Listen, I have no doubt you love me, but I know you are not completely over here. I'm fine with that, but I will not marry you until you call out my name instead of hers. I'm willing to wait."

He slid his hand down the side of her neck, brushed aside the collar, and buried his face at the nook of her neck. "I need you and want you like hell. I want to marry you, but for now, I'm content having you at my side." His kisses continued in between his short declarations. He slid his hand up her thigh and brushed aside her panties.

"Oh, keep that..." she gasped, "...up and you can call me by any name you want."

"I'm sorry I disappointed you."

"Disappointed?"

"The whole Sage thing. I should be over her by now."

"Loss of someone we love takes time, and I'm willing to invest the time for you to heal. But for now, I need you to finish what you started. She leaned up and whispered in his ear, "Take me now or forever lose me." She lifted her muslin mini-dress over her head, climbed onto his lap, and melted into his arms.

2

SAKATO AND ROMONOV

The morning arrived exposing its vulnerable underbelly, as Ayase Sakato stepped into the sunlight. Every day was a store full of possibilities like a candy store only the candy she craved was in her opinion, virtually inaccessible. She and Nadia took residence in a small ranch house outside of the Free Zone, yet close enough to Harmony that they could visit anytime. The two often traveled to the city for entertainment and the blossoming nightlife. Nadia normally ended the night with a gentleman on her arm while Ayase lay alone listening to the sounds of unbridled passion from her room. Hearing her with other men was agonizing because all she wanted was to be the one pleasuring her, to be the one responsible for furnishing the many nights of passion that she overheard through the thin walls.

Ayase stepped inside still wrapped in her sleeping attire, wrapped in her blue, terry bathrobe and panda slippers. The previous night was an active evening for Nadia. She arrived home well after bedtime and her moans woke Ayase around two in the morning. Her partner must have been adept at fucking since it was only the second time that she remembered Nadia having a screaming orgasm and the first to cause her to seemingly speak in tongues. The whole production brought back memories of being trapped inside a cave a little over a year ago with Nadia wondering if they were going to live through the night. It was at that time she shared in confidence that the only time she ever spoke Russian was when she was blessed with, as she put it, a prodigious climax. Hearing Nadia's passionate cries the previous night was the second.

Ayase had two cups of coffee, took a shower, and brushed her teeth but Nadia never emerged from her room. After an additional hour, she carried a tray of fruit and a steaming hot plate of flapjacks into her room. "Rise and shine, sexy." She pulled the curtains open sending bright rays of sunshine teeming through the room. Nadia lay nude, spread eagle on the bed, a smile still pasted on her face. Ayase took a moment to admire her long, lean legs, washboard abs, and sizable, quintessential breasts. Her hormones were sent ablaze or more specifically, were reignited after seeing her so vulnerable and ostensibly innocent.

"What are you staring at, silly? You've seen me naked a million times and nothing's changed."

"Except you're more beautiful" Ayase whispered.

"Come here!" She playfully pulled Ayase on top of her and gave her a tight hug. "I hope we didn't keep you awake last night. Six times! I came at least six times. He was insatiable which was exactly what I needed. He's the first man to ever keep pace with me. And wow! He was well-endowed. Like I never..."

"Enough! I don't want to hear about your sexual escapades. I hear enough of it throughout the week."

"Sorry. I didn't mean to upset you. I just think you need to get laid, Ayase. I should have sent him into your room last night.

You're so uptight that when you finally do orgasm, I hate to be the man on the other end. Talk about explosions," She laughed.

"Can we change the subject? I thought the two of us could go out for lunch and maybe stop by Marcus's after. It's been weeks since we've seen him and the gang. Go on, get dressed. We're leaving in twenty minutes." She threw a pair of panties and a bra on, slipped into her pants, and a Rolling Stones t-shirt.

"Hurry, I'll be waiting," Ayase requested.

Outside it was early afternoon by the time they departed. Slowly, the heat and thick humidity enveloped them. Despite many hot days, the humidity following last year's floods seemed forever present. They walked in silence. The back of their hands inadvertently touched, and they both smiled. Ayase wondered if Nadia had any idea that she was in love with her. At the same time, she knew that a relationship was an impossibility. One thing she learned was that Nadia didn't have a queer bone in her body.

They stopped at a small pizzeria that recently opened near the newly built city hall. Citizens walked by one after the other oblivious to the evils that threatened them, families, men, women, and children.

"Pepperoni or sausage?" Ayase inquired.

"I had enough sausage last night," Nadia chuckled. "Let's go with pepperoni."

"By the way, I have someone I want you to meet. A friend of mine who works at Mercy General."

"Who?"

"You'll know that once I introduce you. I met her through Selima. She's wanted to meet ever since I mentioned you."

"Whatever! Marcus's place is up ahead." They climbed a steep hill and emerged from a copse of oak and silver birch trees. His new home stood on top of an inactive volcano, more specifically in the caldera basin bordered by lanky, forested ridges on three sides while the wall of the third collapsed, and was overgrown with vegetation. Marcus carefully carved steps into the igneous rock formations that led to his home. Up ahead, a child and a woman toiled in a large green garden, soaking in the sunshine, oblivious to them. The home itself stood tall like it had bloomed from the fertile land along with the surrounding greenery. On one side, a stunning waterfall stretching ten meters across cascaded from one tier of the ridgeline to the next until venting into a crystal-clear estuary that fed into a swiftly flowing brook that zigzagged and drained into a hilltop draw.

They had descended nearly three-quarters of the steps when the little girl raised her head and stared while her mother languidly plucked away at weeds. Ayase waved and the child swooped behind her mother hugging her thigh tightly.

"What is it, Joanna? We're safe here, sweetie," Selima assured. Joanna's tiny arm stretched out from between Selima's thighs and pointed.

"Nadia! How nice to see you," she shouted. "Come, Joanna. We have company."

Selima double-timed until she was standing in front of Nadia. "It's about time you visited. We've missed you."

"Well, we're here now. This is my best friend, Ayase Sakato."

"So nice to meet you, Ayase. Nadia has shared so much about you. You are as adorable as she explained. Please come inside." As she turned towards the house, Selima just as quickly stopped. "Oh, Joanna, don't be so shy!" She peeled her from her leg. Nadia, Ayase, I'd like you to meet Marcus's daughter, Joanna."

"Nice to meet you, Joanna. How old are you?"

Joanna hid her face on Selima's shoulder.

"She's shy but will open up once she's comfortable. Let's get inside to see Marcus."

"They ascended the steps and walked inside. "Marcus, visitors!" She yelled and shortly after Marcus emerged from a back room. "Hey, ladies! It has been a long time. I remember you Ayase although you may not recall meeting me during the Second Nil War. Ferris used to tell me about the adventures he had with you in the cave complex. He thought highly of you. And of course, Romonov! You and I fought many battles together. Have a seat. Would you like some coffee or lemonade?" he asked.

"Lemonade sounds great for the both of us."

"Selima, do you mind? I'm a bit winded."

"Of course."

"I'm still trying to recover from being shot. It damaged the lower quadrant of my right lung, and I sometimes need a minute to catch my breath."

"Any news about Sophi's recovery?"

Selima set three glasses of lemonade on the coffee table and took a seat next to Marcus.

"Sophi is coming along well according to Dr. House. She's still going through speech therapy and can stand on her own. He is hopeful that she will be walking within the year."

"She's been through so much. If anyone can recover from a traumatic brain injury, Sophi can. Ayase and I are stopping by the hospital on the way home."

"You're going to see Sophi?"

"Yes, but our main goal is to meet with Nayla and Adiva. We haven't seen them in a while, and I hope to introduce Ayase to Nayla."

"Are you playing matchmaker?" Selima asked.

Nadia glared in her direction signaling her to shut up. Selima quickly changed the subject. "Have you seen the new hospital?"

"No, I heard one was being built, but had no idea it was complete."

"It's not completed but getting very close. The towns' people decided to name it *Ferris Medical Center*," Marcus walked across the room and returned with a picture. "Here, take a look. It's even nicer than I imagined it."

Nadia glanced at the picture and handed it to Ayase. "Beautiful!"

"We hope to be self-sufficient as a city by the end of the year. Sergeant Ballard has been recruiting for the military, and Angela is taking point for hiring medical personnel for the hospital. She said we should be fully staffed by next month. You mentioned that you are going to Mercy General. Both Adiva and Nayla have agreed to transfer to the new hospital once it opens. They're going to stay with us until their house is built. Nurse Houlihan and her staff will stay at Mercy."

"Have the two of you considered moving closer, Nadia?"

"We do have an eye on a small cottage about a mile from here if it hasn't already been claimed."

"You must be talking about the Goddard place. Still empty and since Selima has been appointed the Minister of Property and Acquisitions, the home is yours if you want it."

"I'd be glad to do that for you," Selima cut in. "I can make the arrangements. It'll be nice to have neighbors. Will the both of you be moving in together?" Selima inquired.

"Naturally! We'll always be roomies. We're best friends, and we share everything."

"Not everything," Ayase longingly thought to herself at the same time, she was excited about the move.

Following lunch, Nadia and Ayase set off for Mercy General Hospital. They crossed the Bentley River and arrived by nightfall. "Here we are. Sorry, it took so long. I got a little disoriented."

They stepped inside and walked to reception. "Hello, we're here to see Nurse Nayla." Nadia finished and glanced down the hall. "There she is. Nayla!" she hollered.

Nayla was speaking with Dr. House and held up her finger signaling one minute.

"Isn't she cute, Ayase?" Nadia asked as they walked towards her.

"You better not be trying to set me up!"

"Me, never! I can't believe you would think that. She's just a good friend that I want you to meet. That's all. Ahh, here she comes now. Hey, Nayla. Where's Adiva?"

She hugged Nadia and held out her hand. "Hi, I'm Nayla, nice to meet you. Nadia has told me a lot about you."

"Oh, she has?" She glared at Nadia. "Can we go to the cafeteria and sit down?"

"Sure, follow me. After a few minutes, Nayla took a seat while Ayase sat across from her. "I'm sorry, but I have to go to the bathroom." Nadia quickly departed leaving them alone as if planned.

Ayase quickly assessed Nayla. She was one of the prettiest, most enthralling females she had met since Maria and shared many of her features. She wore her hair braided and wore a white hospital scrub shirt and pants, but her attractive body shined right through the generic uniform. She admired her perfectly round cheeks and oh, those lips, plump, full, rose-red, and glossy.

"Ayase, did you hear me?"

"Sorry, I zoned out for a minute. What did you say?"

"I just said that it's nice to finally meet you. Nadia tells me more about you every time I see her and to be honest, I was excited to meet you. It's nice to finally put a face with the name."

"I hope I'm not a disappointment."

"Disappointed, no, not in the slightest. You are much more than I anticipated."

"More in a good or bad way?"

"More in an excellent way." Nayla had never been the type to thrust her opinion or share her intimate thoughts with others, but Ayase was particularly receptive, and she felt at ease speaking with her. "You're captivating." Nayla finished as her cheeks reddened. She couldn't believe the words escaped her lips.

"Oh, you're just being nice, and I appreciate that you're trying to make me feel better about myself, but I realized I'm nothing special a long time ago. You, on the other hand, personify beauty. You must have been a model at some point in your life, right?"

"So, what are your plans once you leave? Will you be staying nearby?" Nayla asked.

"I share a cottage with Nadia."

"You two aren't...?"

Ayase anticipated her question. "No, we are best friends. Besides, Nadia has a very healthy and active sex life with many lovers. As for me, I'm more of a stay-at-home, gardening type of girl. I've never been in a serious relationship. You?"

"One. She was murdered by the Nill. I have been spiraling through a minefield of depression ever since but have been out on a couple of dates with a colleague, but that didn't work out."

"Here comes Nadia. I know she's going to want to get going because it's getting dark. Quickly, before she gets here; would you like to go out sometime, just you and I?" Ayase waited for a reply.

Nayla held Ayase's hand under the table.

"I'd love to. Let me know where and when—I'll be there."

"Be where?" Nadia asked.

"Nothing. Just talking about places that we have been."

"You ready to get going?" Nadia asked. "It's getting late."

They said their goodbyes and were home by ten. Adiva quickly dressed, went out, and later that evening, returned with not one but two men. "I'll try to keep it down, Ayase. Good night."

3

NAYLA & AYASE

Nayla came out of the bathroom to find Ayase in the same spot reading a book. She was lying down but didn't look relaxed. Her body was tense, wound tight, and while she was clearly in the room, she wasn't there in spirit.

After meeting Nayla at the hospital over a week ago, Ayase had a difficult time thinking of anything or anyone else. Their first date occurred only a day after meeting one another.

Nayla was about to knock when the door sprung open and a man darted outside.

"Hey, Nayla. Come on in. You look absolutely delicious! She's going to eat you up. What do you have planned anyway?" Nadia asked.

"We're going to get some dinner and go to my place for a movie."

"That's nice, but is tonight going to be the night? She's so uptight, is wound tighter than a top, and needs some serious intimate time. I don't know the last time she was laid. Shoot, for all I know, she might be a virgin."

Nayla's cheeks flushed. "Nadia, you're so bad! "We're going to have a nice evening and whatever happens, happens. You don't plan intimacy."

"You are so wrong, girl. Intimate situations must be meticulously planned; you have to set the mood, prep your goods for inspection, and take time to envision the moment leading to the first kiss."

"What do you mean by "Inspection; that seems extremely visceral?"

"Get your mind out of the gutter! I simply meant wet your whistle, have a drink to loosen up, put on makeup, and a nice perfume. I enjoy a glass or two of a good Cabernet before any date. Always plan for sex. The ultimate goal of any date should be a meaningful coital exchange. There's nothing in the world as magnificent as the activities leading up to the ultimate act of orgasm."

"I sense that Ayase is delicate and she needs to be treated that way. I just want to show her a good time and if sex is what she desires, then so be it, but I'm not going to force the issue. She has to be ready."

"Come on, Nayla. You've been on at least three dates already. It's time and if you have to, push the issue because there is one thing I know, she is primed and ready to get laid. Ayase is a fierce and fearless soldier, but when it comes to sex, she is like a self-conscious child; afraid to initiate anything. You have to be the aggressor. Take the initiative and screw her brains out or whatever it is that lesbians do. If you don't, she may just self-destruct."

"I get your point."

Ayase pranced into the room wearing a curve-hugging mini dress. The sheer scarlet material draped from her shoulders, and gaunt bands reached one over each breast exposing the runway of flesh between while the remainder of the dress hugged her hips barely covering the uppermost portion of her thighs. The dress did exactly what she hoped. Both Nayla and Nadia's jaws dropped. Of course, she wanted to look good for her date, but she had a secondary motive. She wanted Nadia to question her sexuality, to wonder what she was missing out on, to be sorry she wasted her time with all the meaningless men that passed through her bedroom door when she could have had something real and meaningful.

She leaned over being sure to poke her perky butt out just a bit as she looked in the mirror and put on some lipstick. She felt a twinge of excitement when the reflection revealed Nadia staring, practically drooling.

She arranged her dress, walked to Nayla, and gave her a long passionate kiss the whole time observing Nadia's reaction. "Are you ready, Nayla? I'm going to warn you now; you're in for the night of your life. I decided that after dinner we would come back here for a movie. We can watch it in my room. Is that okay?"

She opened the door and stepped outside. "So, where are we going?" Ayase asked.

"It's a surprise."

They walked in silence until Nayla asked a question. "What were you trying to accomplish before we left your house?"

"What do you mean? I was trying to get ready for our date."

"I saw the looks you were giving Nadia. You put on quite a show, and I don't think it was meant for my pleasure."

"I apologize. She constantly reminds me that I'm stiff, boring, and destined to be lonely. I just wanted to show her that

I could be outgoing and sexy too; however, I did hope that you noticed me too. I dressed up for you. I also wanted you to see my sexy side."

"First of all, you don't need to try to be sexy because you are naturally. Secondly, I don't find you boring and if you are lonely, I can address that sentiment if you let me. I'm lonely too and desperately in need of a companion. I would be elated if you agreed to help me end my loneliness and maybe along the way, we may learn to love one another. This may be a bit presumptuous, but I sense a strong bond already."

Ayase pressed Nayla against a large birch tree. "I don't know if I can wait until after dinner. I've wanted you since the moment I first saw you." A soft gust of wind stirred Ayase's dress, and her mind drifted as if propelled by the wistful winds. At the same time, the cool breeze, or perhaps it was the proximity of Ayase's warm body, Nayla's nipples stiffened. Ayase's steamy lips and probing tongue sent lustful thoughts rebounding in her mind.

"You're right. I could do without dinner." Ayase clutched her hand and led her to her home. The house appeared empty. Nayla sat on the bed while Ayase lifted her dress over her head, kneeled at Nayla's feet, peeled off her leggings and panties, and began caressing her thighs with kisses. The more Ayase grazed, the more Nayla's legs hedged open and the more she wiggled in anticipation.

"You are so beautiful, Nayla." Ayase navigated her body feeling every curve while her lips peppered her with kisses until concentrated on her hardened nipples. She grazed, spending extra time suckling each as Nayla's ecstatic moans grew louder and more frequent.

As she pleasured Nayla, Ayase heard the front door close, and followed by footsteps. Now, it was her chance to leave her roommate frustrated and wondering what was going on inside her bedroom; she wanted her to hear the cries of her lover, the sound of her screaming in ecstasy; she wanted Nadia to realize what she missed out on. Nayla whimpered unaware of anything other than the ripples of excitement running through her.

"Don't hold back Nayla. If you feel compelled to scream, then scream, if you want to moan, then moan. I find it exhilarating." She remained focused on her breasts, rolling one nipple between her fingers while suckling the other. Within moments, Nayla's knees began to wobble and her body vibrated in a series of powerful orgasms. At first, she whimpered, then when coaxed, she frantically cried out in unison with the peak of each climax. Eventually, she lay thoroughly relaxed and satisfied.

"You are masterful! I've never been pleasured so thoroughly."

"I'm glad you enjoyed it. I can continue if you like," Ayase waited for an answer.

"I am more than satisfied but I believe you must be anxious. I'm not nearly as experienced as you are, and I hope I don't disappoint you, but I want to please you too. Nearly all my experience is with myself, so I want to introduce you to what pleases me when I am alone." She reached into her purse and removed a sizable vibrator.

Lay back and try to enjoy. Nayla nudged Ayase's legs apart and began to slowly circle her clit. She worked the dildo like a sexual savant and within moments Ayase felt a climax rising and when it happened, she made extra sure to put on a show for Nadia. She moaned, groaned, and screamed Nayla's name throughout the whole affair. Still, Nayla continued driving the phallus in and out, and in tune with Nayla's body, she caressed her clitoris at the perfect time. The release was long-lasting and unthinkably powerful. This time she screamed not to put on a show, but because the tsunamic release was overwhelming and continued rolling from one to the next for several minutes. Nayla touched her wet lips to Ayase's. "I hope that was fulfilling."

She struggled to speak and couldn't get a word out edgewise as she fought to catch her breath which was nearly impossible until her heart stopped fluttering. "I couldn't imagine sex getting much better, Nayla." They cuddled up with one another and drifted off waking at times throughout the night to make love.

The next morning Ayase woke to Nadia working in the kitchen. "Well, good morning. I take it you had a fulfilling night," Nadia's eyes appeared bloodshot as if she didn't sleep a wink.

"Totally fulfilled. I hope I didn't disturb your sleep, but my lord does Nayla know how to navigate the female anatomy? I don't know how many times I came."

"I counted seven, but I might be off by one or two; your cries blended sometimes. I had no idea you were so passionate."

"I guess you kind of know how you sound night after night now. But I hope you also discovered that I'm not the bore you claim I am, and I can be adventurous too. I want you to know that you hurt my feelings."

"I didn't mean to. I was trying to get you to open up and find some happiness instead of locking yourself in your room every day. I want you to be happy, Ayase. I love you."

4

LEEBA & EOWYN

She was impenetrable. It was as if she were encased in an impervious membrane that prevented anyone from ever reaching the Leeba of old. The months of isolation, abundant death, and destruction transformed her into a shell of what she used to be. Over the months since being reunited, she accepted that Eowyn was a living person and not a creepy apparition of her dead lover, but the love they once shared was irrevocably lost. Still, Eowyn cared for her, bathed her, fed her, and did the same for Batya.

Eowyn leaned back on the couch, a glass of wine in hand while Leeba was concluding a tea party with Batya, Wilson, and her other spherical children. She wasn't invited just like she wasn't welcomed back into Leeba's heart.

"How'd the party go?"

"Oh, it was grand! The kids were..." Eowyn drifted. Beyond the bay window through the tied back, lace curtains, she gazed at the bare limbs of a large maple tree. Every minute she remained was grueling; she felt like vultures were pecking away at her flesh. Soon nothing would remain but hollowed eye sockets, bone, and a skeletonized version of herself. "This is how I will live." The words escaped her lips even though meant to be a harmless internal thought.

"You used to love me, didn't you?" Leeba asked as she plopped down next to her.

"Still do."

"Did I love you?"

It was like a dagger through the heart. She realized early on that Leeba's love had faded, but hearing it, the confirmation was excruciating. "You...yes, we loved each other very much. I still love you."

Leeba kissed her on the cheek. "I feel like I remember something, a light tug at my heart. A familiar glimmer flashed in her eye then just as quickly vanished. "Sorry, got to get the kids. Could you do me a favor and let me know when my wife gets home? She's been gone for a long time, and I hope to see her soon."

Eowyn's heart dropped to her stomach. For a moment, there was recognition; Leeba returned, but just as quickly the shroud returned, and she was carried away. It was at that time she realized that Leeba's wounds were far beyond her capacity to heal. She wasn't sure how much longer she could stay and tend to Leeba when her heart was breaking, and she required care herself. She wiped away a stream of tears, finished off her glass of wine, and refilled her cup.

"Knock, knock!" Eowyn jumped to her feet spilling her wine on the floor. "Anyone home?"

Eowyn took a deep breath and brushed the tears from her face. "Come in! I was just having a drink and could use some company." She hugged Selima relieved to have someone to talk to, but her heart skipped a beat when she saw him enter. Suddenly, all her loneliness dissipated. The man she thought about daily, thoughts of him helped her to endure the long nights of solitude and to manage the monumental loneliness that consumed her. When Marcus learned of Waffa's demise, she so wanted to be there for him, to help him through the pain, but that was an impossibility since she was occupied with Leeba. Instead, Selima capitalized on her absence, took care of him, loved him, and supported him through one of the most difficult times of his life, and as a result, he felt obligated to love her.

"So, how's Leeba doing?"

"According to her, she's fine, and I guess that's all that matters."

"And how about you?" Marcus inquired while he wrapped his arms around her. "I've missed you," he whispered.

"Of course, you have. I miss you too. Best friends, right?"

Being near Marcus brought back waves of heated recollections. Making love on the lawn, romantic picnics, and days of cuddling in bed while the rains beat down on the roof. She often fantasized that the torrential rains returned, and they were stranded alone once again.

"So, Eowyn, can I see the baby?" Selima asked.

"Nessa's sleeping, but you can see her. Just don't wake her. She kept me up through the night. I mean, Leeba helps some, but for the most part, I'm on my own."

"We have a suggestion that might remedy that, but we'll talk about it later. You and Marcus speak while I peek in on Nessa." Selima walked softly towards the nursery.

"Nothing has improved with Leeba?" he asked tentatively.

She put up a monumental effort to hold back her tears; she had to maintain the front that she was a strong, autonomous woman who didn't require pity or assistance, but for the first time in her life, she felt defeated, her defenses failed her. "I can't do this alone, Marcus" and all efforts to conceal her pain abruptly surfaced. Tears flowed uncontrollably, and she threw herself into his arms. "I'm so tired. I wake and go to bed each night hoping Leeba will return, but she's not. She's damaged beyond repair; has no idea who I am, doesn't love me. Fuck, she loves a volleyball more than she cares for me."

She looked into Marcus's eyes and began to laugh. "I'm pitiful, ain't I? I bet you never thought you'd see me like this, sobbing like a baby."

"You forget, Eowyn. I know you as well as I know myself. You are the most resilient woman I know; you're ferocious, vivacious, powerful, yet contrastingly, the most feminine, soft-hearted, and passionate person I've ever had the pleasure of knowing."

She removed her head from his shoulder and looked into his eyes. For the moment, nobody else existed in the world. Eowyn moistened her lips, wrapped her arms around the back of his neck, and laced her fingers through his hair. She nibbled at his lower lip for an instant then earnestly molded her lips to his. Marcus pulled her so tight their bodies nearly sculpted as one then just as quickly, he pried himself from her arms.

"We can't do this. Selima is in love with me."

"I don't doubt that, but the one thing I didn't hear you say is that you're in love with her."

"You two look like you are in a deep conversation," Selima emerged from the back room with Nella in her arms. Surprised, Marcus took another step back from Eowyn.

"Just catching up. Revisiting old times and past relationships." Marcus slung his arm around Selima.

"Yep, love that no longer exists." Eowyn poured a glass of wine, took a sip, and sent the glass crashing against the wall."

"You see, my girlfriend would never have done that. She was always even-tempered and patient. This girl is an imposter; probably a Nill spy," Leeba declared while pointing at Eowyn.

"Eowyn ran outside. The door slammed behind her.

"What's with her?" Selima looked at Marcus.

"She's just frustrated and hurt about, well, you know who."

Why don't you go see if she's all right while I speak with Leeba," Selima suggested as she fed Nella a bottle.

Marcus headed for the door but stopped when Selima called his name. "Do you know how much I love you?" She smiled and turned her attention back to the baby.

The happiness she once thought unobtainable, returned when she discovered Marcus was alive. She wasn't going to let the second chance evade her. Selima didn't leave his side while he was recovering at the hospital, and once released, they continued to hang out until Selima made her intentions clear and kissed him. For days, he avoided her unsure if he wanted another relationship until, perhaps, the extreme loneliness affected his judgment, days later, he showed up on her doorstep. She opened the door and he took her in his arms.

He found Eowyn sitting at the banks of a fast-moving brook and took a seat next to her. "Are you, all right?"

"I've lost her—I've lost you, and I don't know what to do with myself. I understand she was stressed and experienced unusually difficult circumstances, but so did I. I would never forget her or write her off. How does a love as strong as what we had simply fade away? I just can't wrap my mind around it."

"I think it's important that—and I realize that this is no consolation—she still loves you. Her love for you never died. Her mind fractured. She believed herself to be the last person on earth. Unlike us, who had each other to lean on, she was on her own. I couldn't imagine what she experienced as she tried to reconcile that."

"I've considered that and thank God, we had one another. I just don't want to be alone. I have so much love to give, and nowhere to displace it."

He wanted nothing more than to sweep her up and make love to her at that very moment, but his sensibilities directed him otherwise. "You won't be alone for long. You are beautiful, intelligent, funny, and it won't be long before another person sweeps you off your feet."

"Right! A single washed-up woman with a baby. Yeah, every man or woman's dream!"

"You are far from washed up; you're still young, energetic, and possess a voracious sexual appetite. Yes, you have a child now, but if anything, that makes you more desirable."

Eowyn rested her head on his shoulder. "Yes, I am a mother now with a child that we need to talk about."

"To be honest, I was surprised to hear that you had a child. I know this sounds narcissistic, but I thought I was the only man in your life. I only learned of your pregnancy two months ago and do you know what I immediately thought?"

"No."

"How could she do this to me? How did you forget me so quickly and run into another man's arms? I know it's selfish to think that way, and I should have been happy you moved on, but I wasn't. Knowing I was the only man you ever chose to be with made me feel special. Knowing that you chose me of all people to love you was one of the greatest moments of my life. To be loved by you was amazing; you're amazing, and you should never forget that."

"The baby wasn't planned, and I would never burden the father with the responsibility. I love her so much, Marcus. I guess she should be my focus going forward. I don't need to be in a relationship, right?"

"Exactly! Focus on you. Heal and only worry about a relationship when the time feels right. Leeba is self-sufficient, right?"

"Yes, she can take care of herself and Batya."

"Maybe it's time to move out, maybe into my guest house. Make it your own and build a new life with Nella. Selima wanted to see if you wanted to move in with us anyway. The guest house is right next to our home, and you could come and go as you please. No matter where you decide to stay, I promise, I'll be there to support you whenever you need a friend. As long as I am on this earth, you have a friend, and I won't fail you."

Eowyn smiled. "There is something you can do for me right now."

"I've got a real good idea of what that might be." He reached into his pocket and pulled out a vial of morphine. "I thought you were trying to wean yourself off of this?"

"I thought you said the same thing."

He pulled back on the plunger and filled the syringe. "Hold your arm out." He carefully nudged the needle into her vein and pushed the plunger. "That's more like it! Your turn."

Marcus held out his arm, Eowyn kissed him lightly, and inserted the needle sending the warmth of its contents cascaded from head to toe. "You remember what this does to us?"

"How could I forget, but we can't. Come on; let's get back to the house."

I do have some packing to do and a new life to begin." They walked hand-in-hand, had dinner, and parted ways later that evening.

5

SELIMA AND MARCUS

Marcus admired her sinewy legs, lean flanks, teardrop breasts, and firm, round butt in the mirror as she undressed. The burns monopolized most of the left side of her body, her cheek, shoulder, chest, flank, and hip, yet, the scars failed to rob her of her beauty although she strongly disagreed.

She turned towards him while covering herself. "I understand if you find me displeasing, and I would accept if you chose to shun me. I hoped that if this day ever arrived, I would be an unblemished specimen for your pleasure, but instead, I come to you maimed, and unsightly, yet I remain chaste and willing to dedicate myself to you."

He ran his thumb over her full red lips and kissed her lovingly. "Your scars make you more desirable. They tell the story of a gallant, noble woman who repeatedly put her life on the line for the benefit of others; they disclose your courage, resilience, and kind-heartedness. At this moment, not another woman on this earth could be more alluring."

Marcus draped a bathrobe around her shoulders, walked her to the bed, and sat down. He swept the hair from her eyes, but she quickly covered her face, attempting to shield the pockmarked skin and excised ear. He kissed her on the cheek then slowly navigated to the marred area of her ear. "You're stunning."

Selima didn't answer but instead let her long hair fall over her scarred face while she tentatively began removing her robe.

"Why are you shaking? There's nothing to be nervous about. It's just you and I; two people who love one another, nobody else." Marcus slipped the robe back over her shoulder.

"You don't want me?" she asked. A single tear zigzagged down her cheek.

"Of course, I do, but when you're ready. When the time is right, you won't be nervous or apprehensive. I don't want you to be the least bit uncertain, and you must be invested when the time is right. For now, I am thoroughly content just holding you."

Selima peered into his eyes. "I want nothing more than to be yours, Marcus. As far as I'm concerned, I was yours from the time we first met. Something draws me to you, something intriguing about you that attracts me."

"You know I've always cared for you, Selima and I promise to cherish you for as long as you'll have me. Now, with that out of the way, what do you say to a picnic? We could go for a swim and let Joanna and Tiny have some time in the sun."

"Yes, the outdoors would be nice. After spending that week in the hospital, I know I'm ready for an adventure or in this case, some time with my family."

"Get in your bathing suit, and I'll get some snacks together."

"Joanna!" Marcus yelled. After a minute, she emerged from the back room.

"Yes, Dad."

"Get your shoes on. We're going to have a picnic and go swimming."

"Selima too, right?" she excitedly asked.

"Of course, baby. Hurry now!"

An hour later, Marcus sat along the shore gazing at Selima and Joanna frolicking in the water while Tiny curled in his lap. He smiled in admiration as he thought about how well Joanna turned out despite the many tragedies in her short life. Selima was a good mother to her, much better than Marcus would have ever guessed. He smiled as she splashed water while Joanna giggled. The sun shined brightly above as he took a drink of water and his eyes fluttered. His mind immediately journeyed not by choice but more out of practice to Eowyn; the last time they made love before returning to society. He tried to vanquish the thought but unsuccessfully. They both ended up in the Free Zone under less-than-optimal conditions. Both were seriously wounded and fought for their lives after the confrontation with Lieutenant Raleys' forces.

After weeks of hospitalization, they were both released, Marcus a week before Eowyn. Knowing their relationship was going to change so drastically was disconcerting. For days, he remained depressed and wondered what his next step would be. He was torn. On one hand, he owed his life to Selima. She saved both him and Eowyn from a sure death just weeks ago and he thought he might love her. On the other hand, he wanted nothing more than to be in Eowyn's arms, loving her day and night.

Once Eowyn was discharged from the hospital, she sought Marcus out, eventually finding him in the same abandoned home they shacked up in during the epic rains. When she stepped inside, she found him in a deep sleep, a half-empty vial of morphine on the floor next to him. She lit a fire and warmed some soup. The whole time, the morphine in the next room was on her mind. She hadn't used it since her hospital stay and promised herself she was finished with the drug, but now that she was alone and the materials were in front of her, she contemplated using it one last time.

She had just sat down and was beginning to eat when he woke.

"How did you find me?"

"Oh, it took a while but then I remembered the time we spent together here and just hoped I was right. And here you are."

"I've missed you so much. I can't keep my mind off of you, and I thought a little time away might help me to be stronger. I know you love Leeba and that I have to give you space as you rebuild your life, but damn, I love you."

"I feel the same way, but we have to return to our families. Selima has been worried sick about you. Your friends are just as worried. You have to get home to them, but at the same time, I know how you feel. You're crazy if you don't think I am struggling too. I love you with all my heart, but I am committed to Leeba. We both have to be strong."

After a lengthy pause, Marcus replied, "I know you're right but you're here. There's not another living soul to disturb us, no discernible reason why we can't share one last night together...just one more night, right?"

"Honestly, Marcus that will only make things more difficult." She sat next to him and brushed his hair from his eyes. Being so close to him weakened her resolve.

"Dad...dad?" Joanna's voice snapped him out of his stupor. "Swim with me and Selima."

Marcus slung Joanna over his shoulder and slowly waded into the water. "Roarrrr!" he pretended to be a sea monster, lurching towards Selima who screamed and fled. With his free arm, he scooped her up. "I'm going to eat you up!"

"No, Daddy! No!" Don't eat mommy," she hollered.

"But I'm a big ornery sea monster. What should I do?"

Selima smiled, pleased by Joanna's choice of words.

"Would it be better if I was a kissing monster? Roar! Come to me while I kiss you with my big, gooey lips!" Selima pretended to run but he corralled her in his arms and attacked with a barrage of slimy kisses.

"My turn, daddy! Let the monster get me," Joanna requested as he lowered her into the shallow water. "Roar! I'm going to capture and kiss you until you never want to be kissed again." Janey did her best to flee but only made it a few steps when he hoisted her into the air and plastered her belly with kisses.

"Ha, ha, ha," Joanna giggled. "No, no! No more kisses!"

"Please monster, don't take my baby. Set her free; you can kiss me instead."

Selima leaned into him; her chest pressed against his. She gazed into his eyes. "Is this what love feels like?"

"This is just a small aspect of love, baby. I promise there is so much more, and I hope we can explore all aspects together."

They returned home after a long day of swimming. The sun hung low on the horizon, and darkness set in shortly after their arrival. Selima bathed Joanna, tucked her in, and sat next to Marcus who busily read from an old magazine.

"This was a good day."

"I had a great time, and I'm glad you did too. You deserve some peace and lots of happiness. You are happy, right?"

"Of course, I am. I just sometimes don't know how to act. I mean, I've never been part of a close-knit family. And did you hear Joanna today? She called me mom!"

"How'd that make you feel?"

"Elated. I love her so much. I'm going to like being a mother."

"I have no doubt. I feel fortunate to have you in my life."

After a long pause, she broke the silence. "I'm ready, Marcus. I want to make love to you, but I'll need your instruction."

He walked to her toward the bedroom.

Knowing she was anxious, he simply held her close at first. "Are you sure?"

"I want to make you happy."

He softly began peppering her with kisses and ever so slightly moved from her neck until his lips explored her cleavage. "Are you okay?" he whispered as she lay in the bed.

"Make love to me, Marcus."

He loomed over her on all fours, slipped his hand into her blouse, and cupped her breast while lifting her shirt over her head. She gazed at him as his lips enveloped her nipple while he playfully tweaked the other.

She whimpered each time he touched her. She pressed her lips tightly against his neck trying to keep pace with him as he oscillated from one breast to the next while one hand lightly stroked her through her jeans.

Unexpectedly, her body tightened and slightly quaked until she went limp.

"Oh my, I couldn't breathe. My body felt like bolts of lightning were shooting through me. Scary and liberating at the same time."

"You've never felt something like that before?"

"I never knew that pleasure before now. Was that sex?"

"That was foreplay which I guess is a part of sex, but it is just the beginning." Marcus began peeling her panties from her legs.

"Marcus, can we please stop? While I found that exceptionally pleasing, I would like to wait for more. Is that okay? I need to process. I just need to lie down after this eventful day."

Over the months to follow, she repeatedly avoided intimacy; at times, she passionately sought him out, but never once did she ever allow things to advance beyond kissing, touching, and elements of foreplay. While a major disconnect existed sexually, their relationship blossomed otherwise.

"Of course, get some rest." Marcus sat down on the couch extremely frustrated but at the same time, he tried to understand her hesitancy, however, his mind quickly returned to thoughts of Eowyn.

He replayed the same scene repeatedly. Eowyn ran her fingers through his hair until no longer content, she began kissing him passionately. At the same time, she pulled a vial from her pocket.

"I thought we both decided to stop using?"

"I just used it to help me get over you. Anything to get you out of my mind. I can't do it on my own."

Without answering, she filled a syringe and unhesitatingly, injected herself. "I forgot how good this feels." After a few minutes, she took his hand and led him to the bedroom.

6

THE EXTENDED FAMILY

The town of Harmony flourished over the years that followed. The city functioned autonomously of the Free Zone, formed its own governing element, and promoted a system of self-sustaining agriculture, but remained forever allied with the Free Zone. While Staff Sergeant Ballard assumed command of the military forces, Selima and Adiva served as administrators of Ferris General Hospital. The heart of the city revolved around a group of six homes, those of Marcus, Joanna, Sophi, Selima & Eowyn; Raghba and Dimitry; Ayase Sakato and Nayla; Nadia Romonov; and Leeba and Batya Lebedev who chose to live in a more remote region of the district.

Life in Harmony remained free of war and peace-loving for the decades that followed. Families grew, producing many children and grandchildren. Raghba's family sprouted from two to five including two daughters and a son. Adiva had two children with Ned Petry. Despite never marrying, they grew old loving one another unconditionally for the remainder of their lives. Nayla and Ayase lived a blissful life, eventually married and adopted a child. Joanna followed Selima's example and grew to be a Princess whom the entire town admired. She became active in politics and later, used her position to become a renowned human rights advocate. Leeba never fully recovered but lived in a state of relative happiness with her growing family of spherical children. Batya cared for her mother until she, finely of age, married and started a family of her own. She and Joanna remained best of friends and worked in their free time documenting the history of the Free Zone and Harmony in a series of encyclopedic publications.

Finally, the day arrived. Marcus and Eowyn had started a tradition of holding an annual family reunion for a day of fun and fellowship. Each year the group grew in size. On this particular day, Selima, Leeba, Raghba, and Adiva sat around a fire pit peddling gossip about the happenings of the Cooperative while monitoring the many children who played kickball, hopscotch, and the older boys who played football. Dimitry and Ned grilled burgers and hot dogs while having a beer.

"Joanna, do you have a moment to talk?"

"Dad, we don't want to miss the celebration, do we?"

"This will only take a few minutes. What I tell you must remain between you and I. Do you understand? Nobody else needs to know."

"Not even Mom?"

"Especially her."

"You're scaring me, Dad. You're not getting divorced, are you?"

"Of course not! I love your mom very much. This is something that occurred before Selima and I committed to one another, and I only recently discovered this myself. I've been wondering how to tell you this for a long time."

"Okay, you've managed to pique my interest,"

"You have a sister, Joanna; Nella is your sister."

Joanna nearly fell to the ground and steadied herself against a large rock. "Nella is my sister. That means that you and Eowyn...?" She looked at her father with inquisitive eyes.

"Yes, Eowyn and I. You know the story of how the Great Flood isolated us all from one another. Eowyn and I spent many months together unsure if anyone survived besides us, and we fell in love."

"If you were in love with Eowyn then how did you end up with Mom?"

"Once the storm ended, we returned and discovered that so many others survived. Well, Eowyn returned to Leeba and I— well, I moved on and fell in love with Selima. I spent weeks in the hospital, and she was at my side every step of my recovery. I learned to love her and here we are today. Regardless, Nella is your sister. Nobody else knows this but Eowyn, me, and now, you."

"Why so secretive? You weren't with mom at that time."

"That's a good question and something that Eowyn and I debated about for a long time. When we returned, Leeba was in a very fragile state and Eowyn thought the news could fracture her already delicate psyche. As for Selima, I recalled how she reacted to my relationship with Waffa. You were very young and probably don't remember, but she was president at the time and used her authority to kidnap Waffa. People died as a result of her actions including your sister Janey, so I chose not to share the news with her to avoid any potential problems."

"Do you still love her?"

"Of course, I love your mom! I'll always love her."

"I meant Auntie Eowyn. Do you still love her?"

"Always will. What we shared during those dark times will always and forever link us. That doesn't mean I don't love your mother any less. She's my soul mate who cared for you when I couldn't and for that, I will always be indebted to her."

"Why don't we ever see Eowyn? She never attends family events, and I rarely see her in town. Why?"

"She made that choice. Eowyn has experienced suffering that most will never even come close to encountering in their lifetime. The freedom we enjoy today is in many ways a direct result of her heroism and sacrifice. I don't believe that this world would be what it is today without the presence of Eowyn and of course, Ferris. At the same time, what they managed to accomplish took a great toll on them."

"It took a great toll on you, Dad. I hear the stories about you. Batya and I have documented many of the battles of the Nill Wars and your name comes up repeatedly alongside theirs, and another name I recently uncovered, Allura Amor. Did you know her?"

Hearing her name jabbed at his heart. A smile crossed his face and for a moment, his mind was swept away by memories of their love, her beautiful smile, then drifted to her death, blood running from between his fingers as he tried to stop the bleeding and the declaration of love as her eyes closed for the very last time.

"Dad—Dad!"

"Oh, sorry."

"Where did you go to?"

"Her...Allura. We met many years ago during the initial deportations. We were only teenagers packed into railcars like cattle. We helped one another live through some very dark times."

"And don't tell me! You loved her too."

"She would have been my wife if the Nill hadn't killed her. You would have liked her so much, Joanna. She was so much like you; funny, intelligent, strong, and full of passion. If your research isn't filled with stories of her, then you need to do more research. She was majestic."

"It's difficult to find people that can provide a firsthand account of the First Nill War."

"I'm right here, Joanna! I lived through it from the start of the Nill occupation to their ultimate surrender. Besides me, ask your mother. She was there from the First Nill War onward and she can provide a unique perspective from the Nill point of view. We fought side by side once she saw through the Nihilistic State's lies and propaganda."

"I thought you wouldn't want to talk about it and Mom, well she seems like she just wants to forget."

"I think your mom is much like me in that she rather not revisit the difficult times, but I think documenting history is more important than personal feelings. Many people should never be forgotten like Sergeant Major King, Fila, Staff Sergeant Dougherty, Corporal Carr, Katya, your sisters, Veil and Janey, your Uncle Glenn, and so many more. Most don't even remember their names. I would love to be part of your project. Besides, I have nothing but time on my hands since I'm semi-retired. Your mom is rarely home during the day anymore, so I would like nothing more than to spend time with you. Do you know who else would be a great source of information?"

"Who?"

"Eowyn. We ought to include her in this project. It might get her to open up and come out of her shell. I'll talk to her about it and let you know what she says. I'm going to check on her tomorrow morning if you'd like to tag along."

"Normally, yes, but I am scheduled to conduct some interviews at the capitol. Soon though. I want to get to know my sister, Nella. Thanks for being honest with me."

"Remember to keep it to yourself. I want your mom to avoid any undue stress."

"I love you daddy."

Early the next morning, Marcus arrived at a small cottage tucked away in the mountainside, knocked on the door, stepped inside, and made his way into the bedroom where he found her sleeping. He sat in a chair at the back of the room. A diffused light showed through the thin curtains revealing the silhouette of Eowyn fast asleep in bed. Marcus leaned back and closed his eyes. Still tired from the previous evening, he quickly fell asleep. Hours later, he was jarred awake by someone shaking him. He woke feeling much more rested than he had been in days. She greeted him with a kiss on the cheek. He didn't want her to stop, but she hadn't had company in many days and was desperate for some conversation.

"When did you get here silly? Come into the dining room. I'm making some coffee and you can have a blueberry muffin. You're hungry, right?"

"Famished." As they entered the kitchen; she leaned her back against the counter facing Marcus and smiled. He couldn't help but notice the outline of her breasts peeking through her silk gown.

"So, what brings you out this way?" she poured them each a cup of coffee, raised hers to her lips, and sipped. "Watch, it's hot!"

"I was worried about you. You didn't show up at the reunion last night, so of course, I was concerned. Why didn't you come?"

"I'm sure I wasn't missed!"

"Actually, several people asked about you the least of not which was Joanna. She misses you. By the way, where are those blueberry muffins you were talking about?"

"Oh, yeah. She slipped on a glove and pulled the pan from the oven. They'll have to cool for a few minutes. Drink your coffee and tell me about everyone while you wait."

"They were all there. Well, except you. Shoot, even Ballard and Angela showed."

"Leeba?"

"There but no change. She seems to be perfectly happy, yet, clearly has no grasp of what's going on around her. Joanna said to say hi. She misses you and get this, she and Batya are documenting the history of the Cooperative, Harmony, and the Nihilistic Wars. She wants the two of us to help. What do you think about you and me working together like old times?"

Eowyn dumped the muffins from the tin into a wicker basket, grabbed one, and broke a piece off. "Open up!" She shoved a piece into his mouth.

"Could be fun. I'd love to work next to you again," She grabbed a napkin, wiped a crumb from his lip, and slipped another piece into his mouth. He took a drink of his coffee.

"You are so dorky!" She raised the napkin again only this time she pressed up against him as she swept away the crumbs.

"Dam, I miss you! You monopolize my every thought. I think of you out here all alone, and all I want to do is run and hold you."

"What's stopping you? I'm here, you're here, and I am more than willing. You tell me your stories about how Selima is afraid to be intimate. The whole time I wish that I could be there for you. I'm not afraid, and I want nobody but you." She picked up her coffee, walked out to the front porch, and leaned on the railing as she admired the sunrise. A moment later, she heard Marcus step outside behind her. He placed his hands on her waist.

"It's okay, Marcus. I'm yours if you want me. I'll always be yours."

He lifted her nightgown, nudged her panties to the side, and slowly inched into her.

Her cup shattered on the ground as she placed her hands on the railing to steady herself. Marcus used his knees to pry her legs further apart and they vigorously made love; she worked with him in perfect cadence until they were both satisfied.

Several minutes later, Eowyn sat next to Marcus on the top step of the porch. She lowered her chin on his shoulder. "We can't keep this up, Marcus. I feel guilty."

"Me too, but I'm going to talk to Selima tonight; I'm going to tell her the truth. Before she left for the capitol this morning, she said she wanted to talk to me tonight, so I'll use that time to tell her about Nella and inform her I'm in love with you."

"I want to be there too, Marcus. She is my friend, and I want to be able to explain and be there for her."

"That's fine. She normally arrives around seven, seven-thirty. Remember, Eowyn, if it comes down to my marriage or you, I have no choice but to remain with her. She's my wife, and I love her too, but I will always be there for Nella and to support you—always!"

Eowyn took his hand and guided him to the bedroom. "I need another taste before you leave." An hour later, Marcus closed the door behind him and set off for home. He arrived home to find Joanna sitting inside.

"Oh, hey! What are you doing here?"

"Hello to you too, Dad! I finished at the capitol early and thought I would check in on you. Are you okay?"

"Fine, sweetheart! I promise."

"You don't seem happy."

"No worries. I do have some things on my mind, but I hope to work them out tonight with your mother."

"Does it have anything to do with Eowyn?" Marcus plopped down next to her.

"You are a most intuitive person. Is it that obvious."

"It's hard not to notice the way your eyes light up whenever you mention her name. When you speak about her, I can't but help see the smile on your face, your longing eyes. You're not too good at hiding things. Do you love her?"

"Very much."

"Mom?"

"Very much."

"You're in quite a pickle. You need to be honest with mom about everything to include Nella."

"I'll be speaking with her tonight, and I promise I will share everything. I just hope I don't hurt her too badly with the news. I don't want to lose her."

"She loves you so much. I can't see her possibly leaving you. You're her life."

"I wouldn't go that far. Her job is her life as of lately. She seems perfectly content spending all of her time at the capitol and to be honest, I rarely see her anymore. In many ways, she's become a stranger to me, a version of herself I don't recognize."

"I haven't seen much of her either, and yes, I have noticed a big change in her too, but one thing I am sure of is that she will always love you. You're not going to leave her, are you?"

"God no! I know she loves me, and I do her, but I hope I'm not oversharing; she shies away from intimacy. I just don't understand. Everything will be going well and then she suddenly shuts down. It's like she's trying to hide something."

"I don't know what to tell you, Dad. She's very private and doesn't share too much with me. You need to discuss it with her. Now, I didn't come here to be your therapist. I wanted to see if you wanted to do some fishing at Bentley's like we used to. Just you and me. What do you say?"

"There's nothing I rather do! Just give me a minute to get the rods and gear together." Marcus disappeared into a back room and returned minutes later pushing Sophi in a wheelchair with Tiny on his heels."

"Hey, Joa..nna. Missed you."

"Sophi! When did you get here?" She hugged her.

"Two days ago. No mo..more hospital for me. And watch this." She placed her hands on the armrests and hoisted herself to her feet. She took a step followed by another and another until she walked across the room and embraced Marcus. I can wal... walk now and check out my new sp..spikes," she pointed to her hair and smiled.

"You're amazing! I knew you would walk again. Where are you going to be staying?"

"Here. Selima and your dad wanted me he...here."

"Great! I'll get to see you more often. Do you want to go fishing with us?"

"N...n...no, physical ther...thera..py. Have fun though."

"Marcus sat Sophi on the couch. Is there anything you need before we leave?"

"No, have fun."

An hour later they arrived at the Bentley River and waded into the water. "So, Sophi is doing well?" Joanna asked as she cast her line into the rapidly moving current.

"As well as can be expected, I guess. Amazingly, she is doing as well as she is. Doctors gave her little to no chance of ever walking or functioning independently. Her recovery is a tribute to her resilience and determination. She ranks right up there with the toughest people I know. She's unbreakable."

"So are you Dad. No matter what happens with Mom, I'm proud to be your daughter."

"Thanks, sweetie. It goes without saying that you are the most important person in my life. I couldn't have a better daughter, and you've had many amazing sisters."

"What do you say to doing some fishing and stopping all the chit-chat? I could use a good trout dinner tonight," Joanna quipped.

When they ended their fishing trip they were surprised to see Selima and Eowyn chatting on the couch when they walked in.

"Well, what an honor it is to have you visit, stranger! Joanna walked in with a stringer of trout thrown over her shoulder while Marcus trailed behind.

"Yes, I've been hibernating deep in the woods and was enjoying the silence. I know I should have visited more, but I had to work some things out first."

"Hey, ladies. What a surprise. You're both early." Marcus kissed Selima, went to the kitchen, and returned with a glass of water. "How did you manage to get out of work so early?" He sat next to Selima. "You haven't been home this early in months."

"You said you wanted to talk and what's more important than our family, right? Besides, I've been a nervous wreck waiting to see what you have to say. But I'd rather we speak in private; I'm only going to talk to you in private."

"Joanna, are you up to throwing on an apron and preparing some fish with me?" Eowyn inquired.

"I'll be there in a few. I need to clean up."

Once alone, Marcus clutched Selima's hand. A tear slid from the corner of her eye, trickled along the side of her nose, and dotted the floor below. "Tell me Marcus; tell me what I already know."

"Just what do you think you know?"

"You want to leave me. You're frustrated with my inability to be intimate, and you need someone who can love you the way you deserve."

"First, you're wrong. I would never leave you. Second, I am frustrated and wonder why you can't be honest and tell me why, what is preventing you from committing yourself one hundred percent?"

"I couldn't possibly be more committed to you, my love. I have something to share with you. Something very personal that explains why I have been so fickle."

"If it's something I'm doing, just tell me."

"Not you, Marcus. It's me. Something happened to me during the first Nill War that I have never shared with anyone, something horrendous."

"Tell me everything, Selima."

"Remember, after my brother was executed, Abbas had me arrested. He tried to force me to be his wife and I refused. And he..." she took a deep breath while tears continued streaming. "Have you ever learned of the practice of female circumcision?"

"Never heard of it."

"Well, it's an archaic, ritualized cutting of the genitals only in my case, he had them completely exorcised..." She could no longer hold back the tears and sobbed on Marcus's shoulder.

"It's okay, sweetheart. Go ahead and tell me."

"They mutilated my genitalia. I am forever scarred and no longer able to receive pleasure from intercourse. I have forever been ruined."

"But when we are together you did orgasm. I know you do. I felt it—you did too, right?"

"I felt something amazing, but I'll never be able to have sex like a normal person. I'm sorry. I should have told you, but I was afraid I'd lose you."

"You're not going to lose me." Marcus tried to hug her, but she pushed away.

"I'm not dumb, Marcus. I know about Eowyn. You are not good at hiding it. At the same time, I don't blame you. I've been distant and disengaged. I just wonder how long you have been in love with her."

She wiped away her tears. "You don't have to answer that. I also figured out that Nella is yours. She has many of your features and of course, you and Eowyn were cooped up together for months. All I had to do was do the math. I want you to know that I am not going to stand in the way of your love or your child. I will be leaving in the morning."

"Leaving, no—why? If it comes down to you or her, there's no choice to be made. Of course, I choose you. Please don't leave, unless you're unable to forgive me for my betrayal. You have to understand that Eowyn and I were together for months and thought you and Leeba were dead. As far as we knew, we were the last two people on earth. At the same time, we openly shared our love for you and Leeba and we took a vow to return to our previous lives once we returned."

"You shared much more than that!"

"We did and that's where Nella comes in. Yes, she is our daughter, but I didn't know that until just recently."

"You can be so dumb sometimes, Marcus! She looks just like you. Anyway, I think I have a better understanding of why you fell in love with her. I don't blame you for what happened, but the question that remains is do you truly love me?"

"I've always loved you, Selima."

"I want to be with you, Marcus, but I wonder how we can move on when you are in love with someone else."

"So, you're not leaving? I mean, I'm begging you to stay."

Selima fell silent for several minutes, whisked away more tears, and began, "Not only am I not leaving, but I propose that we make an addition to our blissful bower. I proffer that we invite Eowyn into our relationship. You are indisputably in love with her, and she is very dear to me, my stalwart friend. What do you say to the three of us together, an amatory triumvirate? The three of us in a polygynous, scandalous liaison that the whole town will be gossiping about."

Marcus was speechless, amazed at Selima's selfless solution and her dedication to him. He considered his selfishness, his infidelity, and the narcissistic betrayal, and yet, she looked beyond his foibles and tendered the ultimate act of benevolence.

"You're sure you want to do this because you make the decision simple for me. I love you, and I love Eowyn. I couldn't possibly say no. I've never been so sure. Of course, we need to see how Eowyn feels about this devious plot."

Selima stood. "Good, then I'll get her." She was about to step into the adjacent room when Marcus called to her.

"You know that this proposal will inevitably lead to difficulties. It won't be easy, and I want you to thoroughly think this through before going to Eowyn. You're my wife, and I am perfectly happy in our relationship whether we have an intimate relationship or not. When you are ready to be intimate, I am here. If that time never comes, I will live with that as long as you are by my side. You never need to be ashamed of your body, your wounds, and the scars around me. I love you as you are; to me, you are flawlessly beautiful."

"I am sure and have put much thought into my decision. You deserve intimacy and if I can't fulfill my wifely duties then it's my job to see to it that you are taken care of. Eowyn is the natural person to fill that role."

Selima left and returned a minute later with Eowyn. "Please be seated."

Eowyn was expecting the worst. She knew that one day Selima would discover their clandestine relationship, and she figured this was that moment.

"I—we have a proposition for you. First, I know that you are in love with Marcus, and I also know about Nella."

"But..." Eowyn tried to reply but Selima continued. "It's okay. I'm not angry. The two of you were stranded together for many months probably wondering if your significant other was still alive. It is only natural that the two of you sought refuge in the arms of one another. I thought Marcus was dead and yet, another miracle occurred when God reunited us."

"I promise that I will leave right now, go to my home, and never see Marcus again if that will salvage our friendship. I do love him, but I value our friendship as well. Please forgive me."

"There is nothing to forgive. I love Marcus with all my heart, and I love you as well. You were there to comfort him when he needed someone the most when I couldn't possibly be there for him, and I am grateful for that. Now, I have a proposition for you, a proposition of great weight and responsibility. I do not want to get into detail, but when I was held prisoner by the Nill, I was tortured in many ways. I have shared most of those stories with the two of you, but I did not share everything. I held back things that I should have shared with Marcus before we were married, but I was too scared to do so. My injuries prevent me from being intimate with a man or it may be better said that I am no longer able to derive pleasure from traditional intercourse. I have been maimed for life," Selima labored to fight off a new barrage of grief.

"I am so sorry, Selima. There's nothing that can be done surgically?"

"In the future perhaps, but with the hospital's limited abilities and the lack of plastic surgeons, the chances are hopeless. Even with surgery, I am told that the chances of regaining the sensitivity and feeling are little to none, but this isn't about pitying me. I want this to be more about the three of us. I love Marcus, and I assume you love him as well," She paused and looked to her for a reply.

"With all my heart."

"And, Marcus, my husband, you love her too, correct?"

"I do."

"Normally, this would be a very precarious position to be in but due to mitigating circumstances, while quite awkward and very risqué, I find there is a natural solution to our current predicament. I've already explained my culture's common practice of polygamy to Marcus. Are you familiar?"

"Afraid not," Eowyn wondered what she might be suggesting.

"Polygyny is the practice of a husband sharing two or more wives which leads me to my proposal. I have suggested to Marcus that we invite you into our relationship. We want you to join us as a member of a triumvirate."

Selima didn't hesitate to answer. "The answer is no! I'm not going to be a third wheel nor am I going to interfere in your relationship more than I already have. I am in love with Marcus, but if being with him means hurting you, then I'll move on."

"You don't understand, Eowyn. We would all hold equal positions; we would be one wheel all joined by our love. It is your thoughtfulness, your desire to not hurt me that convinced me this would be a feasible arrangement. You are the only person in this world that I would ever invite into our lives. If you think about it, you've already given your answer even before I asked."

"How's that?" Eowyn looked confused.

While unsuccessful, the two of you have been covertly meeting and loving one another thinking that I am oblivious to your love affair. The two of you are good at many things but hiding your love isn't one of them. I love you, Marcus, and I love you, Eowyn, and believe that both of you love me. I am not able to be there for Marcus in every way I should be as a wife, but the three of us together will bring us all happiness. This triad will fulfill all of our desires and needs. You are my best friend, and I love you enough to open the door for you to become my partner as well as Marcus's. The decision should be an easy one."

"And Marcus, I haven't heard anything from you. How do you feel about this arrangement?" Eowyn awaited his answer.

"I have nothing to lose in this arrangement. I love both of you. The real question is whether the two of you can do this without ruining your friendship. This won't be easy."

"For me, it's simple. I love you; I love Eowyn, and it's only natural that the three of us are together." Selima waited for Eowyn's response.

"I do love both of you, and I am willing to embark on this experiential journey together, but I hope this whole experiment does not backfire and ruin things instead of making them better."

"So, your answer is, yes?"

"Before I make any decision, I need to know how Joanna might feel about the arrangement. I would like to hear from Sophi as well since she is part of this family too. If the two of them are okay with it, then I am excited to embark on this social experiment, that is as long as you are sure yourself, Selima. Also, be aware that when I commit to someone, I fully commit. Don't get me wrong, I am not just speaking about a commitment to Marcus, but to you also. I don't know how you feel about loving a woman, but I intend to love you as much as I love him. Are you ready for that?"

"I've shared that my dad had three wives, and I am familiar with the lifestyle. I want to share myself with you if you are willing to undertake this radical journey."

7

DENOUEMENT

On the day that the Nihilistic State invaded America, politicians were clueless. The laws they passed meant to end racial profiling, over-riding the in-place Immigration Laws, and opening borders while well intended, exacerbated the situation by leaving the country vulnerable to the ill-driven intent of the few, the terrorists that blended in with the many good, hard-working people desperate to experience the freedoms our country offers. Unlike invasions of the past, this expropriation occurred with stealth, with an atypical self-restraint demonstrated over several years. The assailants masqueraded as everyday Americans with families, attending church, working a nine-to-five job, and posing as law-abiding citizens. Government was infiltrated from the national to the local levels, military leadership compromised, and positions of influence appropriated. Slowly, the pieces fell into place and once the claws sunk in, they tasted blood, coiled around the heart of our Democratic Republic, and choked the life out of our country. Before anyone could react, their pieces were already in place, and they ripped at the soft underbelly of our nation. Politicians unknowingly rolled out the proverbial red carpet and invited the radical terrorists to our doorstep. The trap was set leaving no time for retaliation. And so, the Nill assumed power and began a series of devious acts meant to exterminate the citizenry and impose a new world order. The question that naturally arises is, could something like this ever occur? Who knows, but it's a possibility. While government should be limited, at the same time, there are times that the government must act to protect the citizenry and more importantly, to safeguard our country's sovereignty. This will call for citizens to relinquish some control and permit Legislators the oversight to act for the good of national interests and safety instead of worrying about individual freedoms and being sensitive to everyone's feelings.

Marcus reflected on the past few years of his life as he shared his thoughts with Sophi, Joanna, Selima, and Eowyn. He spoke of his conversations with his father concerning the failure of the government to protect citizens, the attempts of the Nill to eradicate the citizenry, the many people lost as they fought for freedom, and then his mind reverted to a moment in his childhood as his father spoke to him.

"What did you say, Dad?" a much younger Marcus asked.

"Kindness is encouraged in any interaction, but at the same time, don't let kindness get in the way of your civic responsibility to family and community. Kindness is encouraged at all times, but laws are there for a reason, and respecting them is just as important as being kind."

"I got it, Dad. Be kind as a practice but be respectful of laws since they are meant to maintain order, right? We need to be kind but make everyone follow the rules, right?"

"Sort of, Marcus," his dad answered. Just remember that necessity, actuality, and common sense shouldn't be sacrificed in the name of cordiality, pageantry, and in the name of political correctness. Sometimes harsh steps are necessary to ensure the safety and stability of our nation. Efforts to be altruistic should never interfere with efforts to protect our union. No matter what, kindness is encouraged. Just remember, even when dealing with law, kindness is encouraged, but common sense reigns."

"I don't quite understand what your dad was trying to say," Joanna cut in.

Sophi interposed. "The moral of the story is that some... sometimes being politically correct must be sacri...ficed for the safe...safety of our country, citizens, and for the overall well-being of the Repub...lic. Right, Marcus?" Sophi looked to him for confirmation.

"Right on, Soph! Okay, enough of this reflecting. It's late. Good night, ladies." Just as quickly as everyone departed, he was in the shower. Steamy hot water coursed over his body and a thick haze filled the shower stall. He leaned forward, the palms of his hand on the tile letting the teaming water course over his body which sent him into a restful trance. Even the sound of the framed shower door sliding open failed to snap him back to reality but the feel of arms wrapping around his waist drew him back to the present. She stippled his back with kisses. "Marcus, I have some time before I must leave for the capitol."

He turned to face Selima. "Are you sure this is what you want? I don't want you to do something that you might regret later. I'm going to love you no matter if Eowyn is in our lives or not."

"Shhh! Now enough questions. The decision has been unanimously decided. I just wanted to spend a moment alone with you and this seems to be the only place I can do that right now."

Marcus kissed her and pulled her tight.

"There will be a time when I am ready to share my whole body with you," she lightly stroked him as she spoke. "I know that you will be making love to Eowyn and that is okay, but don't neglect me, please. I can please you as well." She continued caressing him and increased her pace. "I still expect you to sleep with me and when the time is right, we will make love, but in the meantime, I promise to tend to your sexual needs," she dropped to her knees. Moments later, Marcus groaned as his body spasmed. "I know how to please you in other ways." She kissed him and exited. "Dinner is almost ready my love."

Joanna and Sophi both approved of the three-way relationship since they already considered Eowyn a part of the family. The experiment succeeded; the bonds of love rooted deep and blossomed.

A year later, Eowyn gave birth to a healthy young boy they named Ferris. Selima, Eowyn, and Marcus went on to have three more children. They lived a happy and fulfilling life alongside their extended family and friends. Selima and Eowyn's love grew from one of great admiration to an intense physical love with Marcus at the center of their world and they at the center of his.

"The family sat down at the ever-growing dining room table. To date, fourteen chairs, one for each member of the extended family, surrounded the specially made mahogany table. Eowyn and Selima sat at the seats of honor at each end of the table at Marcus's insistence while he took a seat between his daughters,

Joanna and Sophi. The babies were safely tucked in bed for the evening while the grandkids sat at a table of their own.

The table was filled with all sorts of food: green bean casserole, cranberry sauce, cornbread, stuffing, candied yams, fried catfish, a steaming hot turkey, and a variety of desserts.

"Marcus, do you mind saying the blessing before we eat?" Selima asked.

"Sure, honey! They joined hands.

"Father, we thank you for the food you have provided. Forgive us for taking our joy and happiness for granted. Bless this food to fuel our bodies so that we may glorify you. We pray that we will be energized and be able to work for the glory of Your Kingdom. Thanks for blessing our family with prosperity, happiness, and love. In Jesus' name, I pray. Amen."

"Let's dig in! Marcus stood to cut the turkey while the others filled their plates and talked.

"One more thing before we eat," Eowyn cut in. "Can I have everyone's attention? Over the past several years, we have all suffered our share of heartache while recently experiencing many triumphs. Our family, and by family, I mean all of you present today, are very fortunate to have one another, and I as well as Marcus and Eowyn will always be here for you. Now, to some miraculous news; I want to announce the coming of an addition to our family. I would like to announce that Selima is with child. Our family is about to have another edition."

Eowyn pulled Selima tight and kissed her. "So, in about six months be ready to meet the latest edition to our family."

Just less than a year ago, Selima was told that she would never have children. After a series of tests, doctors determined that she was infertile. Selima fell into a deep depression and then, on one fateful night while lying with her husband, Eowyn entered. As was typical, she craved intimacy and kissed Marcus then seeing Selima so somber, she turned her attention to her while Marcus left the room. She kissed her softly while unbuttoning her nightgown.

Selima was pulled from her gloom by the attention but when Marcus walked into the room, Eowyn abruptly stopped. "Good luck, Sparky!" She whispered in his ear as she sashayed out the door.

That night, Selima and Marcus made love for the first time, and by the grace of God, she became pregnant.

After a series of hugs and congratulations, the family sat down for dinner. As was the custom, family members were encouraged to share a story of faith, love, loss, or survival. Joanna volunteered to be the first.

"For as long as I can remember, the world that we live in has been in turmoil; that is until recently. We all enjoy a sense of relative peace and happiness due to the sacrifices of so many, some living and some dead. Of course, I was a mere baby when most of this occurred, but I do have some very vivid memories as a child. I have faint memories of my mother, Maria, her beautiful smile and caring ways. It's important to remember that I grew up amid the Second Nihilistic War and yet, and this is a testament to my parents, my memories all revolve around how safe and happy I felt. I was only a child but if I were an adolescent at that time, I wouldn't have sensed the carnage taking place around us because my mom was there to comfort me. I have spotty memories of my dad at the time, but as everyone knows, he was busy like many of you, fighting for freedom. So, here I am today, surrounded by the people that I love most. We are healthy, smiles on our faces, and the future appears bright. Many of the efforts of those present here today, your sacrifices, permit us the freedom to gather and celebrate today. I thank my moms, my dad, all of you, and those who are no longer with us for their sacrifices and efforts to procure the peace we all enjoy today. Maria, Mom, I know you're listening, I love you just as I love each person sitting at this table today."

"Well said, Joanna. You've grown up to be a perfect daughter and that is a direct testament to your mother and Marcus. We all love you," Selima looked around to see who might speak next. When the room remained silent, perhaps people were reflecting on Joanna's profound speech, Selima decided to speak next.

"I am not from your country; in fact, as I look around the table today, I only see three of Nill origins. We, whether by choice or not, were at one time your enemies. Driven by an unfounded hatred, my people endeavored to destroy your culture, eliminate your kind, and appropriate your world but to what end? It turns out, the people that indoctrinated my people into believing you were immoral and innately evil human beings were completely wrong and in fact, were the wicked creatures in disguise that they warned us about.

My father always told me that if you were to mix a cauldron of good and evil, the good would rise to the top while the evil would inevitably fester in the sludge at the bottom. He could not have been more prophetic. Those of you sitting here today whom I am proud to call my family, surged to the top of the proverbial cauldron and represent the very best in goodness, love, and humanity. We not only live in harmony with one another, but going a step further have combined into one joyous family despite our cultural differences and various nationalities.

I apologize, I do not mean to be long-winded nor is it in my nature to speak in front of such a large group. What I am simply trying to say is that God is good and we should all feel blessed that he selected us to meet, become friends, grow into a family, and even in some cases become marital partners. We have risen to the top and now it is our responsibility to continue to make our world a better place for all."

Leeba stood before anyone else could reply. "My family has grown considerably over the past year, and I feel blessed just like Selima so eloquently stated. I lost the woman I loved during the Great Flood and while I despair over the loss, all of you, and my family have made things so much easier. I may not remember much in my current state, but I do recall the horrific violence of the Nihilistic Wars. Many good people were killed, entire families devastated, and communities laid to waste. If it wasn't for people like Allura Amor, Sergeant Major King, his wife Fila, my wife, Eowyn—God rest her soul—and Marcus among others, we would not be here today celebrating. Everyone must remember that many people gave their lives for us to be free and gather here today," she paused then just as suddenly added, "...and oh yes, a little side note...whoever is impersonating my deceased wife, while I think motivated by good intentions, please just let me be. I am at peace with her death. Eowyn is gone but will always remain in my heart."

Some people privately giggled while Eowyn quickly exited the room with Joanna on her heels.

"Thank you, Leeba!" Marcus stood. "Is there anyone else that would like to say a few words?"

The remainder of the people acquiesced. "Well, I do have some things to share with you. Every one of us has lost someone close; most have lost numerous people as a result of the Nihilistic Wars and as victims of the Great Flood or both. As Joanna, Selima, and Leeba have each commented on the peace we share, I believe it is important to remember and never forget those we knew and others that we didn't, who selflessly gave their lives for us to be here today. Many of you were children when the Nill invaded our country. Shoot, I was a child myself, or rather, a teenager who had a mom and dad and even a brother. As we grow as a country, we must remember what made our country vulnerable and ultimately, what led to the Nill invading our great nation and that is the ineptitude of the people. While we should be as inclusive as possible and invite all good people to our country, we must at the same time, be selective and see to it that all those hoping to immigrate into our country pass through a thorough vetting process. We can't afford to let those who mean us harm enter our country again and do us harm. While I say this, we must also be careful to allow those who want to add to or benefit our society a fair chance to become citizens.

But I digress; enough about what our country should be doing; I will be addressing the leaders of the many cooperatives in the coming months specifically about this. Now, I want to rehash the many people who have touched my life as well as many if not all of your lives throughout the Nihilistic War. Leeba mentioned a name that not many people seem to know but her actions were critical to the victory over the Nill. Allura Amor fought valiantly during the first Nill Wars before being killed in action. Her efforts were instrumental in ensuring the freedoms we enjoy today. She along with my brothers, Glenn Martyreon and Ferris gave their lives to secure our freedom. Soldiers like Sergeant Major King, Staff Sergeant Doughty, and others whom I only recall a portion of their names, like Katya, Carr, Token, Rodriguez, Todd, and so many others, selflessly sacrificed themselves for us, to provide us a chance at freedom. My friends Sloane, Ileana, and Mrs. Tobar along with my daughters, Janey Veil, my wives Maria and Waffa, and my parents; all of whom sacrificed their lives so we could live a better one.

Later that night after the guests went on their way and the children were tucked in, Marcus lay in bed with Selima on one side and Eowyn on the other. They each slept soundly with their backs to him. Unable to sleep, he turned to Selima and kissed her on the back then began tracing the deep scars that trailed along her neck, down her spine until concluding at her firm, round ass. He then dedicated his attention to the burns that populated a significant portion of her neck and shoulder.

"What are you doing, silly?" Selima asked.

"Does it still hurt?" Marcus inquired as he ran his finger between her breasts and came to a stop at an especially deep scar just below her waistline. "That's where they stabbed you, right?"

You know that answer to that, Marcus, and no, I don't feel it anymore. All my pain dissipated when I married you," She kissed him and turned to her side. Marcus whispered into her ear as she was sinking into a deep sleep, "I love you with all my heart and no matter what may happen in the future, you are the light of my life." Selima mumbled something inaudible and fell into a deep sleep.

Marcus then shifted his attention to Eowyn's much more sculpted back which was filled with a myriad of gashes crisscrossing throughout her body. One especially severe scar stretched from the small of her spine, took an abrupt left over her side, and ended just below her left breast. He playfully walked his fingers up the side and began gently tweaking her nipple. His mind wandered to the time when the Nill captured them both; Eowyn was tied between two trees while the Nill relentlessly whipped her. The scene quickly morphed into thoughts of Allura, Ferris, Maria, Waffa, and the others, Suddenly, he was thrown into a tailspin of despair. He found himself sobbing uncontrollably. Marcus was well-acquainted with the overwhelming anguish which chipped away at his will.

"Marcus, are you all right, baby?" Eowyn wrapped her arms around him. She often found herself waking up in a cold sweat following a night of horrific nightmares the many years since the Nihilistic Wars. The sense of loss was overwhelming and didn't seem to be getting any easier as the years passed, but the one difference was that she took solace in the presence of Marcus and Selima but Marcus never found a lasting peace.

"Sorry, just thinking about Janey, Veil, and all of the others. I miss them."

"We all miss them, and God knows we all hurt, but we can't lose focus of what is right in front of us at this very moment. We are not alone. You know what helps me when I'm feeling down?"

"I know exactly what helps you, but that's not an option."

"Selima, you awake?" Eowyn whispered and when she didn't receive a reply she walked into the restroom and returned with two syringes. First, she jabbed one into her arm and then handed one to Marcus.

"How do you feel now, Marcus?" She laid back down and pressed herself tightly to Marcus's chest, "Turn onto your back, my love," Eowyn climbed to her knees, hiked a leg over his hips, and lowered herself. "I'm going to take your mind off your pain. Slowly, she undulated.

"Have I ever told you how alluring you are?" Marcus asked as he dropped his hands to her ass and worked to keep pace.

"You two are like bunnies! I need to get some sleep since I have an early meeting at the capitol. Can you please..." She was unable to finish her question when she sensed Eowyn's body tense and the satisfying moans informed her that she had orgasmed. Moments later, Marcus came and then laid between them.

"Good night, Selima. Good night, Marcus. I love both of you."

"I love you too," Selima replied.

Soon after, Selima and Eowyn drifted into a deep sleep, but Marcus had too much on his mind. He walked to the front porch and peered into the night with recurring images of those he loved lying bloody and beaten streaming through his mind. The images haunted him morning, noon, and night despite a desperate effort to forget. In one moment, Allura was bleeding out, the next minute Maria lay dying on the ground, and then the scene transitioned to Ileana's pale body, a stalker gnawing on her arm. Just when he was able to force the horrid images from his mind, his thoughts shifted to Ferris crushed by a tree, fighting to keep his head above the rising water as blood profusely percolated from his mouth until he was eventually whisked away.

Marcus pounded on his head, "I beg you, please let me rest. Make it stop! I am so sorry I let all of you down. Lord, please forgive me," he sobbed uncontrollably.

Just as quickly, an image of Waffa and their baby being sucked under the cataclysmic waters slashed at his psyche. Right after, he purposely sank the needle into his arm and depressed the plunger sending a lethal dose of Morphine into his system. His world began to shrink. He tumbled down the steps and landed staring up at the stars. It seemed to him as if he were there for hours when only minutes had passed. His eyes fluttered as blurred images of Eowyn and Selima frantically calling to him came into view. He smiled. The pain dissipated and for the first time since the Nill Wars, he achieved reaching the level of peace he prayed for multiple times a day. He chuckled as his wives hovered over him; Eowyn slapping his face and Selima cradling her face in her hands. They were unable to see what he did. All of those he mourned stood before him smiling, some with their hands extended and the others simply admiring. Allura kneeled next to him on one side while his brother grabbed his hand and the whole time, Veil, Janey, Ileana, Sergeant Major King, Maria, Waffa, and many others stood with their arms spread wide open.

Eowyn had started CPR while Selima assisted but none of that was important. From behind the growing crowd, his parents stepped into view.

"I missed you, mom and dad."

"Maybe a hallucination?" Selima thought while Eowyn frantically labored.

Selima kneeled and her hand inadvertently came to rest on an empty syringe. Shaking wildly, she held the syringe up. "Eowyn, do you know what he took?"

"Morphine, he's been using Morphine for months, but he told me he quit."

"Fuck, Eowyn, you should have told me. Hurry, there's some Narcan in the medicine cabinet. Hurry!" Selima ordered.

"Hey, little man, I've missed you," Allura whispered into his ear.

"Yeah, Mawcus, where have you been?" Ferris stood smiling.

They were all alive and well, and Marcus experienced immense joy.

Janey and Veil scurried to him next and smothered him with kisses while his mom took his hand, "Welcome home, honey."

"I've never been prouder of anyone in my life, Marcus," His dad proclaimed with a beaming smile.

Ileana stood with her sister, Maria on the outskirts of the crowd as they tended to the baby. Then

an unmistakable voice demanded his attention,

"I knew they'd make a soldier of you eventually! You ought to be a general by now, Martyreon,"

Sergeant Major King joked. In the background Waffa waved from a distance, their baby in her arms.

Here's the Narcan," Eowyn handed it to Selima and she quickly injected it into his nose. "Please, Baby! Please come back to us." In the past, she witnessed others use Narcan, and normally, the patient quickly regained consciousness, but not Marcus. "Is he breathing yet?"

"Our Marcus is dead, my God, don't let this be real," Selima bellowed.

She sprinted back to the bathroom and searched until she discovered one more container of Narcan and quickly tried to revive him again.

"Move, Selima," she shoved her to the side. "I'm not prepared to lose you yet, my love!" Eowyn pressed the plunger, her tears distorting her vision. "We need to get him on his feet," she cried.

"Daddy! What happened to Daddy," Joanna screamed.

Maria stepped in front of Marcus and reached for his hands. No matter how hard Marcus tried, he couldn't seem to reach her.

"Come back to me," Maria yelled.

Suddenly, the light began to fade until he was cast in utter darkness, while the voices of his loved ones echoed through his mind. Eowyn desperately tugged at his hands trying to get him to stand while Marcus was finally able to grasp Maria's hands. He was pulled to his feet and immediately experienced an all-encompassing peace. He hugged his loved ones while feeling overwhelming joy relieved that his journey would continue; Marcus was home.

THE FIRST BOOK OF THE
KINDNESS IS ENCOURAGED
TRILOGY

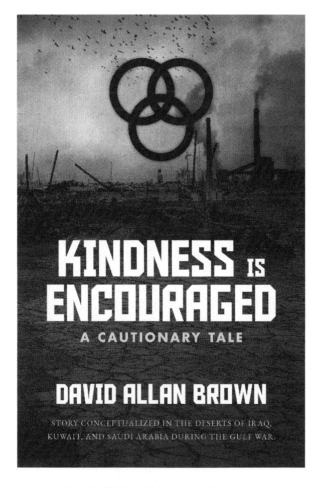

KINDNESS IS
ENCOURAGED
A CAUTIONARY TALE

DAVID ALLAN BROWN

STORY CONCEPTUALIZED IN THE DESERTS OF IRAQ,
KUWAIT, AND SAUDI ARABIA DURING THE GULF WAR.

KINDNESS IS ENCOURAGED:
A CAUTIONARY TALE

THE SECOND BOOK OF THE
KINDNESS IS ENCOURAGED
TRILOGY

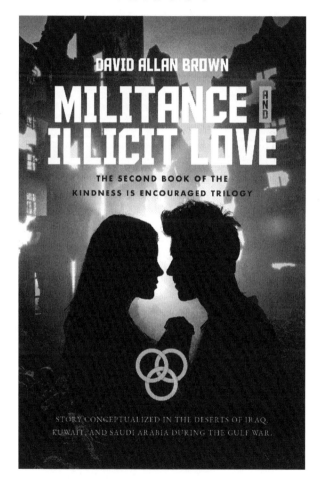

DAVID ALLAN BROWN

MILITANCE AND ILLICIT LOVE

THE SECOND BOOK OF THE
KINDNESS IS ENCOURAGED TRILOGY

STORY CONCEPTUALIZED IN THE DESERTS OF IRAQ,
KUWAIT, AND SAUDI ARABIA DURING THE GULF WAR.

MILITANCE AND ILLICIT LOVE

Made in the USA
Columbia, SC
15 November 2024